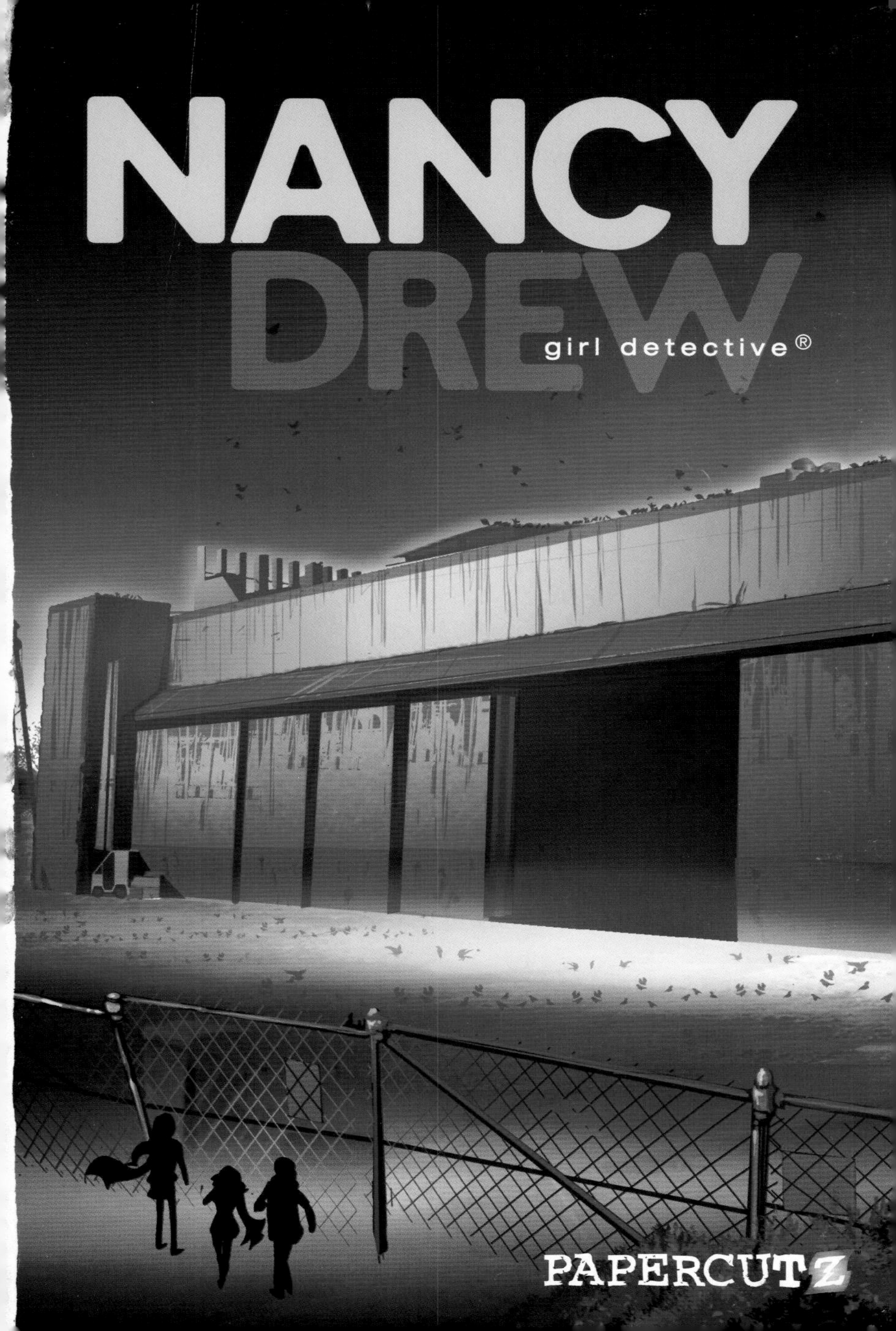
NANCY
DREW
girl detective®
PAPERCUTZ

NANCY DREW GRAPHIC NOVELS AVAILABLE FROM PAPERCUTZ

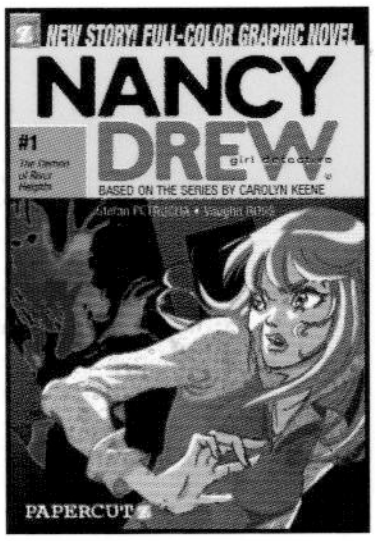
NEW STORY! FULL-COLOR GRAPHIC NOVEL
NANCY
DREW
#1
BASED ON THE SERIES BY CAROLYN KEENE
PAPERCUTZ

Graphic Novel #1
"The Demon of
River Heights"

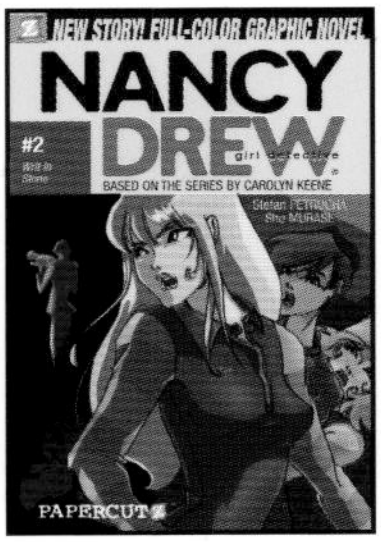
NEW STORY! FULL-COLOR GRAPHIC NOVEL
NANCY
DREW
#2
BASED ON THE SERIES BY CAROLYN KEENE
PAPERCUTZ

Graphic Novel #2
"Writ In Stone"

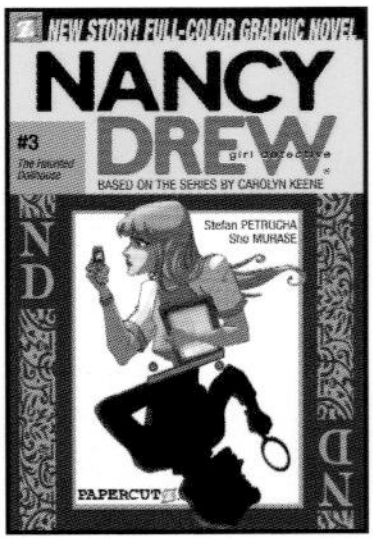
NEW STORY! FULL-COLOR GRAPHIC NOVEL
NANCY
DREW
#3
BASED ON THE SERIES BY CAROLYN KEENE
Stefan PETRUCHA
Sho MURASE
PAPERCUTZ

Graphic Novel #3
"The Haunted
Dollhouse"

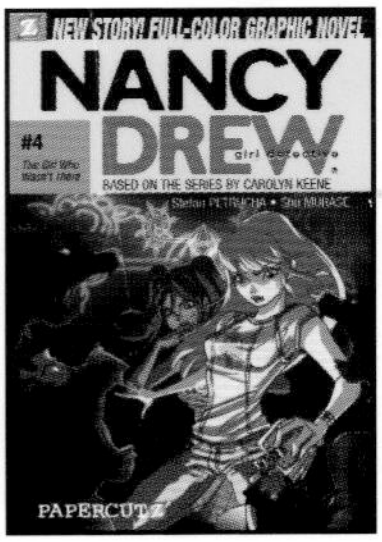
NEW STORY! FULL-COLOR GRAPHIC NOVEL
NANCY
DREW
#4
BASED ON THE SERIES BY CAROLYN KEENE
PAPERCUTZ

Graphic Novel #4
"The Girl Who
Wasn't There"

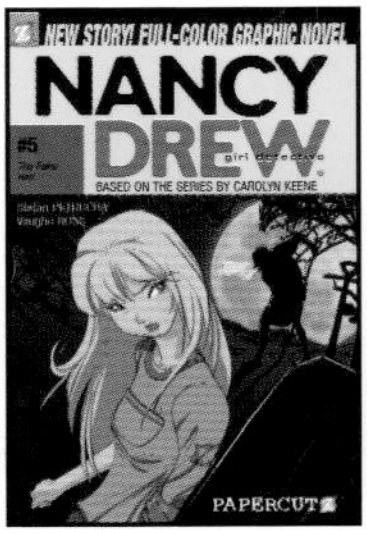
NEW STORY! FULL-COLOR GRAPHIC NOVEL
NANCY
DREW
#5
BASED ON THE SERIES BY CAROLYN KEENE
PAPERCUTZ

Graphic Novel #5
"The Fake Heir"

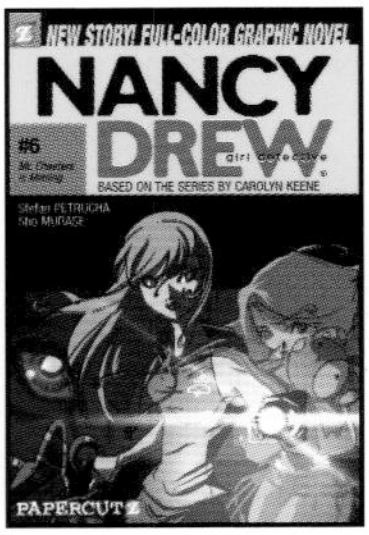
NEW STORY! FULL-COLOR GRAPHIC NOVEL
NANCY
DREW
#6
BASED ON THE SERIES BY CAROLYN KEENE
PAPERCUTZ

Graphic Novel #6
"Mr. Cheeters
Is Missing"

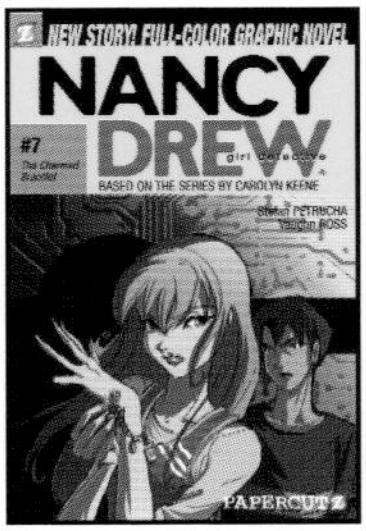
NEW STORY! FULL-COLOR GRAPHIC NOVEL
NANCY
DREW
#7
BASED ON THE SERIES BY CAROLYN KEENE
PAPERCUTZ

Graphic Novel #7
"The Charmed
Bracelet"

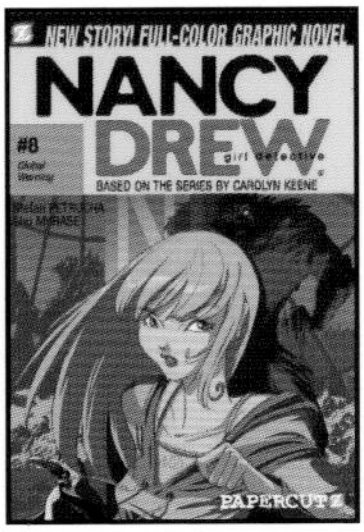
NEW STORY! FULL-COLOR GRAPHIC NOVEL
NANCY
DREW
#8
BASED ON THE SERIES BY CAROLYN KEENE
PAPERCUTZ

Graphic Novel #8
"Global Warning"

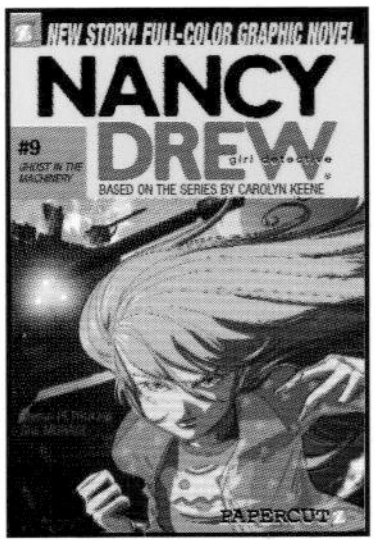
NEW STORY! FULL-COLOR GRAPHIC NOVEL
NANCY
DREW
#9
BASED ON THE SERIES BY CAROLYN KEENE
PAPERCUTZ

Graphic Novel #9
"Ghost In The
Machinery"

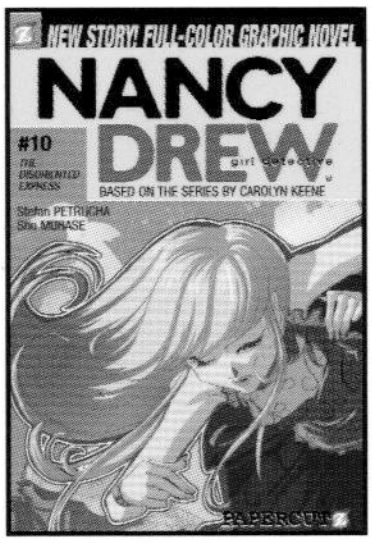
NEW STORY! FULL-COLOR GRAPHIC NOVEL
NANCY
DREW
#10
BASED ON THE SERIES BY CAROLYN KEENE
PAPERCUTZ

Coming in August
Graphic Novel #10
"The Disoriented
Express"

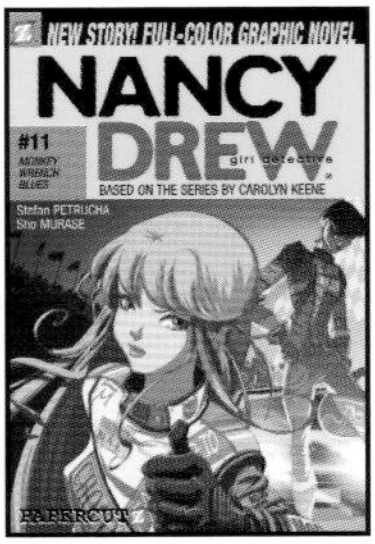
NEW STORY! FULL-COLOR GRAPHIC NOVEL
NANCY
DREW
#11
BASED ON THE SERIES BY CAROLYN KEENE
PAPERCUTZ

Coming in November
Graphic Novel #11
"Monkey Wrench
Blues"

$7.95 each in paperback, $12.95 each in hardcover. Please add $3.00 for postage and handling for the first book, add $1.00 for each additional book.
Please make check payable to NBM Publishing. Send to:

Papercutz, 40 Exchange Place, Suite 1308 New York, NY 10005 • www.papercutz.com

NANCY
#9 DREW
girl detective
®

Ghost In The Machinery

STEFAN PETRUCHA • Writer
SHO MURASE • Artist
with 3D CG elements by CARLOS JOSE GUZMAN
Based on the series by
CAROLYN KEENE

PAPERCUTZ™
New York

The Ghost In The Machinery
STEFAN PETRUCHA – Writer
SHO MURASE – Artist
with 3D CG elements and color by CARLOS JOSE GUZMAN
BRYAN SENKA – Letterer
JIM SALICRUP
Editor-in-Chief

ISBN 10: 1-59707-058-0 paperback edition
ISBN 13: 978-1-59707-058-4 paperback edition
ISBN 10: 1-59707-061-0 hardcover edition
ISBN 13: 978-1-59707-061-4 hardcover edition

Printed in China.
Distributed by Holtzbrinck Publishers.

10 9 8 7 6 5 4 3 2 1

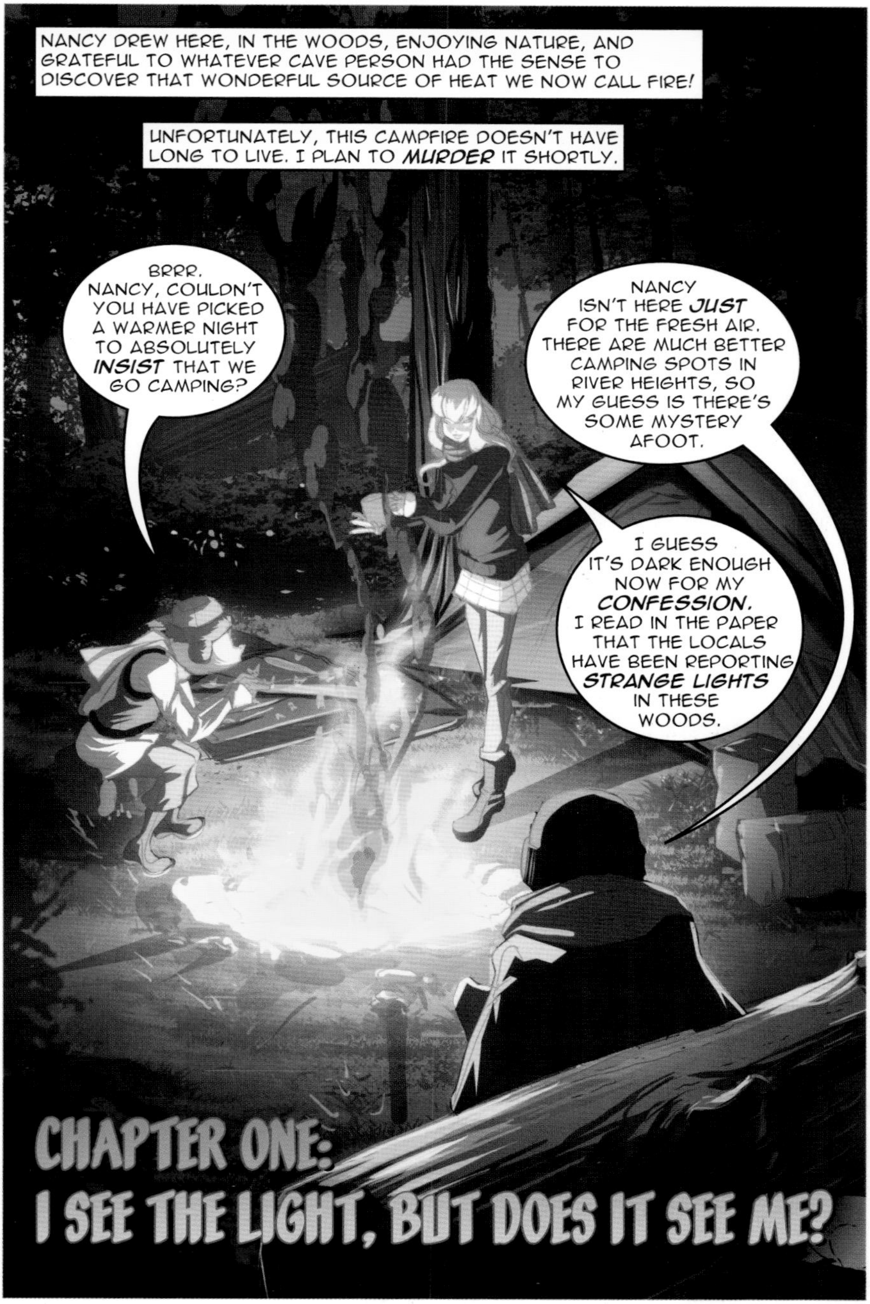

NANCY DREW HERE, IN THE WOODS, ENJOYING NATURE, AND GRATEFUL TO WHATEVER CAVE PERSON HAD THE SENSE TO DISCOVER THAT WONDERFUL SOURCE OF HEAT WE NOW CALL FIRE!
UNFORTUNATELY, THIS CAMPFIRE DOESN'T HAVE LONG TO LIVE. I PLAN TO *MURDER* IT SHORTLY.
BRRR. NANCY, COULDN'T YOU HAVE PICKED A WARMER NIGHT TO ABSOLUTELY *INSIST* THAT WE GO CAMPING?
NANCY ISN'T HERE *JUST* FOR THE FRESH AIR. THERE ARE MUCH BETTER CAMPING SPOTS IN RIVER HEIGHTS, SO MY GUESS IS THERE'S SOME MYSTERY AFOOT.
I GUESS IT'S DARK ENOUGH NOW FOR MY *CONFESSION.* I READ IN THE PAPER THAT THE LOCALS HAVE BEEN REPORTING *STRANGE LIGHTS* IN THESE WOODS.
CHAPTER ONE:
I SEE THE LIGHT, BUT DOES IT SEE ME?

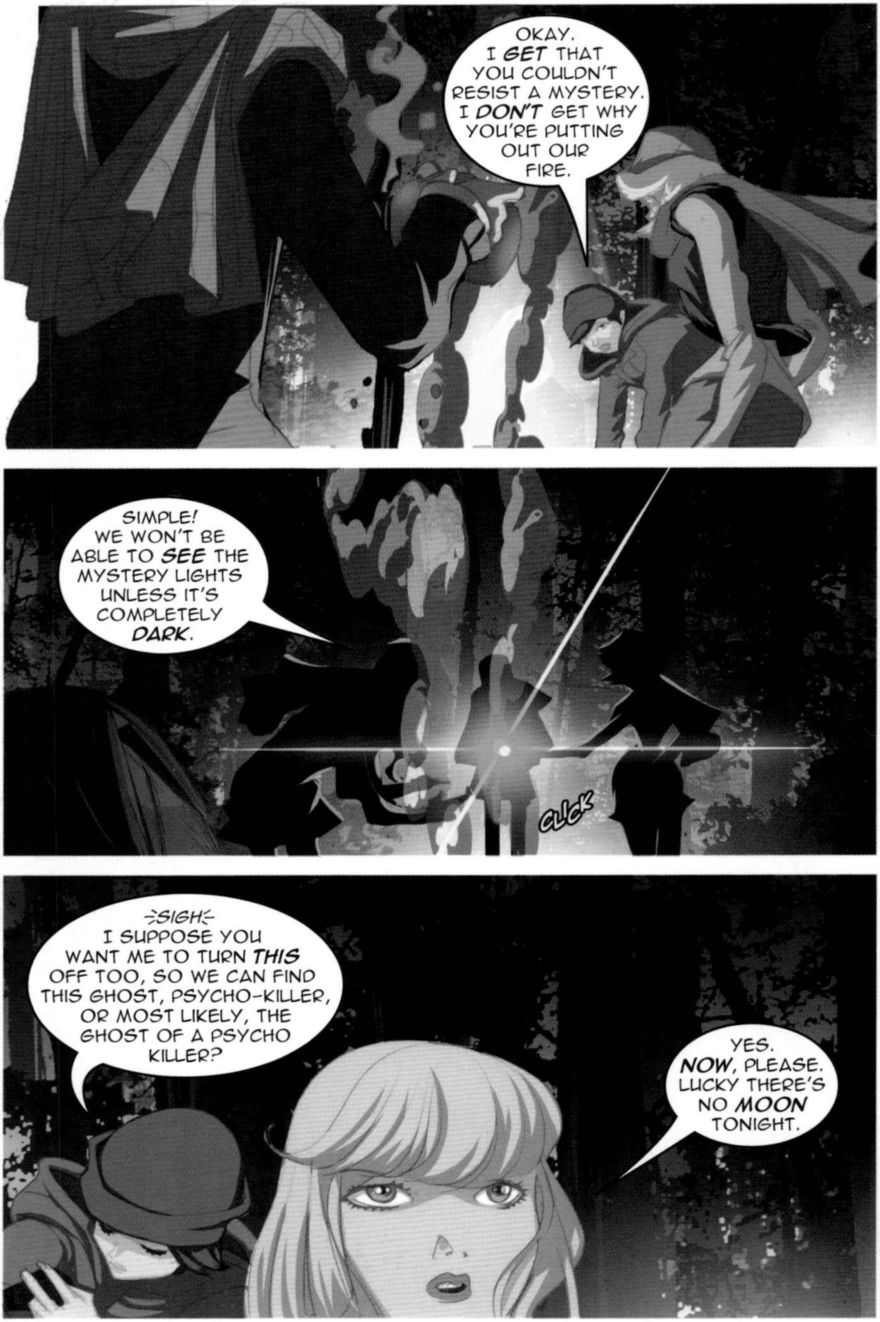
OKAY. I **GET** THAT YOU COULDN'T RESIST A MYSTERY. I **DON'T** GET WHY YOU'RE PUTTING OUT OUR FIRE.
SIMPLE! WE WON'T BE ABLE TO **SEE** THE MYSTERY LIGHTS UNLESS IT'S COMPLETELY **DARK**.
CLICK
SIGH I SUPPOSE YOU WANT ME TO TURN **THIS** OFF TOO, SO WE CAN FIND THIS GHOST, PSYCHO-KILLER, OR MOST LIKELY, THE GHOST OF A PSYCHO KILLER?
YES. **NOW**, PLEASE. LUCKY THERE'S NO **MOON** TONIGHT.

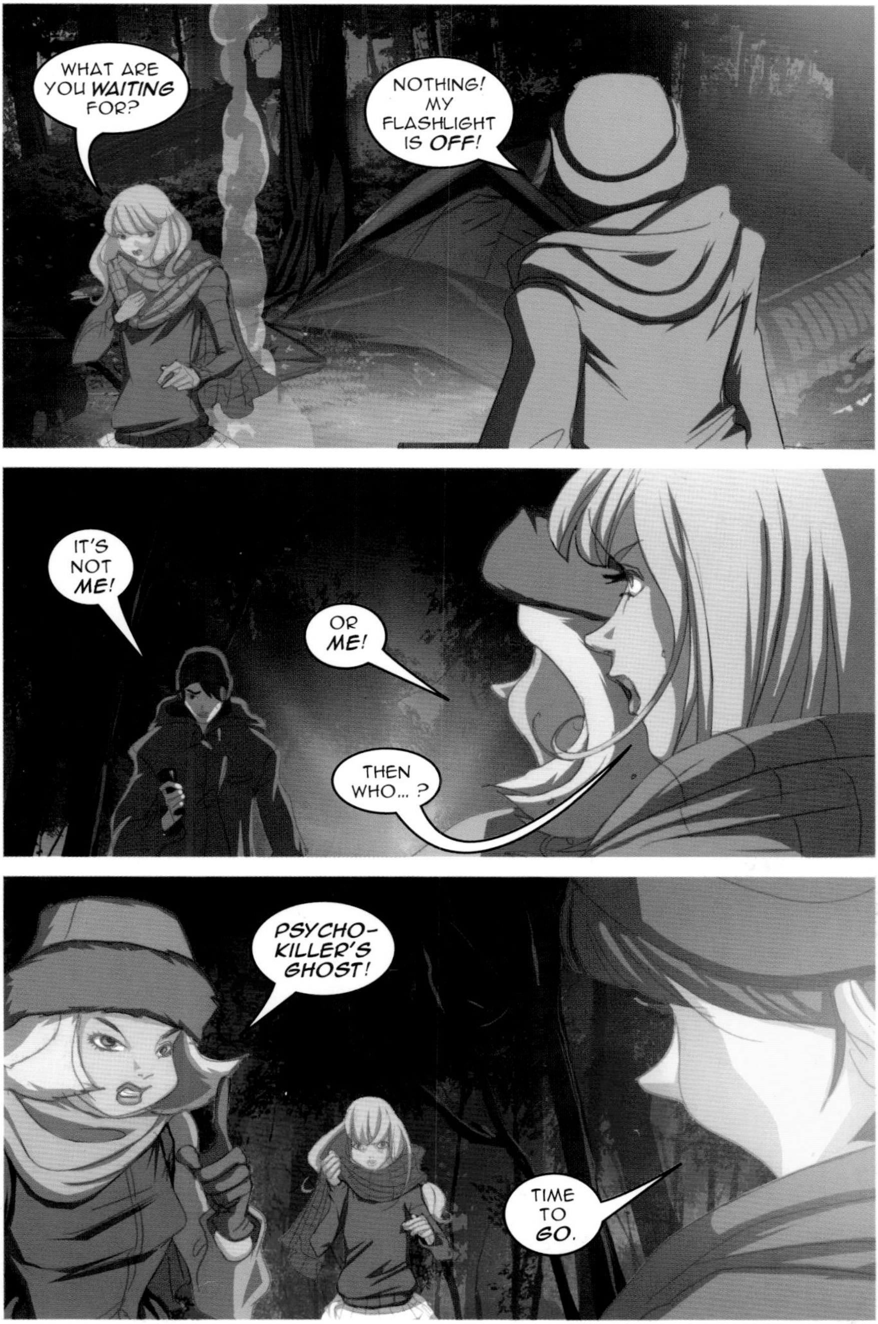
WHAT ARE YOU WAITING FOR?
NOTHING! MY FLASHLIGHT IS OFF!
IT'S NOT ME!
OR ME!
THEN WHO... ?
PSYCHO-KILLER'S GHOST!
TIME TO GO.

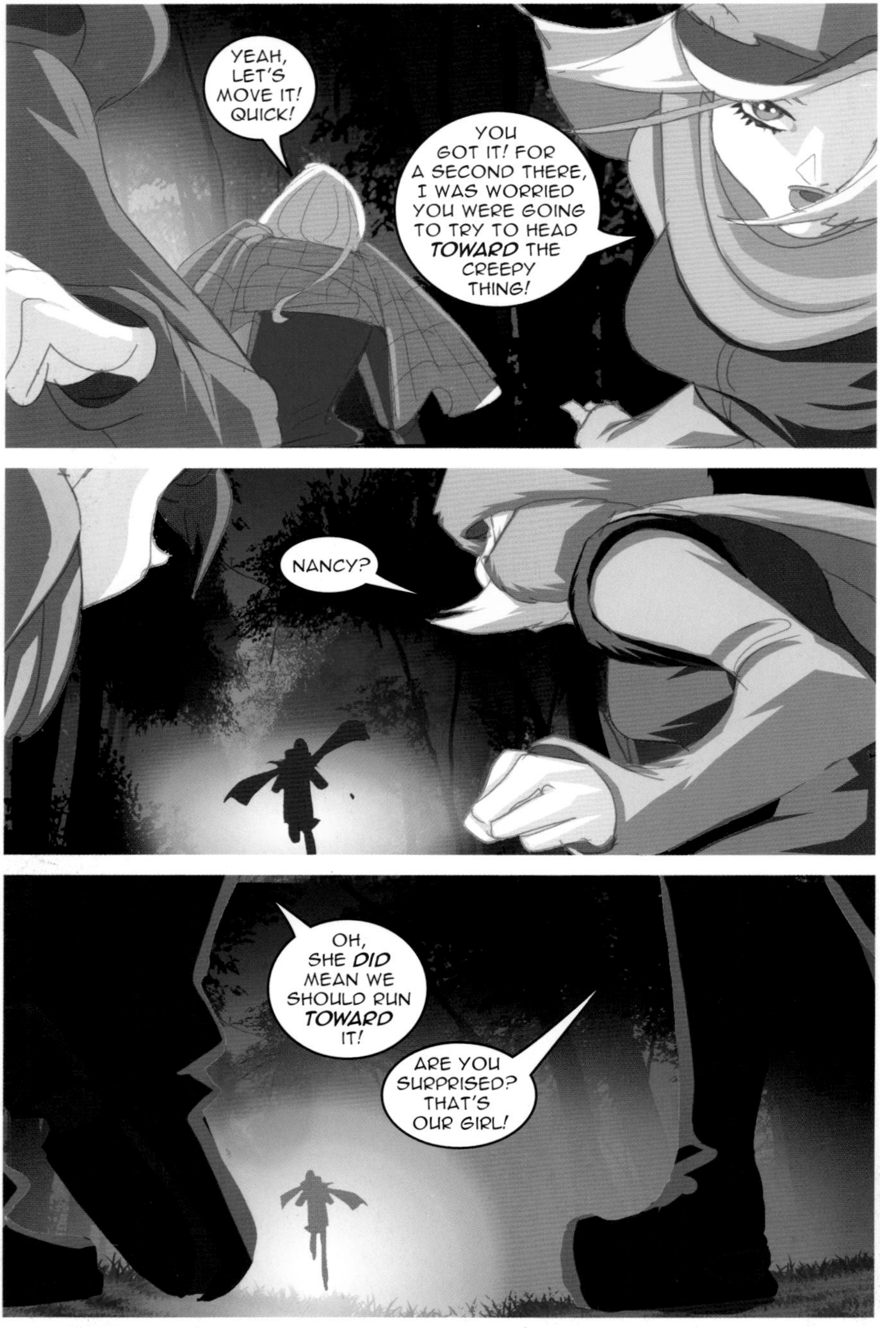
YEAH, LET'S MOVE IT! QUICK!
YOU GOT IT! FOR A SECOND THERE, I WAS WORRIED YOU WERE GOING TO TRY TO HEAD *TOWARD* THE CREEPY THING!
NANCY?
OH, SHE *DID* MEAN WE SHOULD RUN *TOWARD* IT!
ARE YOU SURPRISED? THAT'S OUR GIRL!

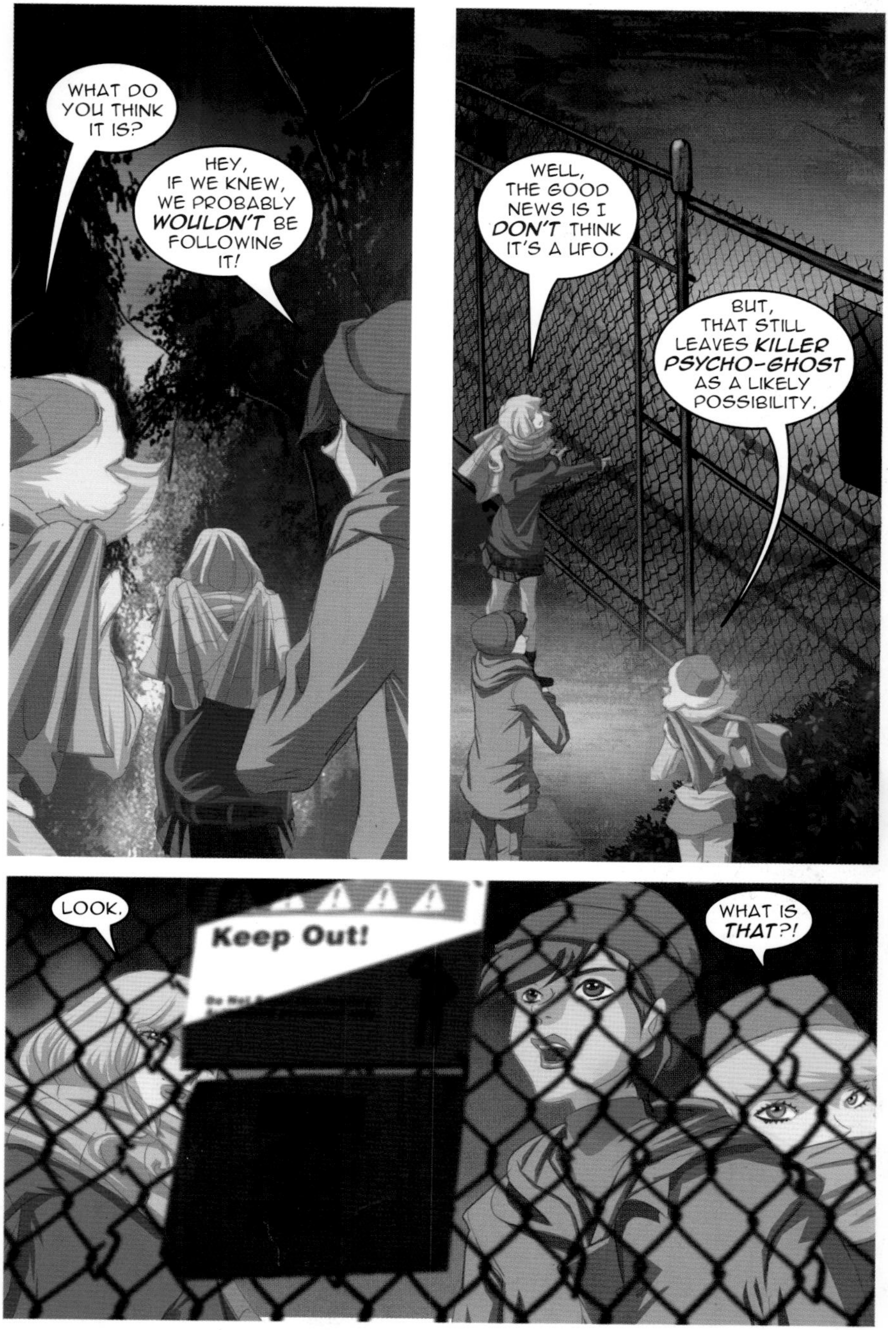
WHAT DO YOU THINK IT IS?
HEY, IF WE KNEW, WE PROBABLY **WOULDN'T** BE FOLLOWING IT!
WELL, THE GOOD NEWS IS I **DON'T** THINK IT'S A UFO.
BUT, THAT STILL LEAVES **KILLER PSYCHO-GHOST** AS A LIKELY POSSIBILITY.
LOOK.
Keep Out!
WHAT IS **THAT**?!

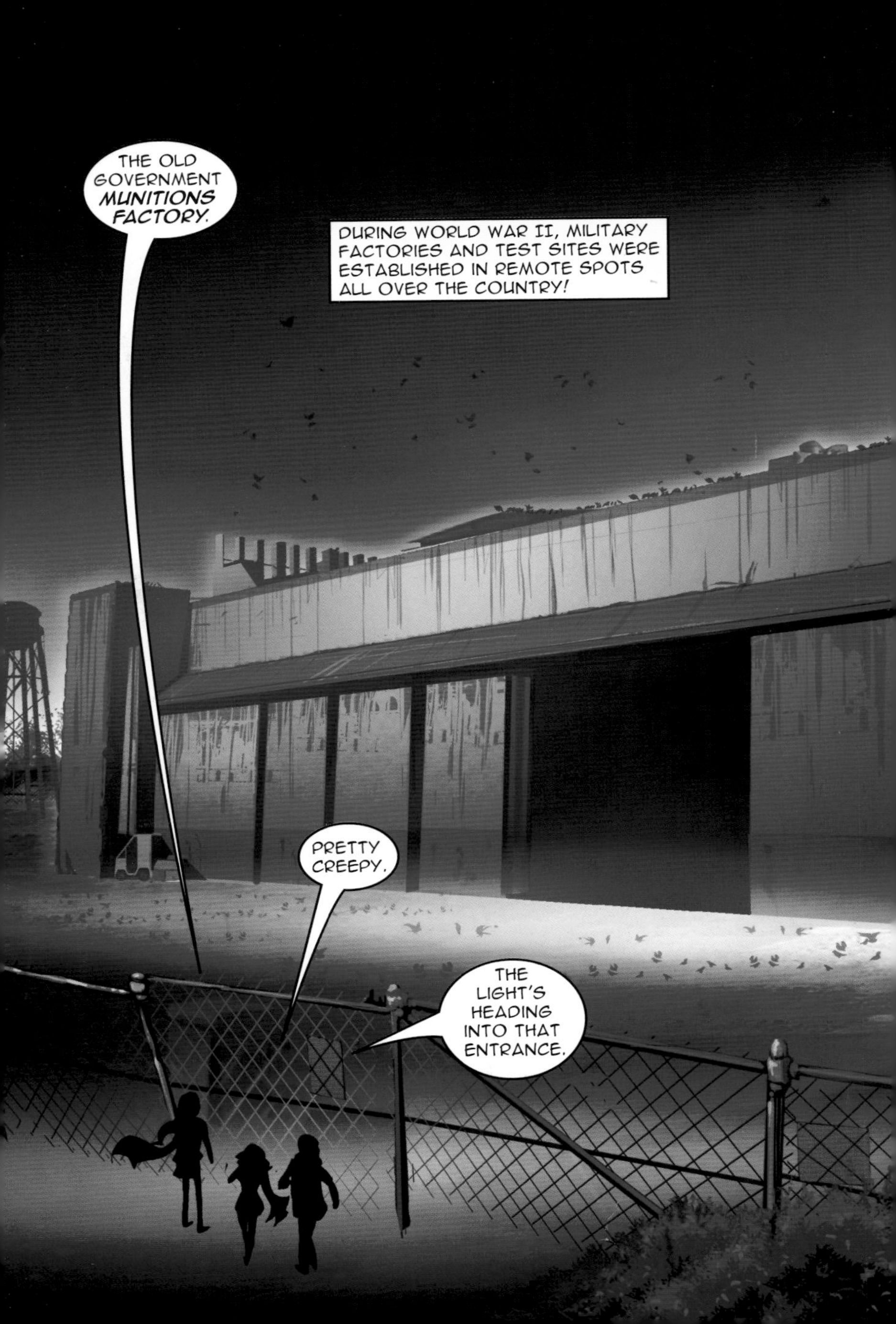
THE OLD GOVERNMENT MUNITIONS FACTORY.
DURING WORLD WAR II, MILITARY FACTORIES AND TEST SITES WERE ESTABLISHED IN REMOTE SPOTS ALL OVER THE COUNTRY!
PRETTY CREEPY.
THE LIGHT'S HEADING INTO THAT ENTRANCE.

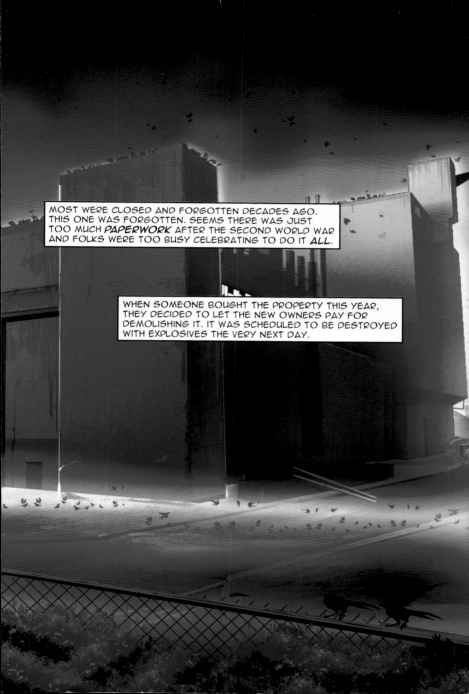

MOST WERE CLOSED AND FORGOTTEN DECADES AGO. THIS ONE WAS FORGOTTEN. SEEMS THERE WAS JUST TOO MUCH *PAPERWORK* AFTER THE SECOND WORLD WAR AND FOLKS WERE TOO BUSY CELEBRATING TO DO IT *ALL*.

WHEN SOMEONE BOUGHT THE PROPERTY THIS YEAR, THEY DECIDED TO LET THE NEW OWNERS PAY FOR DEMOLISHING IT. IT WAS SCHEDULED TO BE DESTROYED WITH EXPLOSIVES THE VERY NEXT DAY.

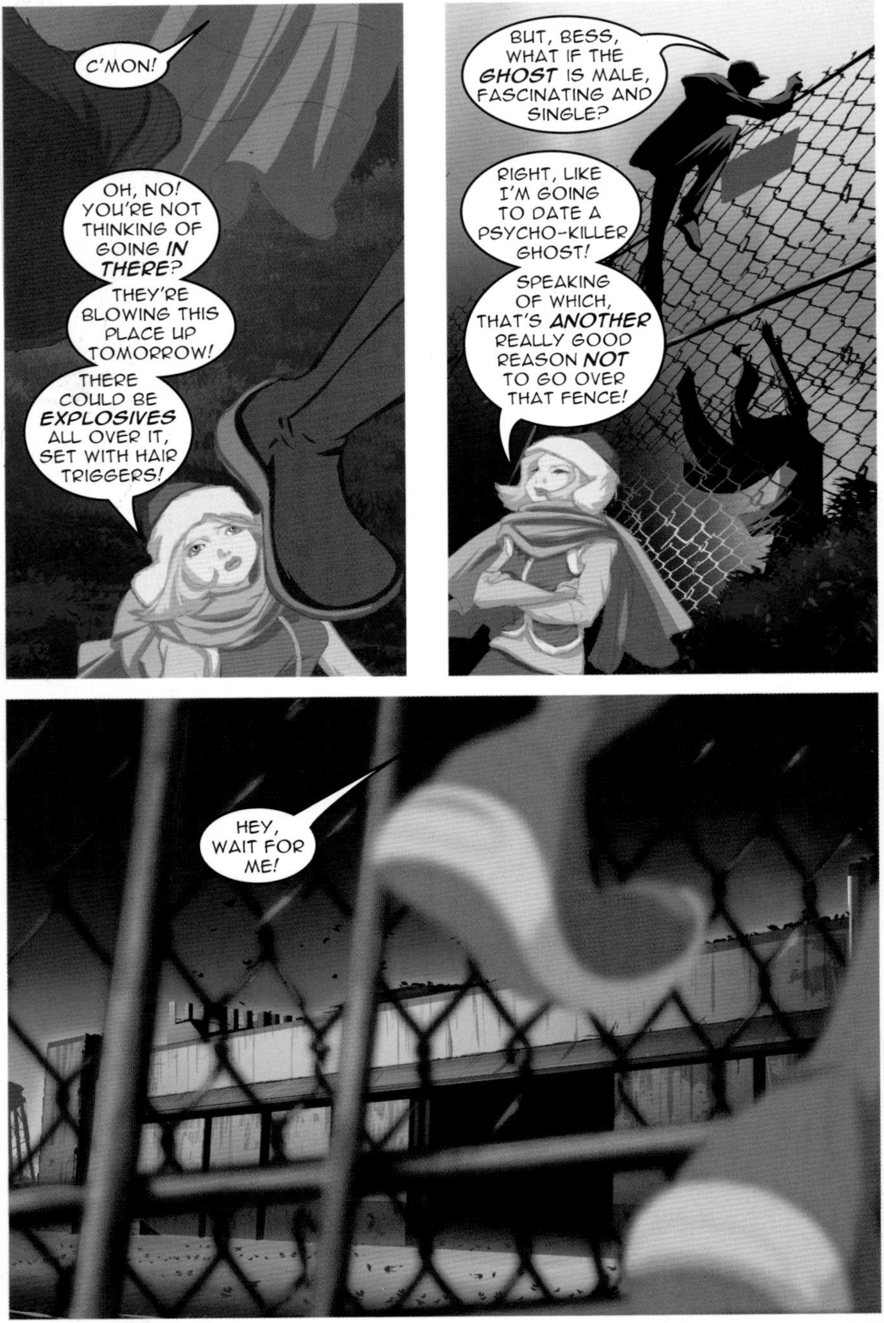
C'MON!
OH, NO! YOU'RE NOT THINKING OF GOING ***IN THERE***?
THEY'RE BLOWING THIS PLACE UP TOMORROW!
THERE COULD BE ***EXPLOSIVES*** ALL OVER IT, SET WITH HAIR TRIGGERS!
BUT, BESS, WHAT IF THE ***GHOST*** IS MALE, FASCINATING AND SINGLE?
RIGHT, LIKE I'M GOING TO DATE A PSYCHO-KILLER GHOST!
SPEAKING OF WHICH, THAT'S ***ANOTHER*** REALLY GOOD REASON ***NOT*** TO GO OVER THAT FENCE!
HEY, WAIT FOR ME!

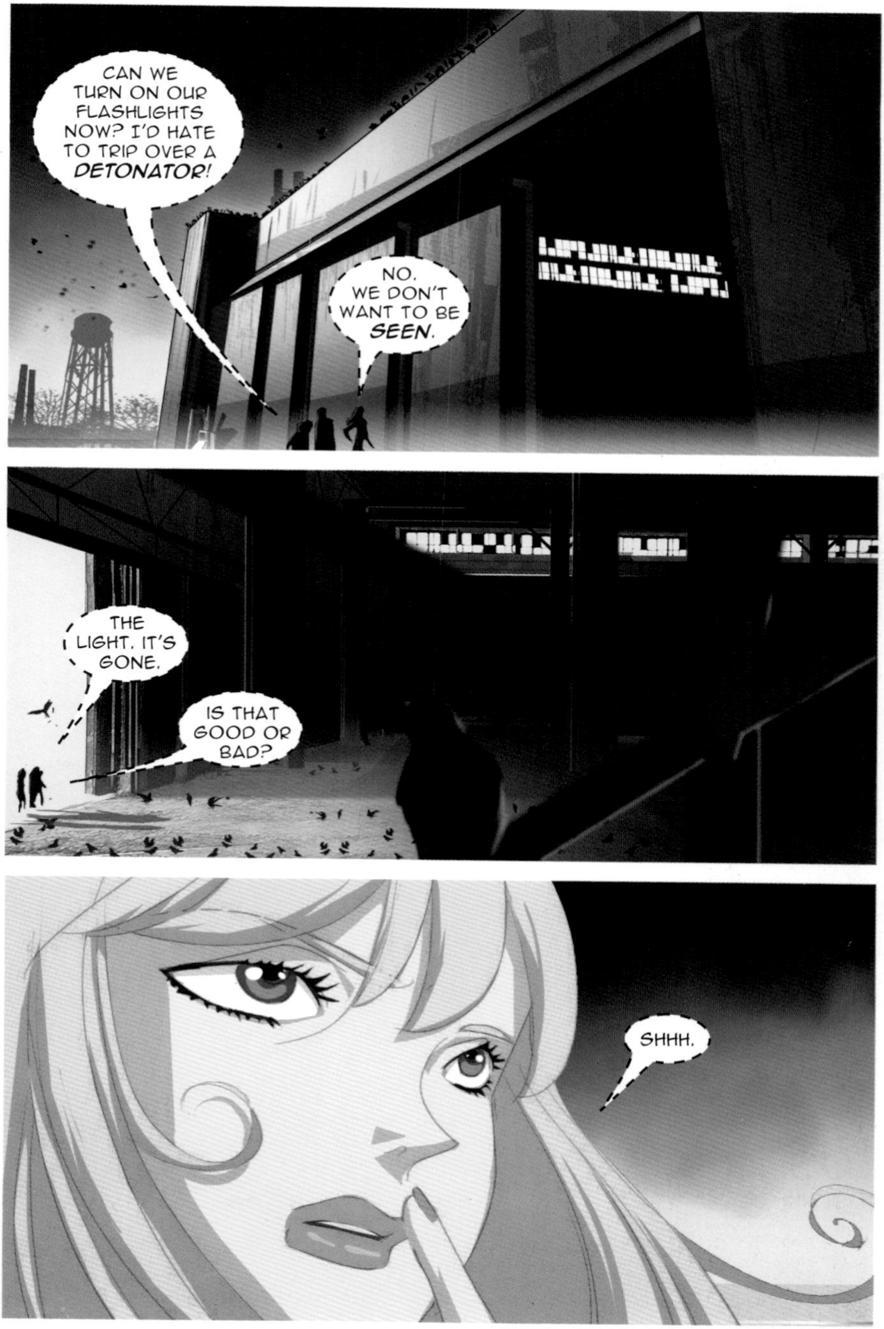
CAN WE TURN ON OUR FLASHLIGHTS NOW? I'D HATE TO TRIP OVER A *DETONATOR*!
NO. WE DON'T WANT TO BE *SEEN*.
THE LIGHT. IT'S GONE.
IS THAT GOOD OR BAD?
SHHH.

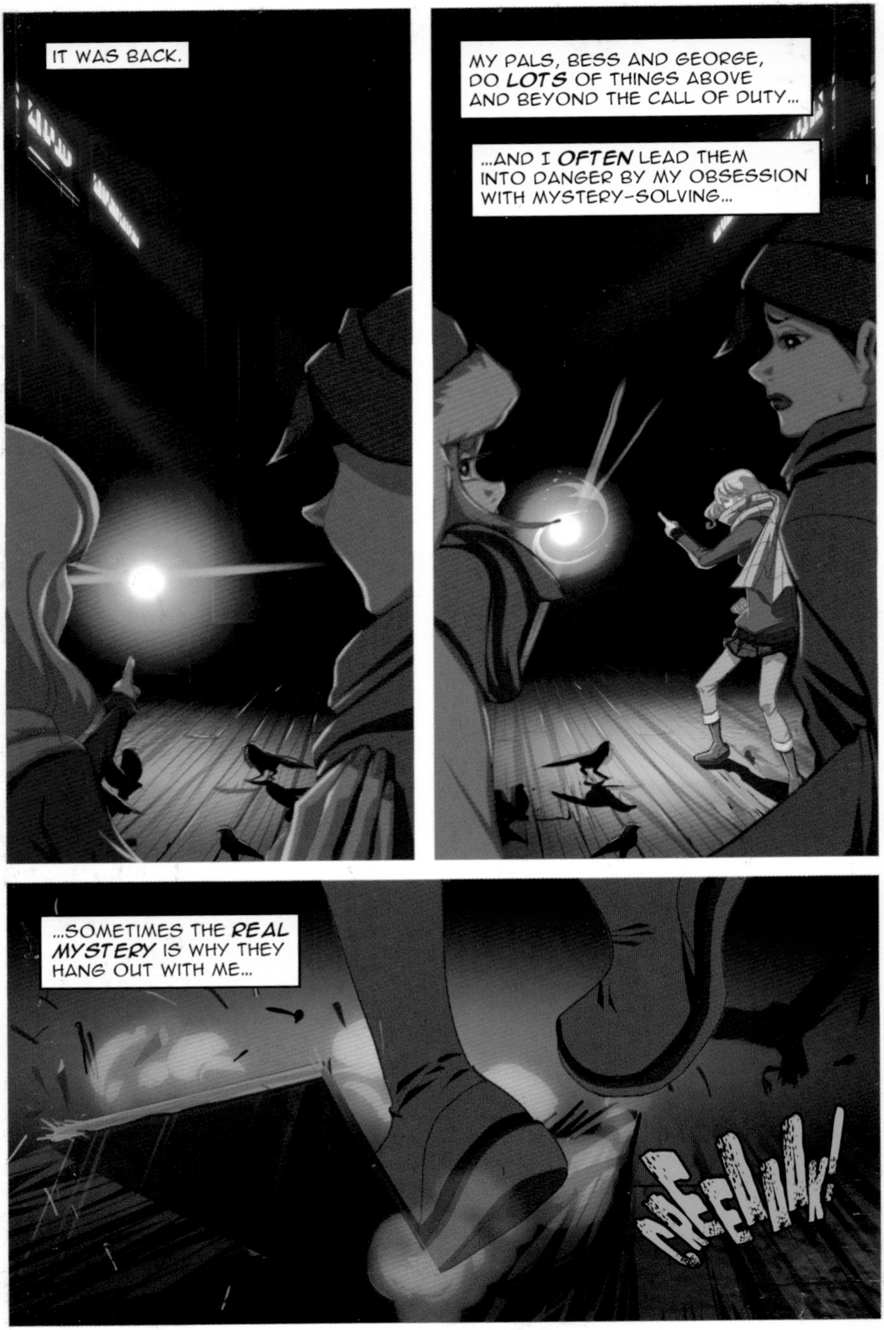
IT WAS BACK.
MY PALS, BESS AND GEORGE, DO LOTS OF THINGS ABOVE AND BEYOND THE CALL OF DUTY...
...AND I OFTEN LEAD THEM INTO DANGER BY MY OBSESSION WITH MYSTERY-SOLVING...
...SOMETIMES THE REAL MYSTERY IS WHY THEY HANG OUT WITH ME...
CREEAAK!

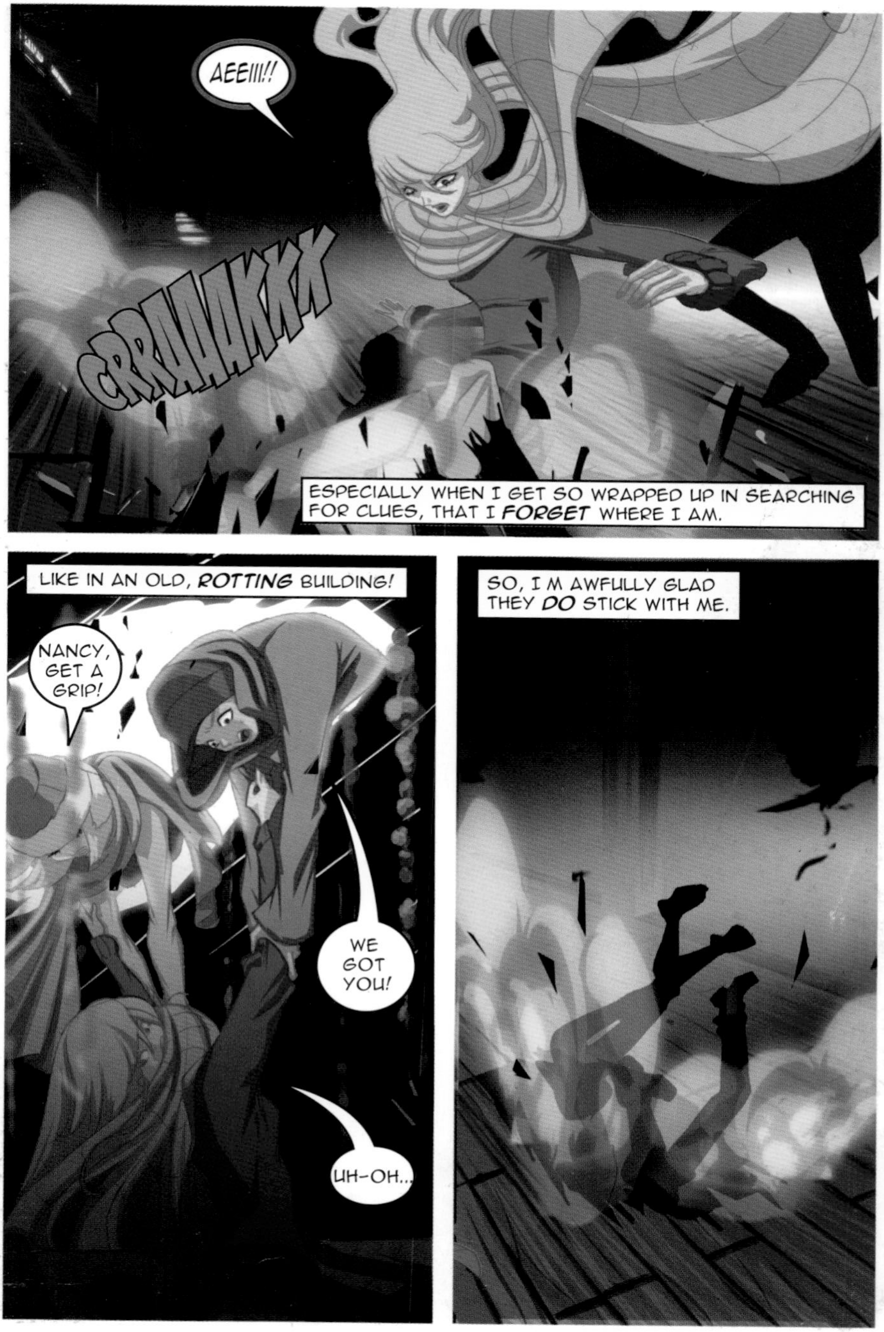
AEEIII!!
CRRAAAKKX
ESPECIALLY WHEN I GET SO WRAPPED UP IN SEARCHING FOR CLUES, THAT I FORGET WHERE I AM.
LIKE IN AN OLD, ROTTING BUILDING!
NANCY, GET A GRIP!
WE GOT YOU!
UH-OH...
SO, I M AWFULLY GLAD THEY DO STICK WITH ME.

BUT I'M NOT SURE IT'S THE *SMARTEST* THING THEY COULD DO.

EEEEAAA!!!!

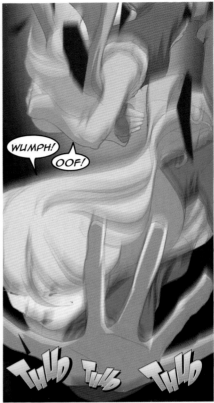

WUMPH!

OOF!

THUD THUD THUD

MAYBE FOLLOWING SOMEONE INTO DEATH-DEFYING ADVENTURES AGAIN AND AGAIN IS WHAT FRIENDSHIP IS ALL ABOUT!

UNNNK.

IN FACT, I WAS THINKING HOW *SWELL* THEY WERE, JUST BEFORE I PASSED OUT! I DON'T KNOW *WHAT* THEY WERE THINKING OF ME.

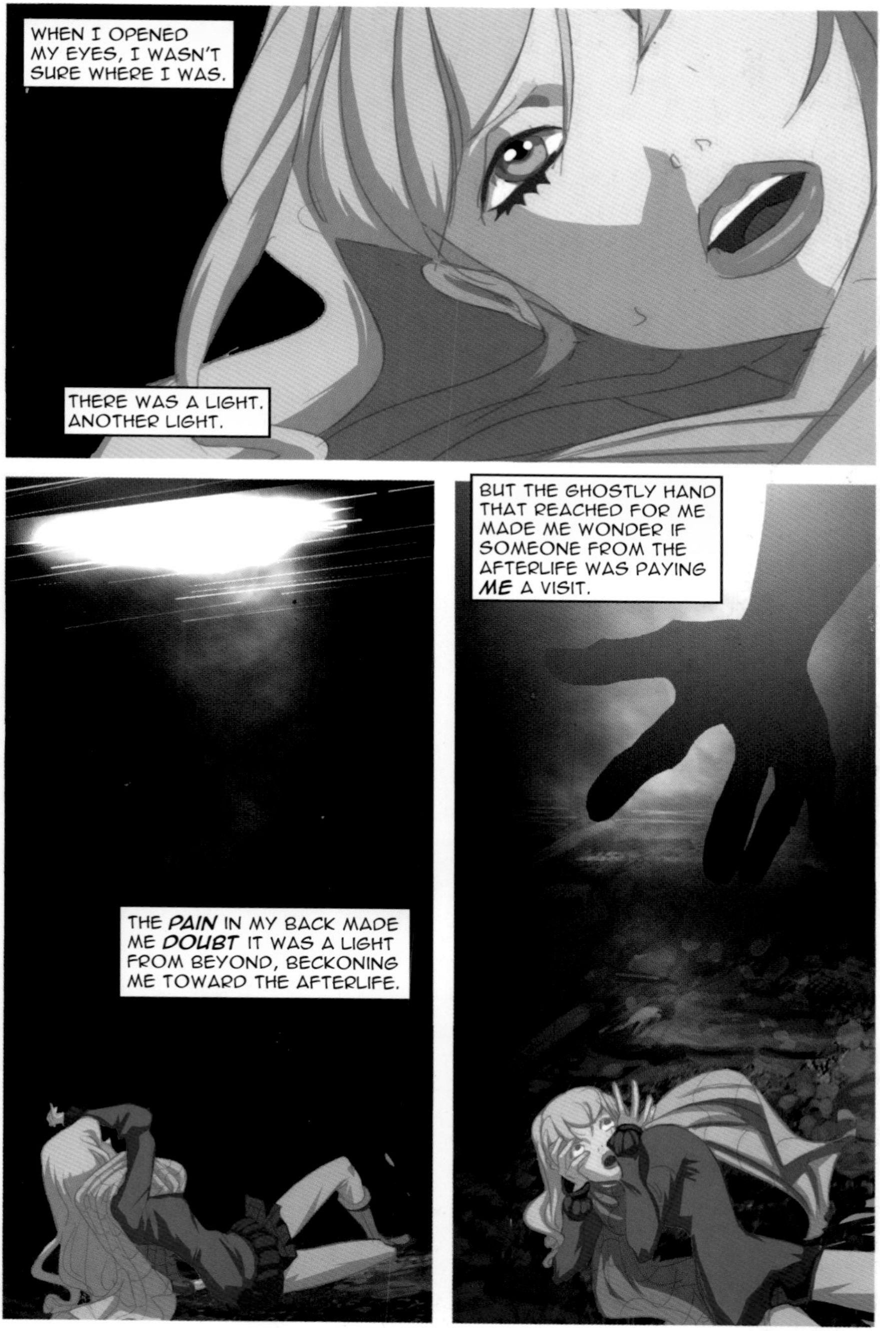
WHEN I OPENED MY EYES, I WASN'T SURE WHERE I WAS.
THERE WAS A LIGHT. ANOTHER LIGHT.
THE PAIN IN MY BACK MADE ME DOUBT IT WAS A LIGHT FROM BEYOND, BECKONING ME TOWARD THE AFTERLIFE.
BUT THE GHOSTLY HAND THAT REACHED FOR ME MADE ME WONDER IF SOMEONE FROM THE AFTERLIFE WAS PAYING ME A VISIT.

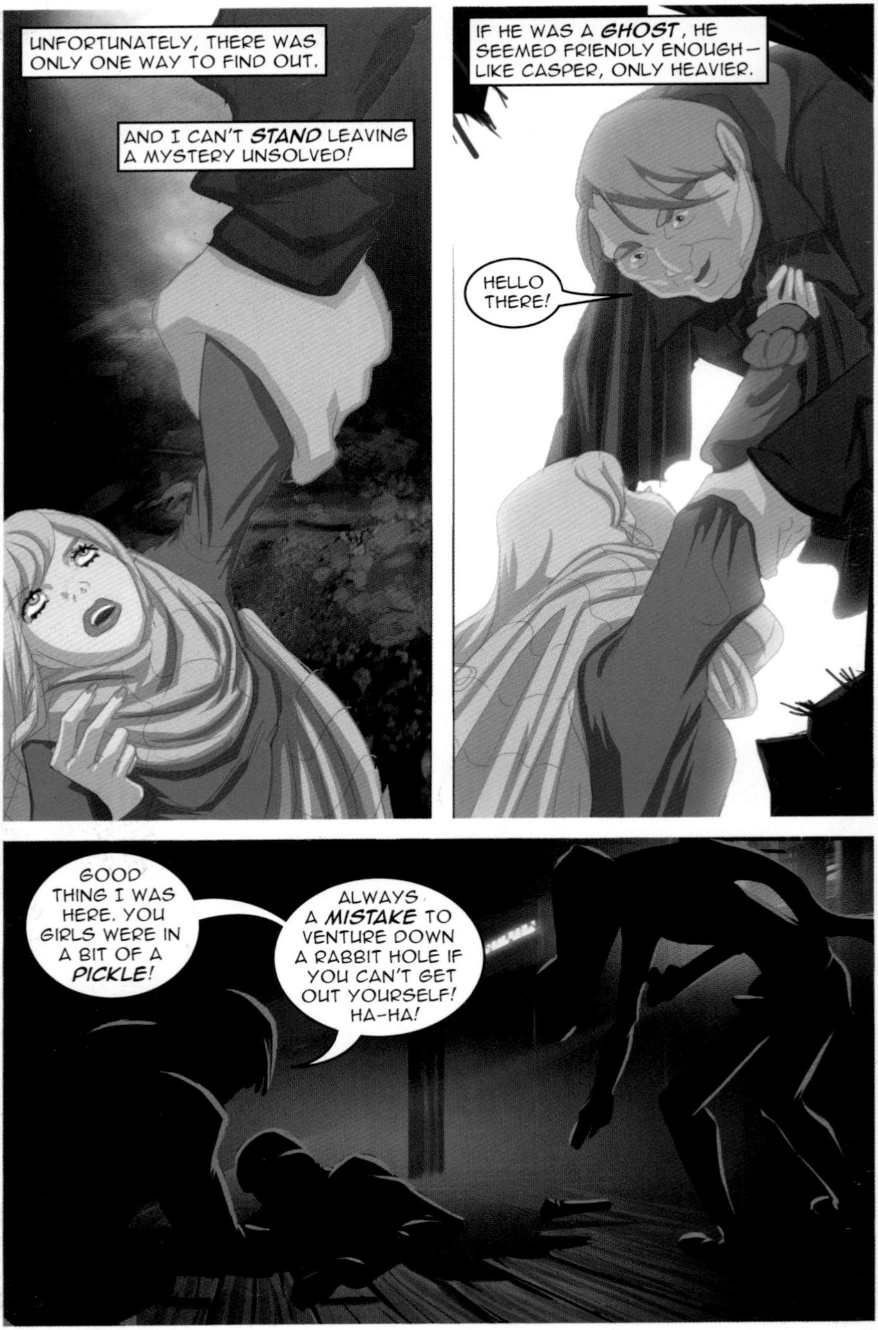
UNFORTUNATELY, THERE WAS ONLY ONE WAY TO FIND OUT.
AND I CAN'T STAND LEAVING A MYSTERY UNSOLVED!
IF HE WAS A GHOST, HE SEEMED FRIENDLY ENOUGH— LIKE CASPER, ONLY HEAVIER.
HELLO THERE!
GOOD THING I WAS HERE. YOU GIRLS WERE IN A BIT OF A PICKLE!
ALWAYS A MISTAKE TO VENTURE DOWN A RABBIT HOLE IF YOU CAN'T GET OUT YOURSELF! HA-HA!

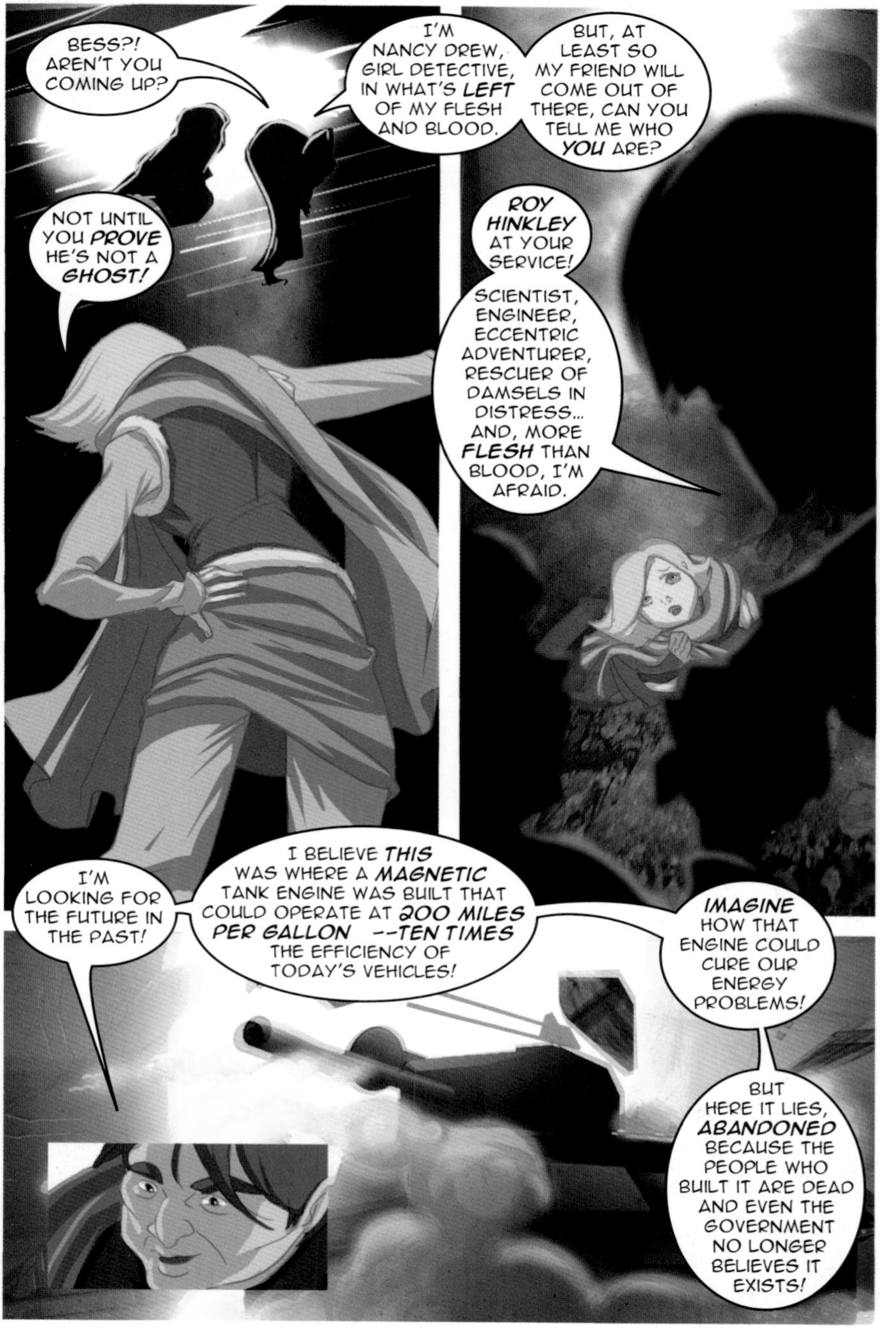
BESS?! AREN'T YOU COMING UP?
I'M NANCY DREW, GIRL DETECTIVE, IN WHAT'S *LEFT* OF MY FLESH AND BLOOD.
NOT UNTIL YOU *PROVE* HE'S NOT A *GHOST!*
BUT, AT LEAST SO MY FRIEND WILL COME OUT OF THERE, CAN YOU TELL ME WHO *YOU* ARE?
ROY HINKLEY AT YOUR SERVICE!
SCIENTIST, ENGINEER, ECCENTRIC ADVENTURER, RESCUER OF DAMSELS IN DISTRESS... AND, MORE *FLESH* THAN BLOOD, I'M AFRAID.
I'M LOOKING FOR THE FUTURE IN THE PAST!
I BELIEVE *THIS* WAS WHERE A *MAGNETIC* TANK ENGINE WAS BUILT THAT COULD OPERATE AT *200 MILES PER GALLON --TEN TIMES* THE EFFICIENCY OF TODAY'S VEHICLES!
IMAGINE HOW THAT ENGINE COULD CURE OUR ENERGY PROBLEMS!
BUT HERE IT LIES, *ABANDONED* BECAUSE THE PEOPLE WHO BUILT IT ARE DEAD AND EVEN THE GOVERNMENT NO LONGER BELIEVES IT EXISTS!

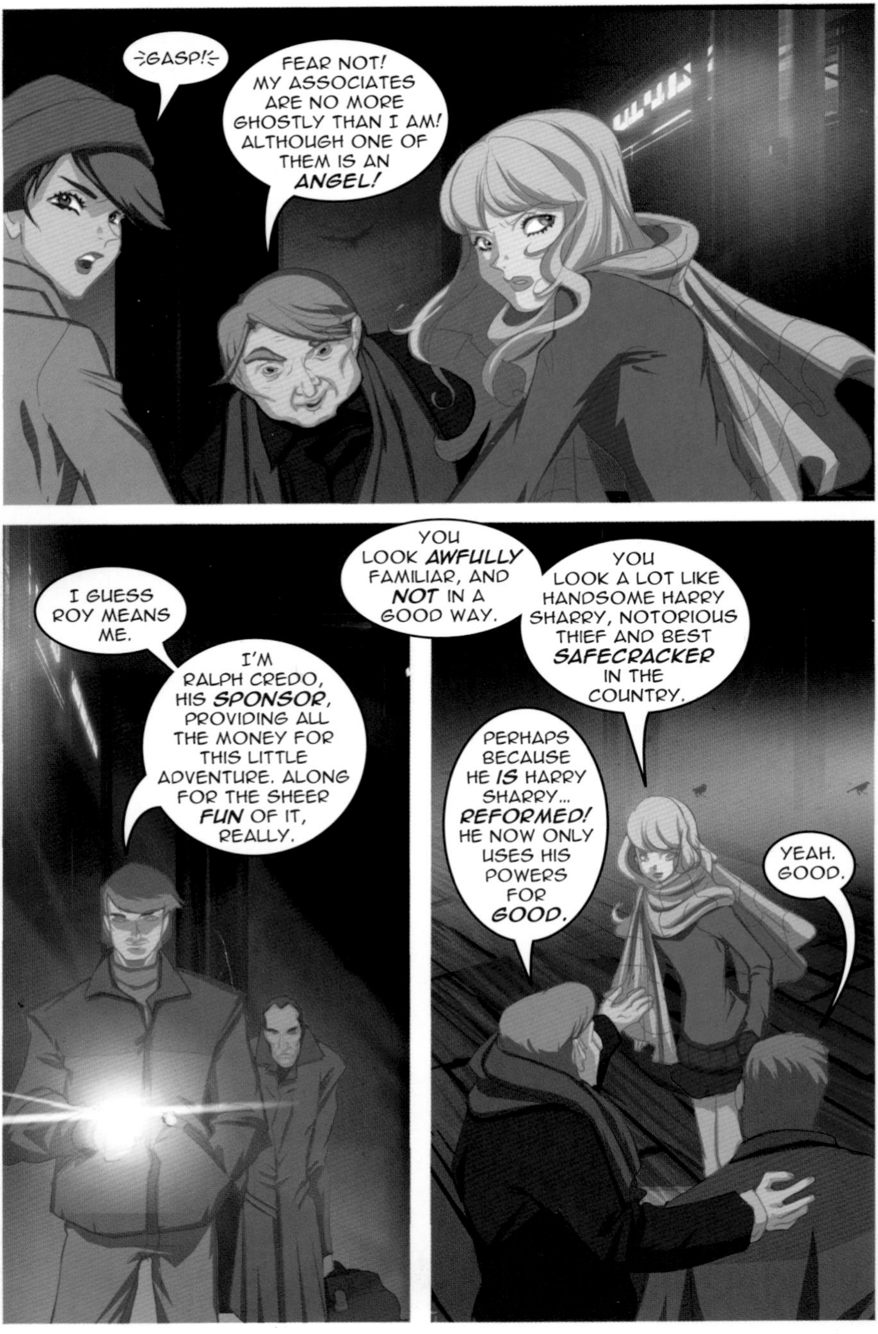

-GASP!-
FEAR NOT! MY ASSOCIATES ARE NO MORE GHOSTLY THAN I AM! ALTHOUGH ONE OF THEM IS AN ANGEL!
I GUESS ROY MEANS ME.
I'M RALPH CREDO, HIS SPONSOR, PROVIDING ALL THE MONEY FOR THIS LITTLE ADVENTURE. ALONG FOR THE SHEER FUN OF IT, REALLY.
YOU LOOK AWFULLY FAMILIAR, AND NOT IN A GOOD WAY.
YOU LOOK A LOT LIKE HANDSOME HARRY SHARRY, NOTORIOUS THIEF AND BEST SAFECRACKER IN THE COUNTRY.
PERHAPS BECAUSE HE IS HARRY SHARRY... REFORMED! HE NOW ONLY USES HIS POWERS FOR GOOD.
YEAH. GOOD.

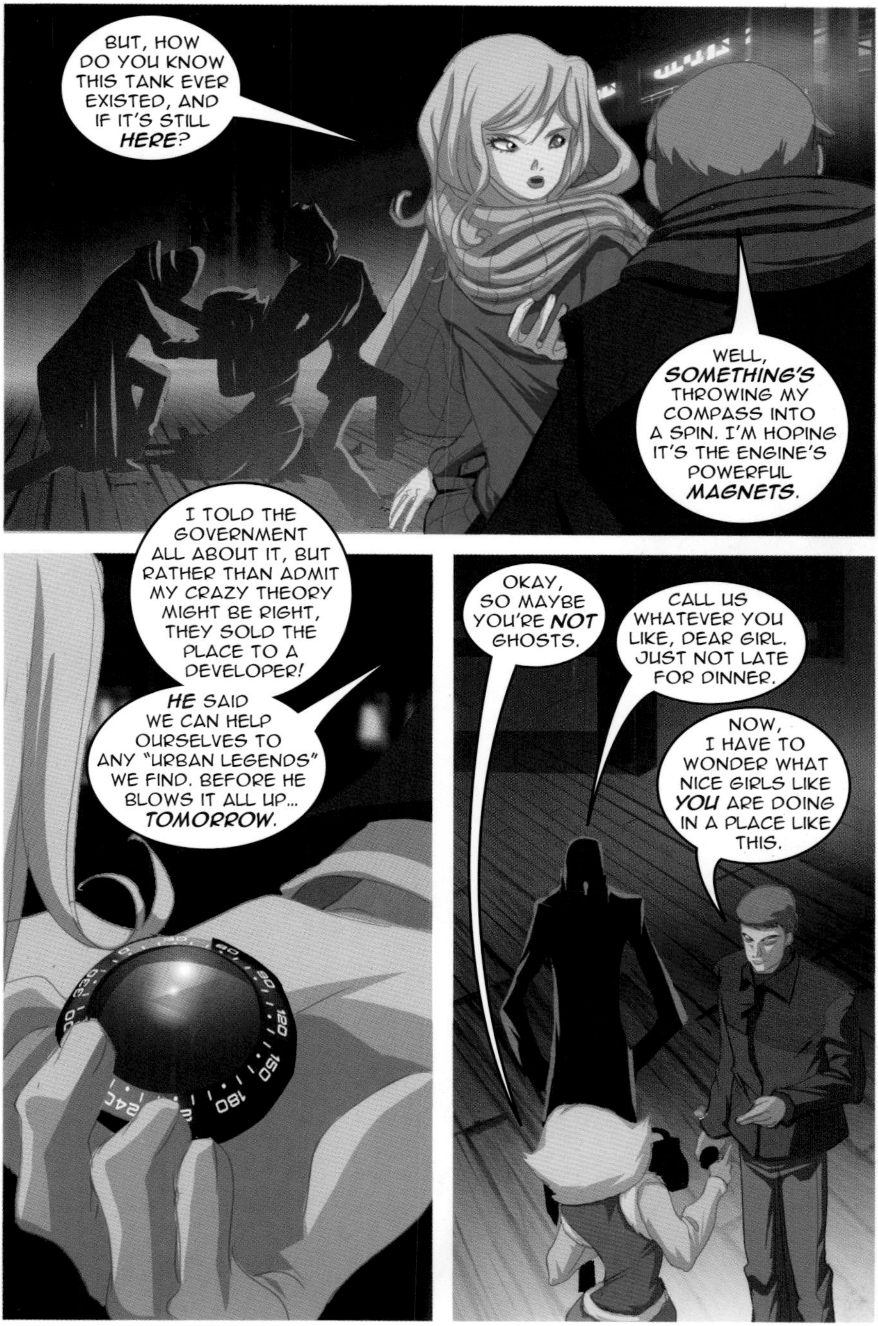
BUT, HOW DO YOU KNOW THIS TANK EVER EXISTED, AND IF IT'S STILL *HERE*?
WELL, *SOMETHING'S* THROWING MY COMPASS INTO A SPIN. I'M HOPING IT'S THE ENGINE'S POWERFUL *MAGNETS*.
I TOLD THE GOVERNMENT ALL ABOUT IT, BUT RATHER THAN ADMIT MY CRAZY THEORY MIGHT BE RIGHT, THEY SOLD THE PLACE TO A DEVELOPER!
HE SAID WE CAN HELP OURSELVES TO ANY "URBAN LEGENDS" WE FIND. BEFORE HE BLOWS IT ALL UP... *TOMORROW*.
OKAY, SO MAYBE YOU'RE *NOT* GHOSTS.
CALL US WHATEVER YOU LIKE, DEAR GIRL. JUST NOT LATE FOR DINNER.
NOW, I HAVE TO WONDER WHAT NICE GIRLS LIKE *YOU* ARE DOING IN A PLACE LIKE THIS.

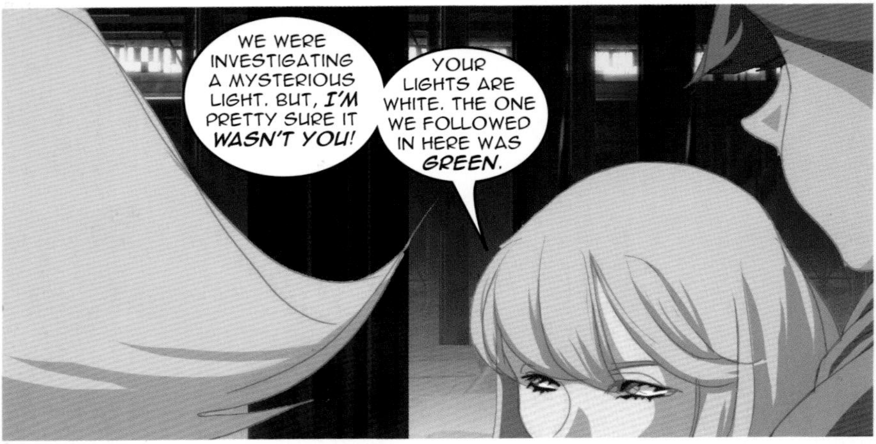
WE WERE INVESTIGATING A MYSTERIOUS LIGHT. BUT, I'M PRETTY SURE IT WASN'T YOU!
YOUR LIGHTS ARE WHITE. THE ONE WE FOLLOWED IN HERE WAS GREEN.

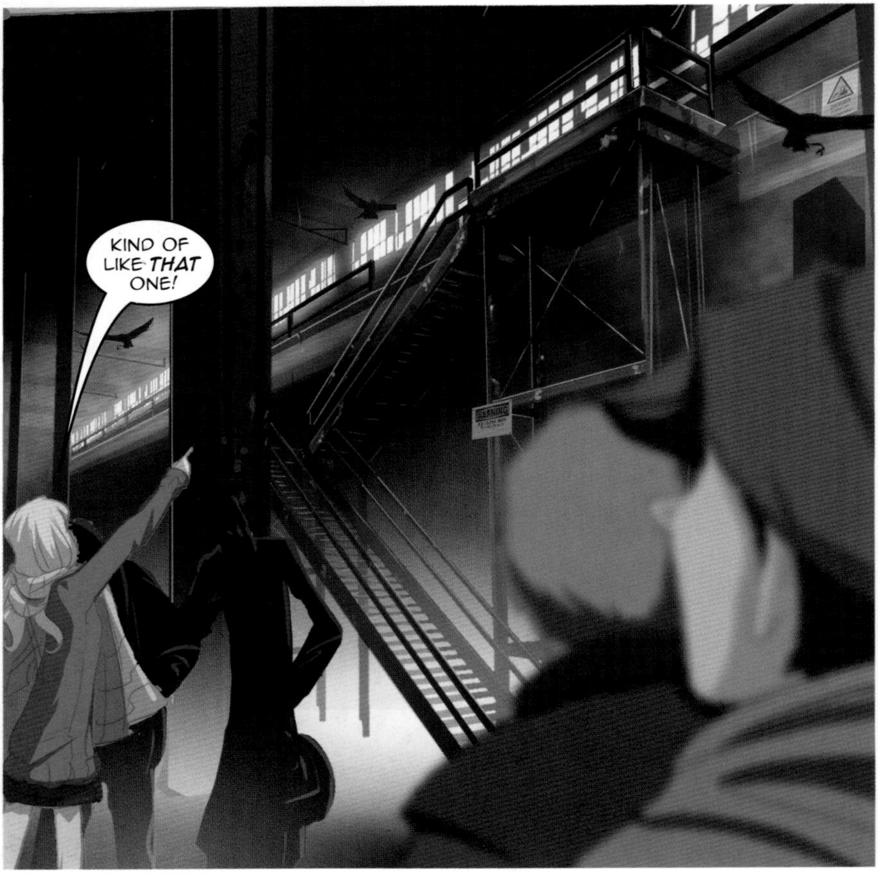
KIND OF LIKE THAT ONE!

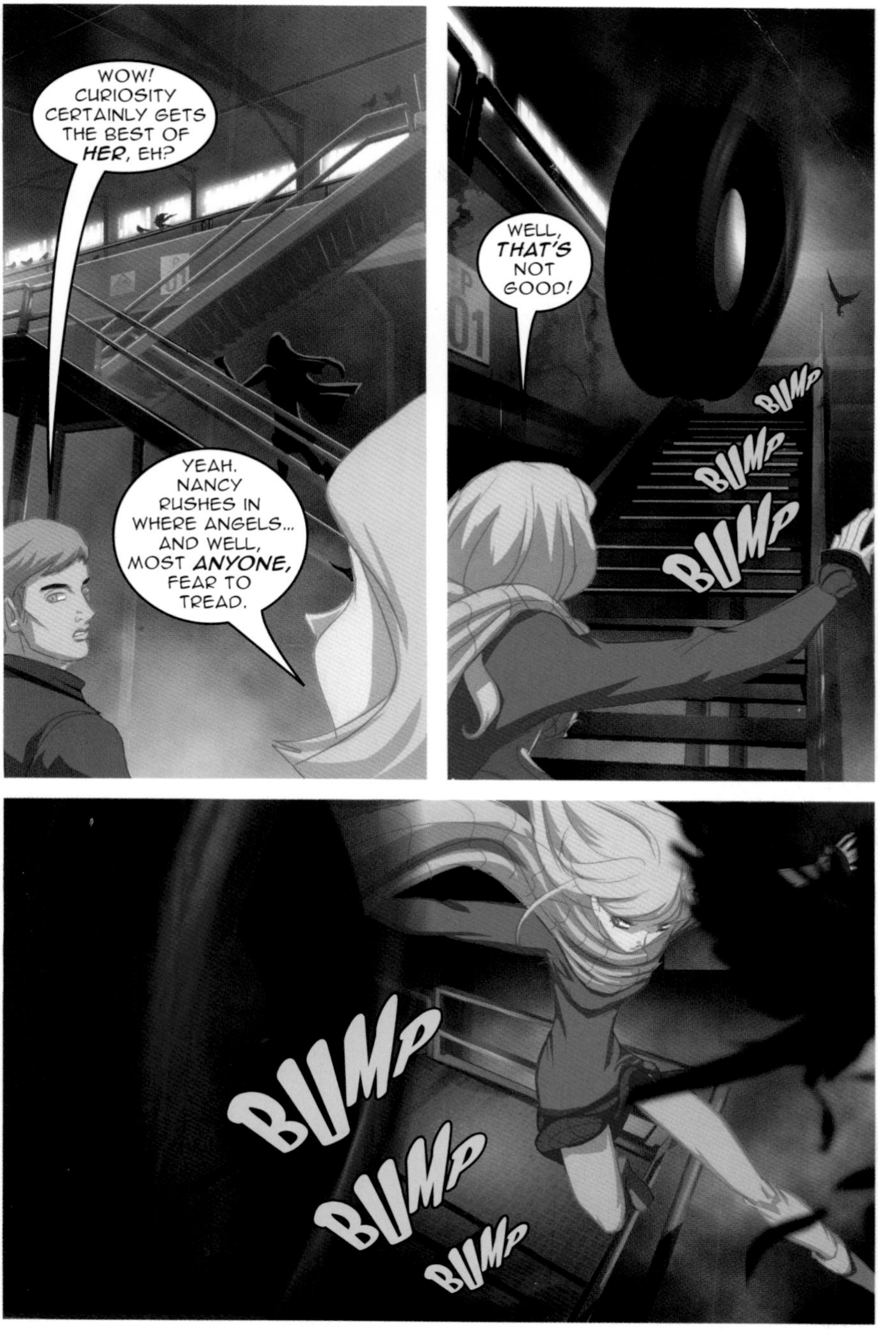
WOW! CURIOSITY CERTAINLY GETS THE BEST OF *HER*, EH?
YEAH. NANCY RUSHES IN WHERE ANGELS... AND WELL, MOST *ANYONE,* FEAR TO TREAD.
WELL, *THAT'S* NOT GOOD!
BUMP
BUMP
BUMP
BUMP
BUMP
BUMP

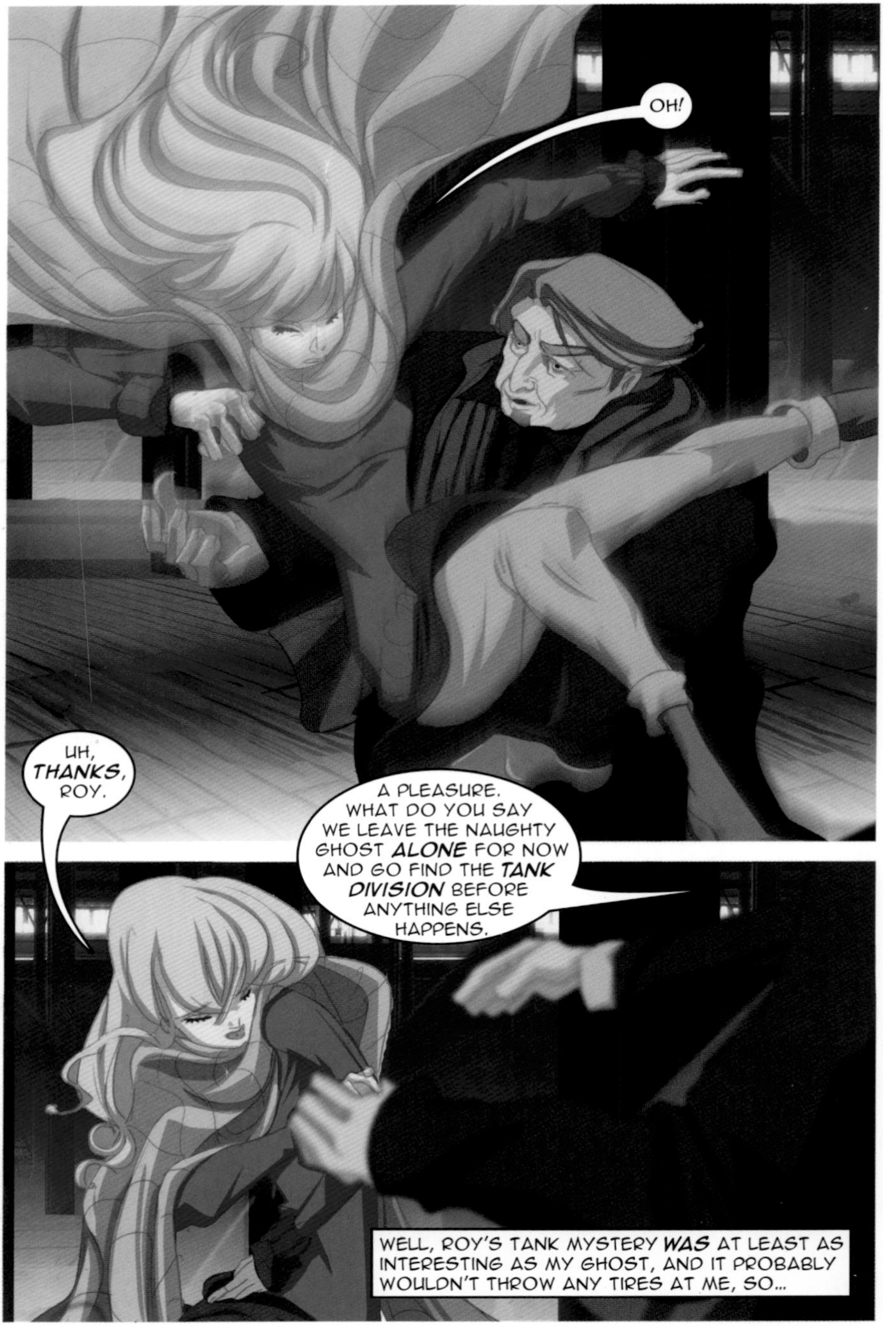
OH!
UH, THANKS, ROY.
A PLEASURE. WHAT DO YOU SAY WE LEAVE THE NAUGHTY GHOST ALONE FOR NOW AND GO FIND THE TANK DIVISION BEFORE ANYTHING ELSE HAPPENS.
WELL, ROY'S TANK MYSTERY WAS AT LEAST AS INTERESTING AS MY GHOST, AND IT PROBABLY WOULDN'T THROW ANY TIRES AT ME, SO...

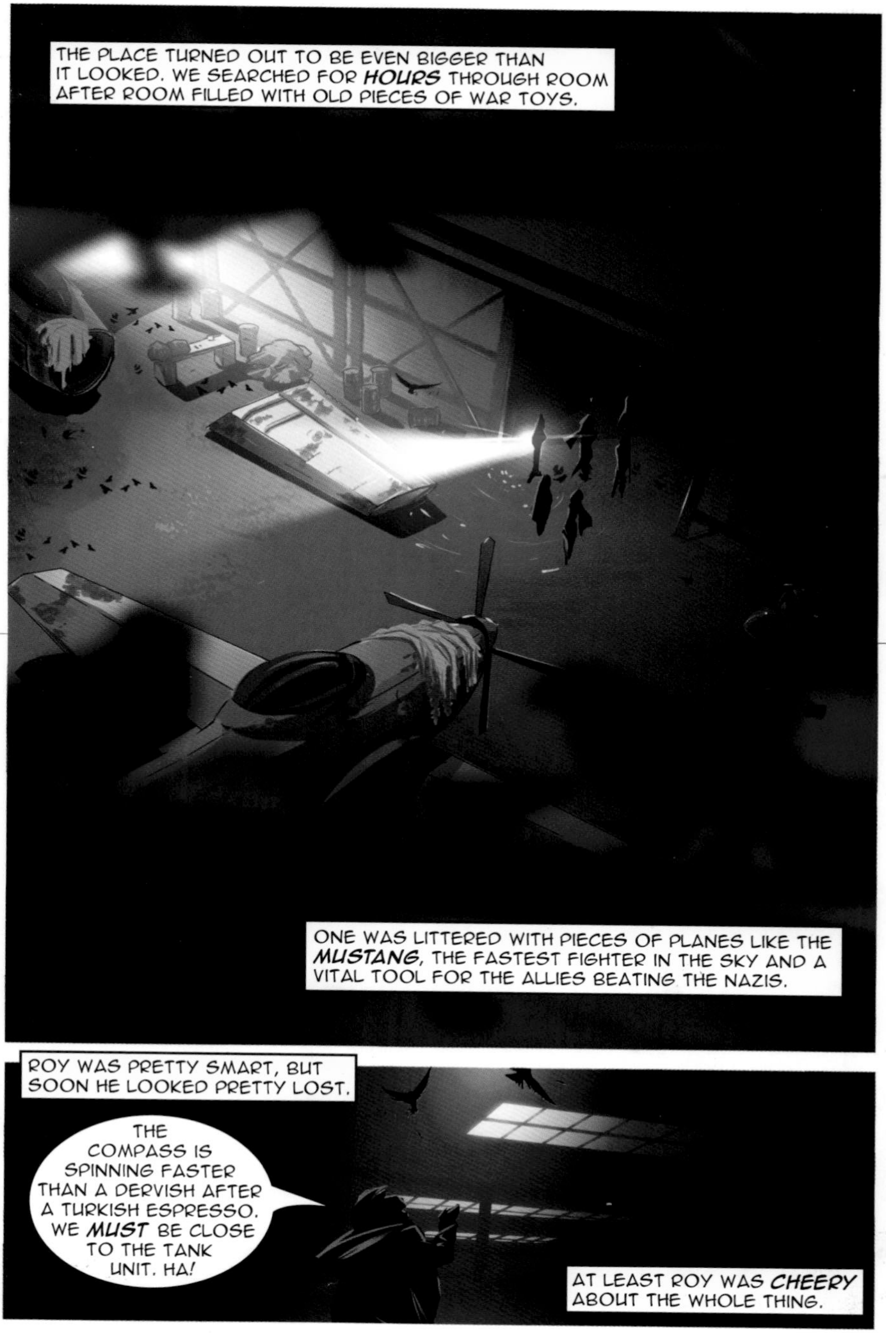
THE PLACE TURNED OUT TO BE EVEN BIGGER THAN IT LOOKED. WE SEARCHED FOR *HOURS* THROUGH ROOM AFTER ROOM FILLED WITH OLD PIECES OF WAR TOYS.
ONE WAS LITTERED WITH PIECES OF PLANES LIKE THE *MUSTANG*, THE FASTEST FIGHTER IN THE SKY AND A VITAL TOOL FOR THE ALLIES BEATING THE NAZIS.
ROY WAS PRETTY SMART, BUT SOON HE LOOKED PRETTY LOST.
THE COMPASS IS SPINNING FASTER THAN A DERVISH AFTER A TURKISH ESPRESSO. WE *MUST* BE CLOSE TO THE TANK UNIT. HA!
AT LEAST ROY WAS *CHEERY* ABOUT THE WHOLE THING.

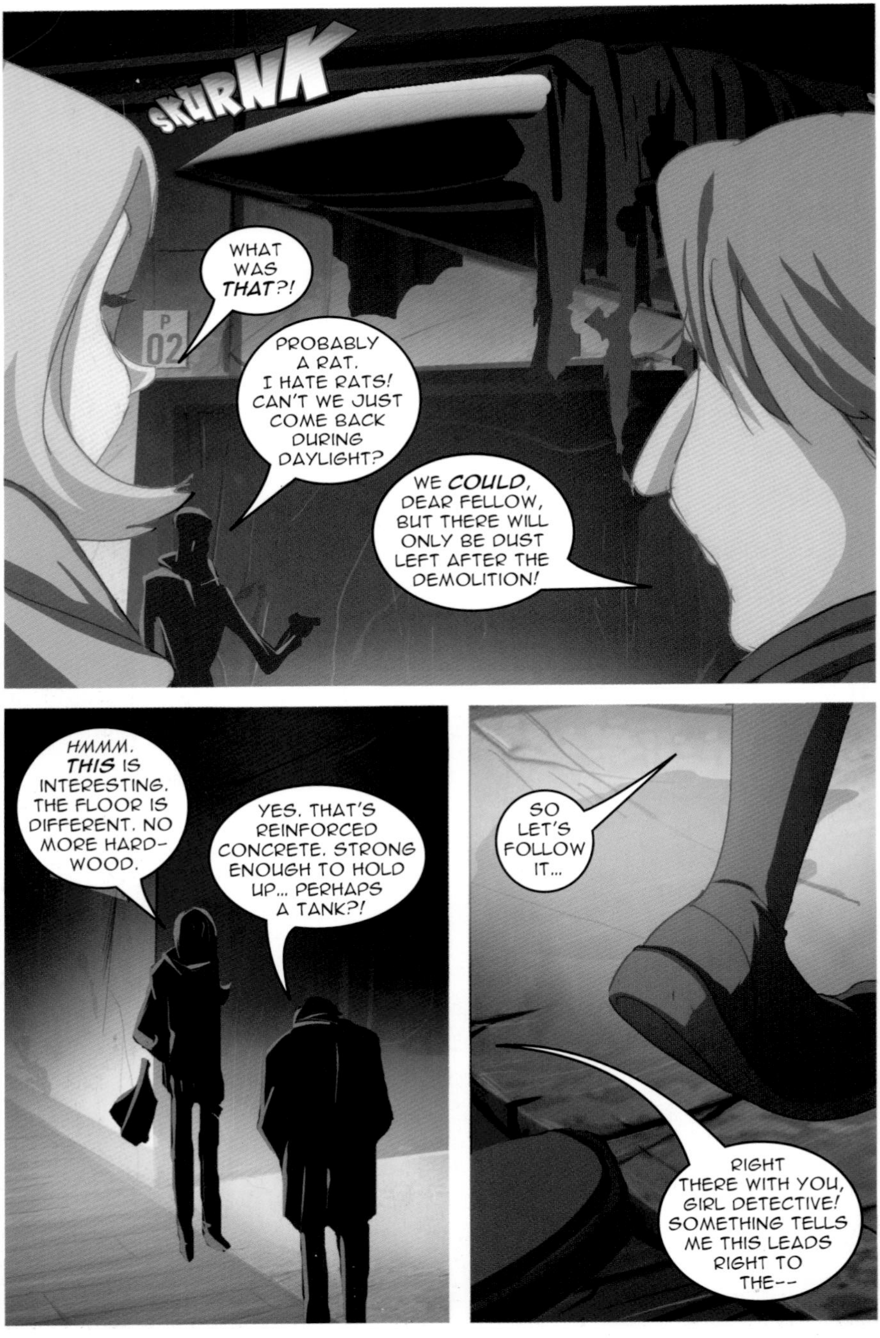
SKURNK
WHAT WAS *THAT*?!
PROBABLY A RAT. I HATE RATS! CAN'T WE JUST COME BACK DURING DAYLIGHT?
WE *COULD*, DEAR FELLOW, BUT THERE WILL ONLY BE DUST LEFT AFTER THE DEMOLITION!
HMMM. *THIS* IS INTERESTING. THE FLOOR IS DIFFERENT. NO MORE HARD-WOOD.
YES. THAT'S REINFORCED CONCRETE. STRONG ENOUGH TO HOLD UP... PERHAPS A TANK?!
SO LET'S FOLLOW IT...
RIGHT THERE WITH YOU, GIRL DETECTIVE! SOMETHING TELLS ME THIS LEADS RIGHT TO THE--

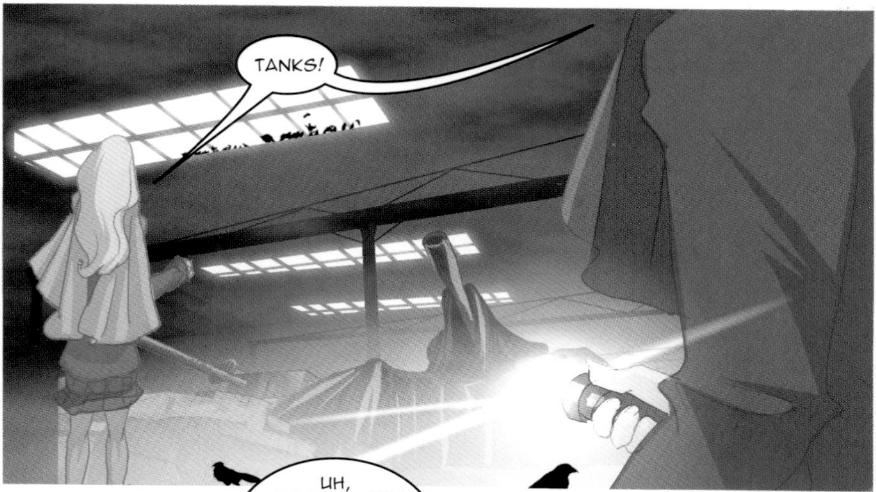
TANKS!

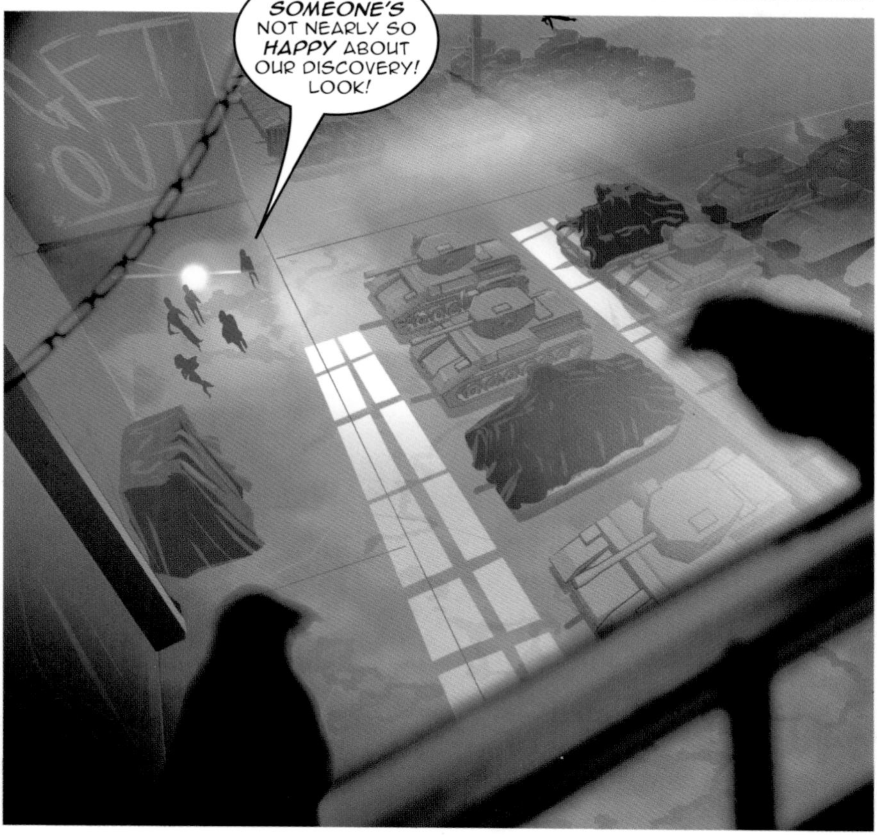
UH, *SOMEONE'S* NOT NEARLY SO *HAPPY* ABOUT OUR DISCOVERY! LOOK!

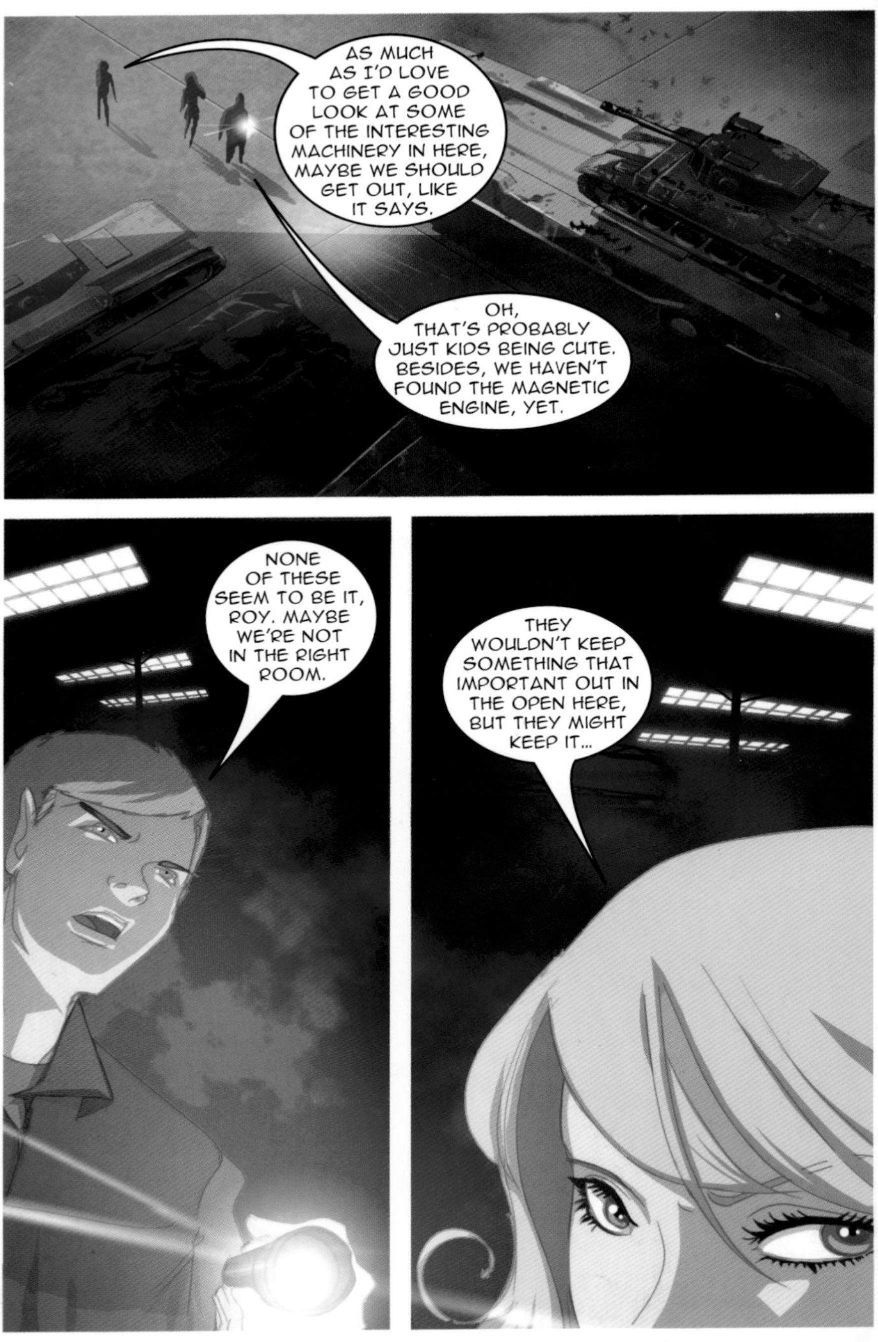
AS MUCH AS I'D LOVE TO GET A GOOD LOOK AT SOME OF THE INTERESTING MACHINERY IN HERE, MAYBE WE SHOULD GET OUT, LIKE IT SAYS.
OH, THAT'S PROBABLY JUST KIDS BEING CUTE. BESIDES, WE HAVEN'T FOUND THE MAGNETIC ENGINE, YET.
NONE OF THESE SEEM TO BE IT, ROY. MAYBE WE'RE NOT IN THE RIGHT ROOM.
THEY WOULDN'T KEEP SOMETHING THAT IMPORTANT OUT IN THE OPEN HERE, BUT THEY MIGHT KEEP IT...

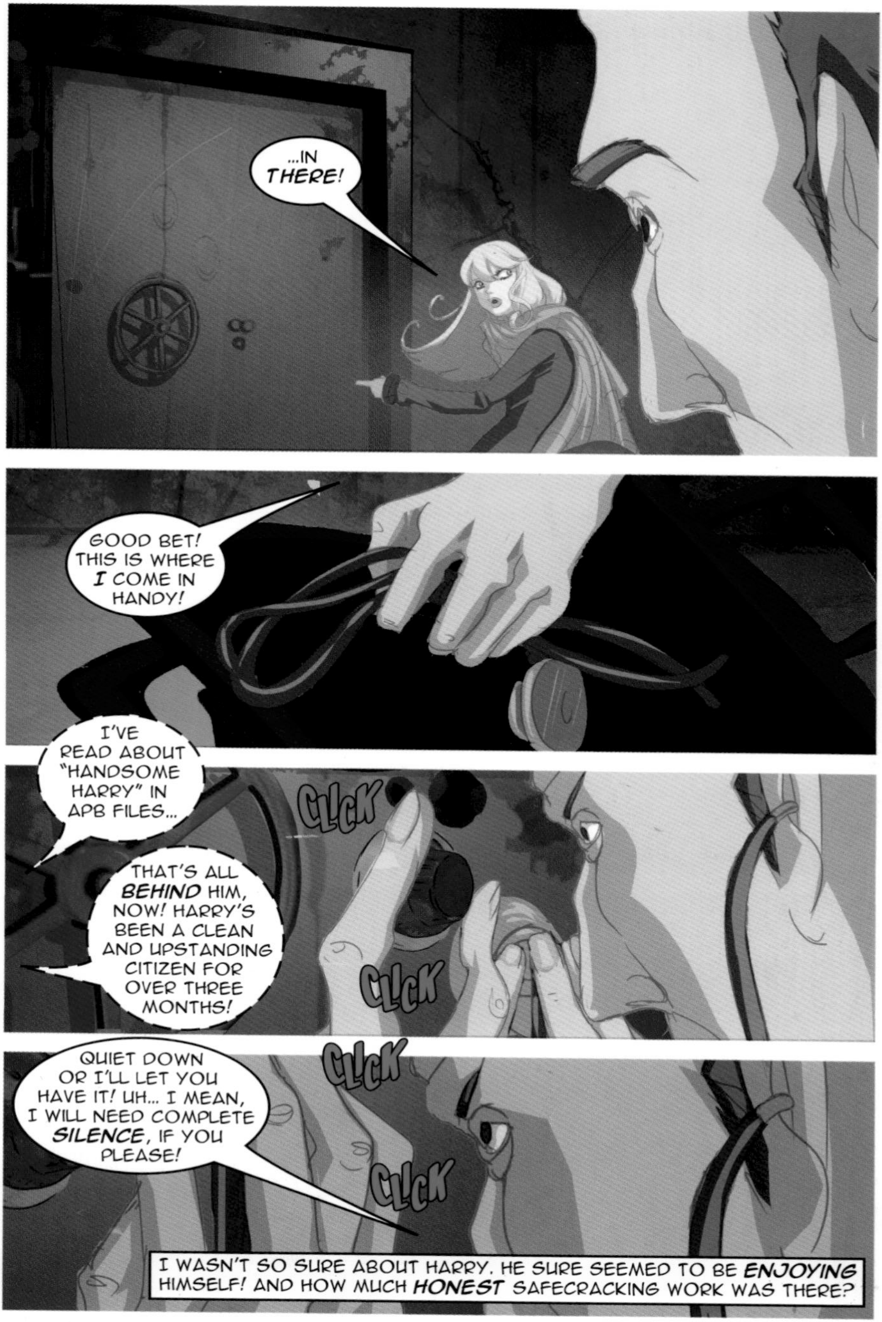
...IN THERE!
GOOD BET! THIS IS WHERE I COME IN HANDY!
I'VE READ ABOUT "HANDSOME HARRY" IN APB FILES...
CLICK
THAT'S ALL BEHIND HIM, NOW! HARRY'S BEEN A CLEAN AND UPSTANDING CITIZEN FOR OVER THREE MONTHS!
CLICK
CLICK
QUIET DOWN OR I'LL LET YOU HAVE IT! UH... I MEAN, I WILL NEED COMPLETE SILENCE, IF YOU PLEASE!
CLICK
I WASN'T SO SURE ABOUT HARRY. HE SURE SEEMED TO BE ENJOYING HIMSELF! AND HOW MUCH HONEST SAFECRACKING WORK WAS THERE?

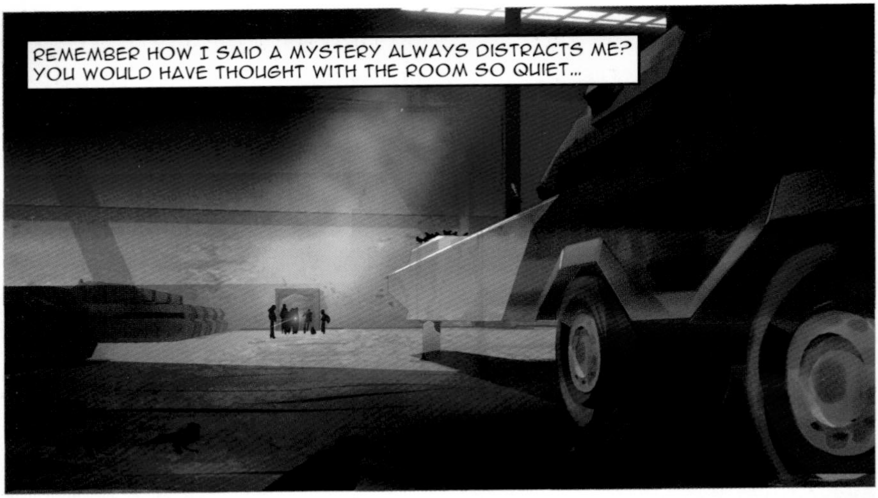
REMEMBER HOW I SAID A MYSTERY ALWAYS DISTRACTS ME? YOU WOULD HAVE THOUGHT WITH THE ROOM SO QUIET...

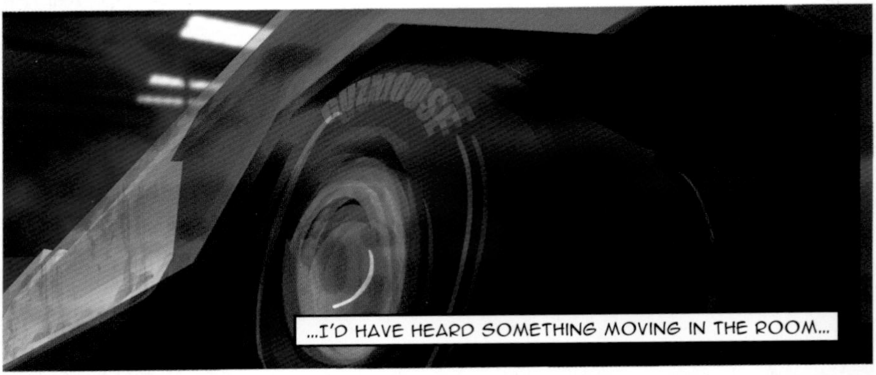
...I'D HAVE HEARD SOMETHING MOVING IN THE ROOM...

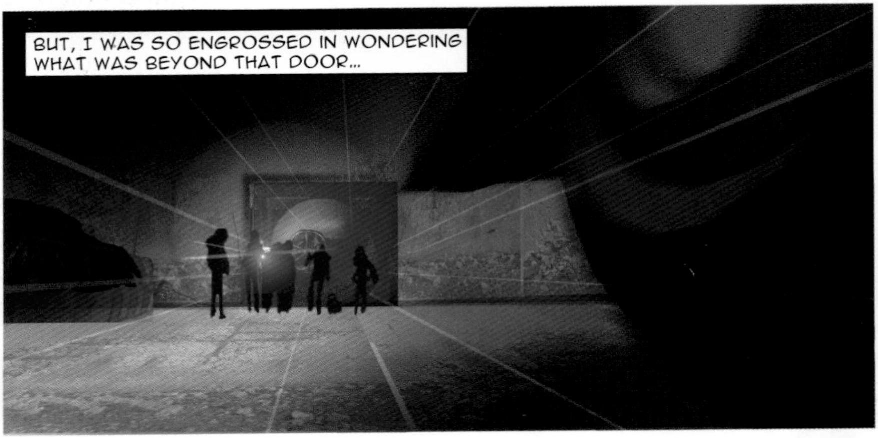
BUT, I WAS SO ENGROSSED IN WONDERING WHAT WAS BEYOND THAT DOOR...

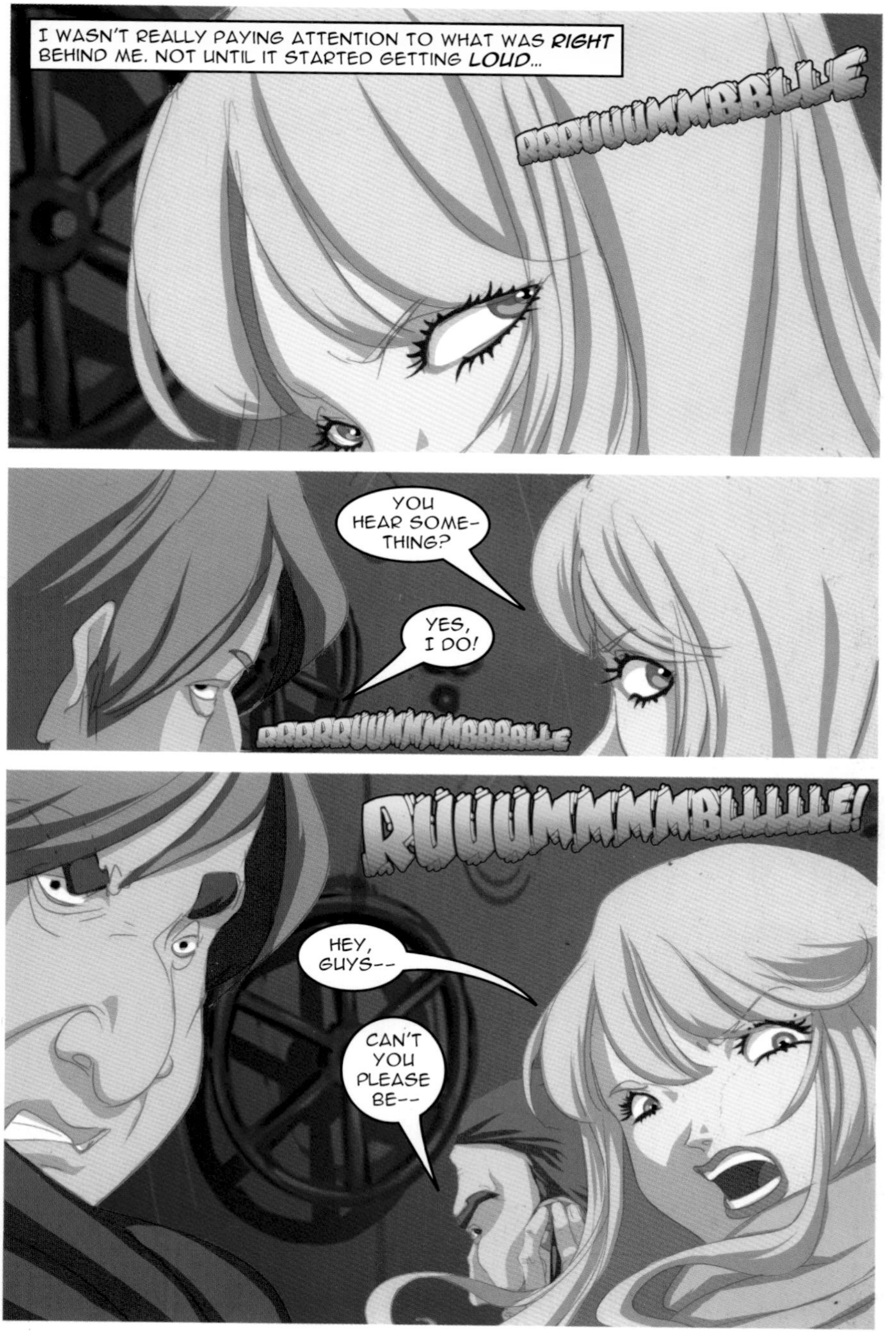
I WASN'T REALLY PAYING ATTENTION TO WHAT WAS *RIGHT* BEHIND ME. NOT UNTIL IT STARTED GETTING *LOUD*...
RRRUUUMMBBLLE
YOU HEAR SOME-THING?
YES, I DO!
RRRRRUUMMMBBBBLLE
RUUUMMMMBLLLLLE!
HEY, GUYS--
CAN'T YOU PLEASE BE--

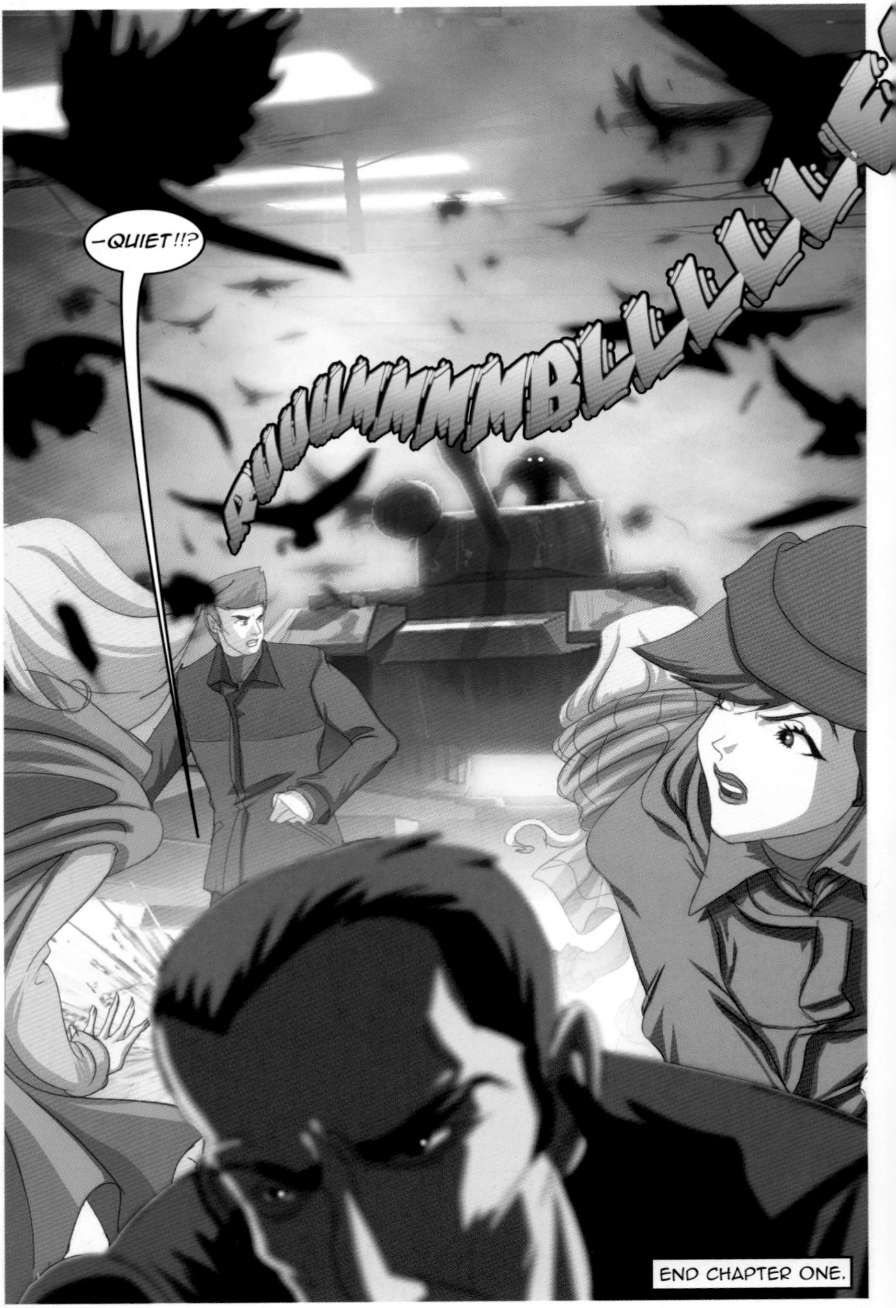
—QUIET!!?
RUUUMMMMBLLLLLE
END CHAPTER ONE.

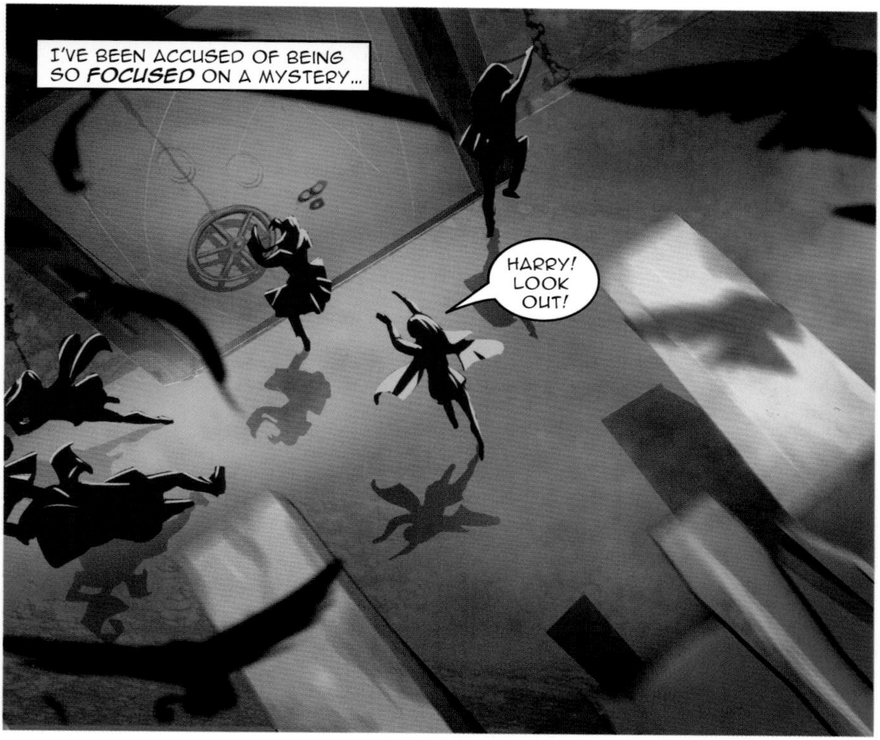
I'VE BEEN ACCUSED OF BEING SO FOCUSED ON A MYSTERY...
HARRY! LOOK OUT!

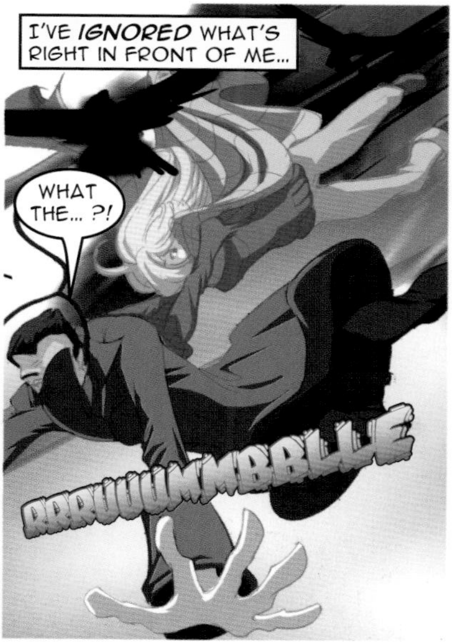
I'VE IGNORED WHAT'S RIGHT IN FRONT OF ME...
WHAT THE... ?!
RRRUUUMMBBLLE

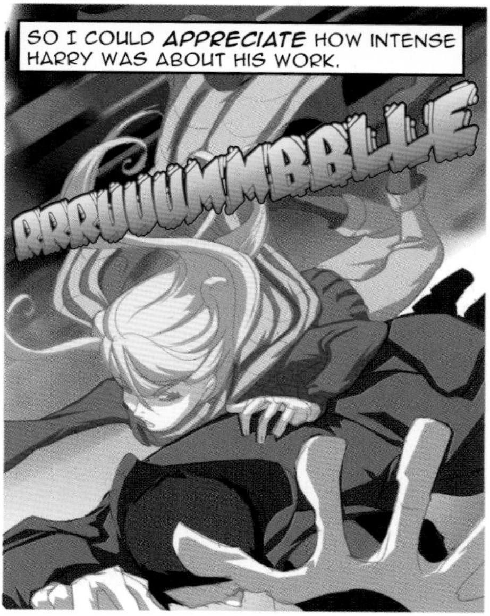
SO I COULD APPRECIATE HOW INTENSE HARRY WAS ABOUT HIS WORK.
RRRUUUMMBBLLE

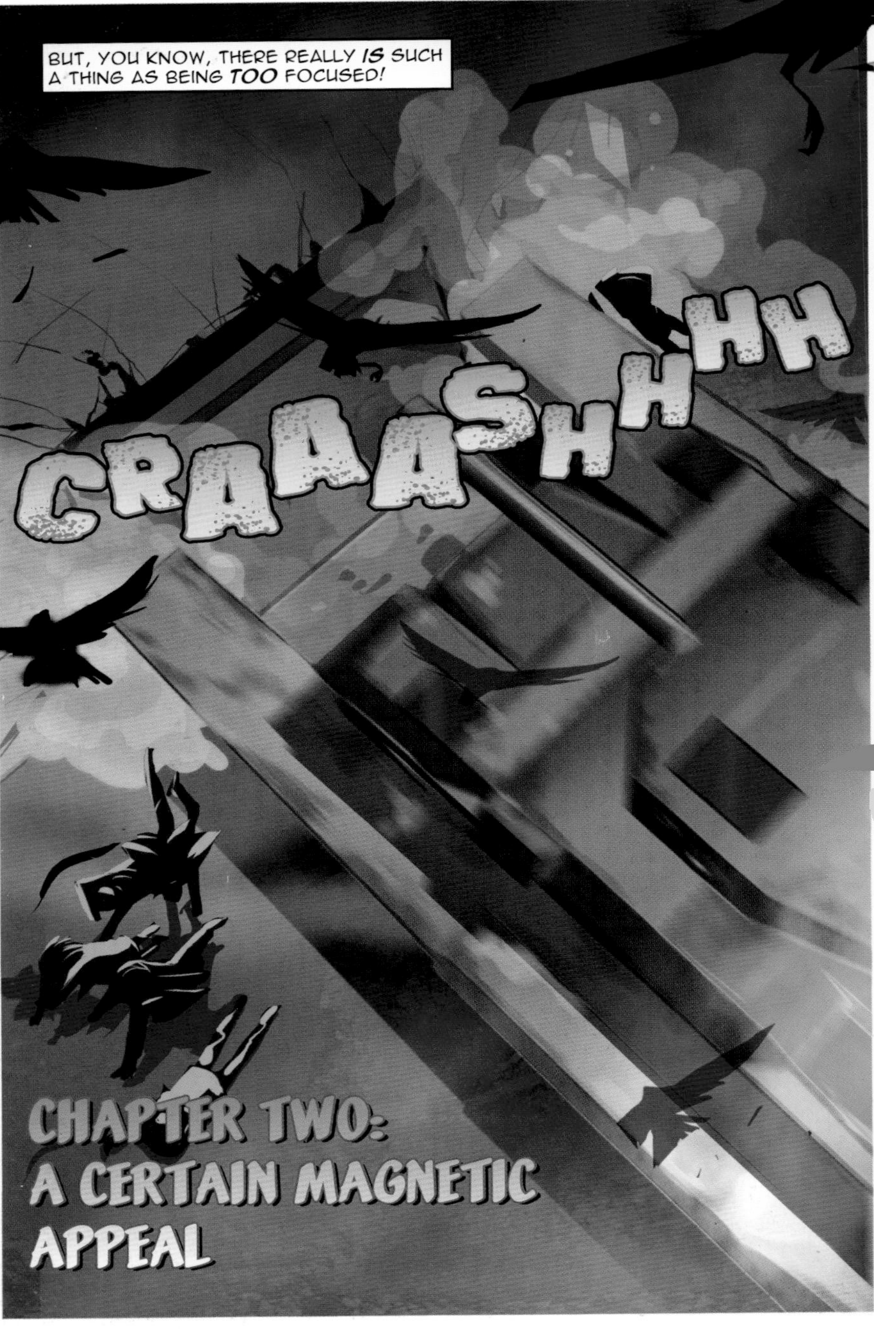
BUT, YOU KNOW, THERE REALLY IS SUCH A THING AS BEING TOO FOCUSED!
CRAAASHHHH
CHAPTER TWO:
A CERTAIN MAGNETIC APPEAL

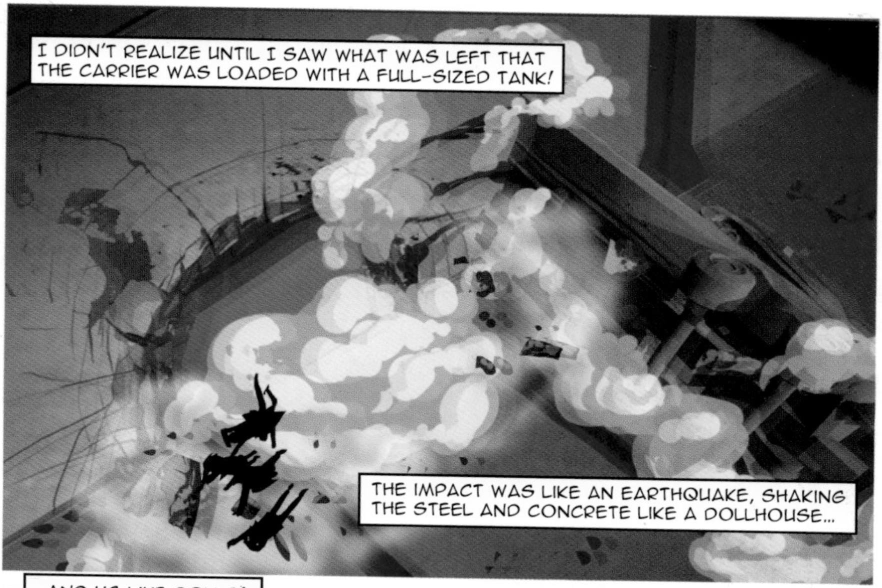
I DIDN'T REALIZE UNTIL I SAW WHAT WAS LEFT THAT THE CARRIER WAS LOADED WITH A FULL-SIZED TANK!
THE IMPACT WAS LIKE AN EARTHQUAKE, SHAKING THE STEEL AND CONCRETE LIKE A DOLLHOUSE...

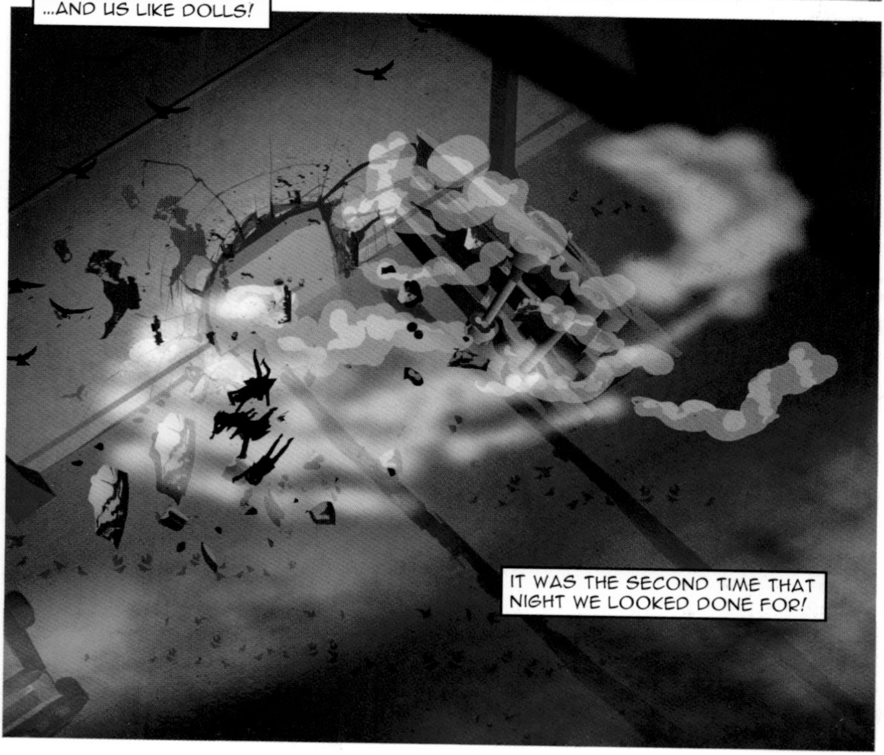
...AND US LIKE DOLLS!
IT WAS THE SECOND TIME THAT NIGHT WE LOOKED DONE FOR!

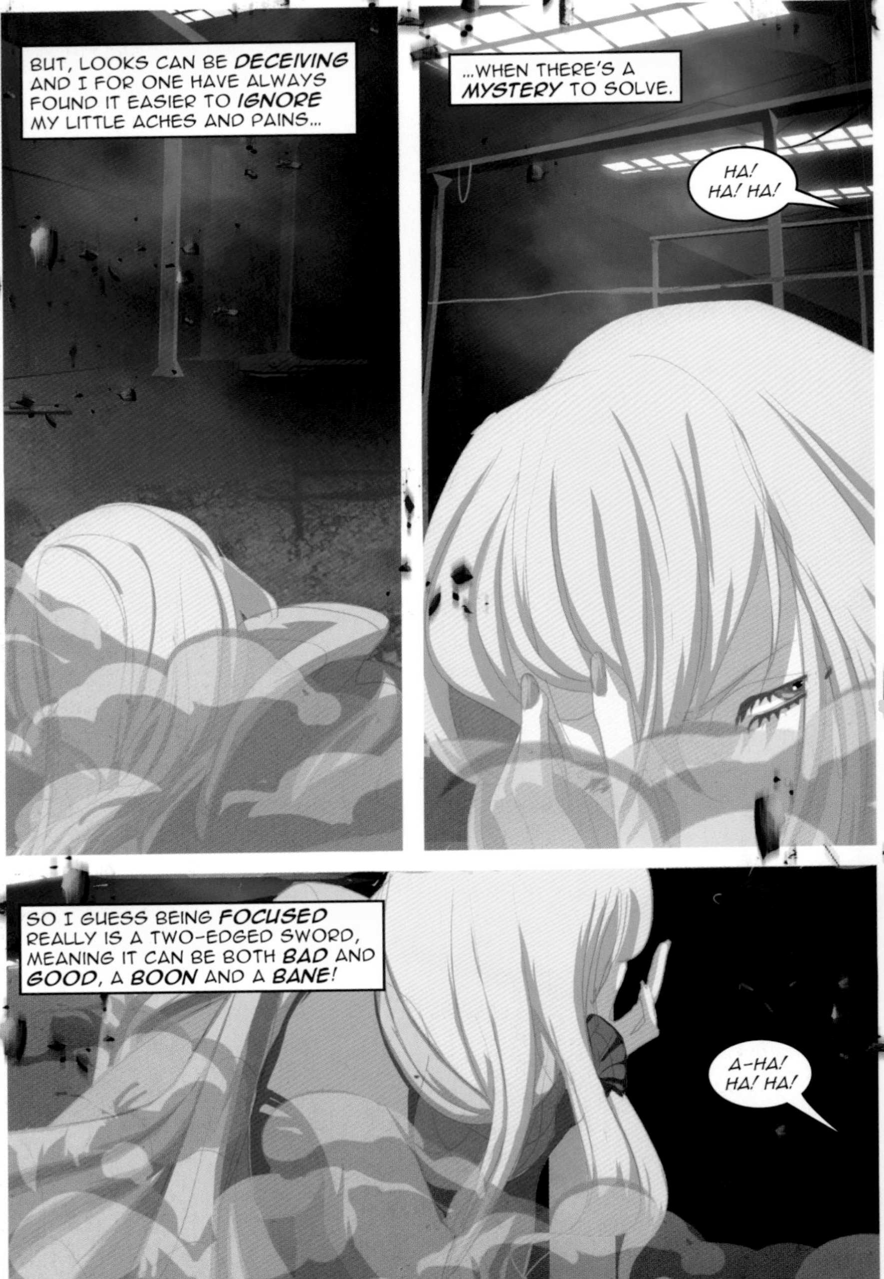
BUT, LOOKS CAN BE DECEIVING AND I FOR ONE HAVE ALWAYS FOUND IT EASIER TO IGNORE MY LITTLE ACHES AND PAINS...
...WHEN THERE'S A MYSTERY TO SOLVE.
HA! HA! HA!
SO I GUESS BEING FOCUSED REALLY IS A TWO-EDGED SWORD, MEANING IT CAN BE BOTH BAD AND GOOD, A BOON AND A BANE!
A-HA! HA! HA!

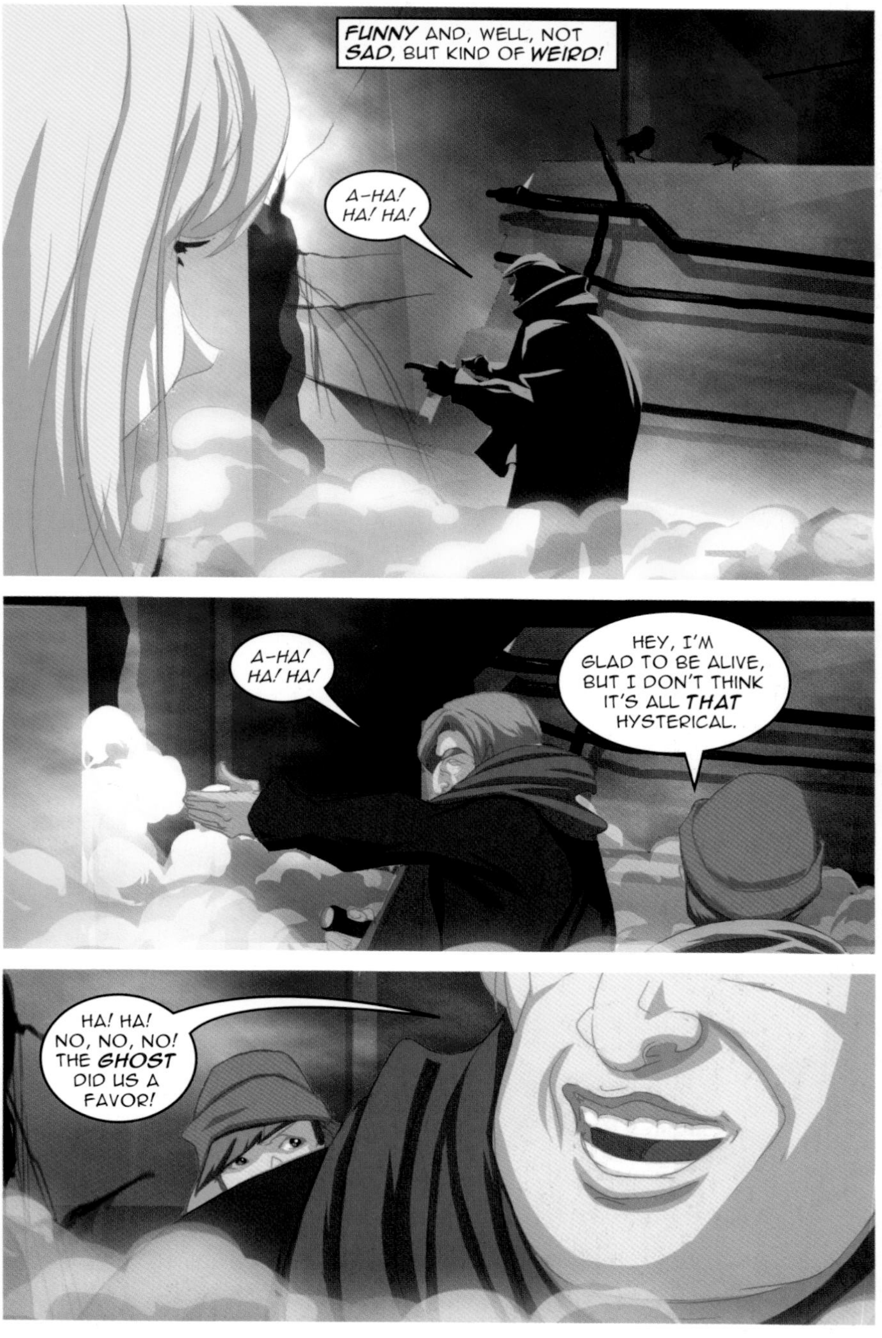
FUNNY AND, WELL, NOT SAD, BUT KIND OF WEIRD!
A-HA! HA! HA!
A-HA! HA! HA!
HEY, I'M GLAD TO BE ALIVE, BUT I DON'T THINK IT'S ALL THAT HYSTERICAL.
HA! HA! NO, NO, NO! THE GHOST DID US A FAVOR!

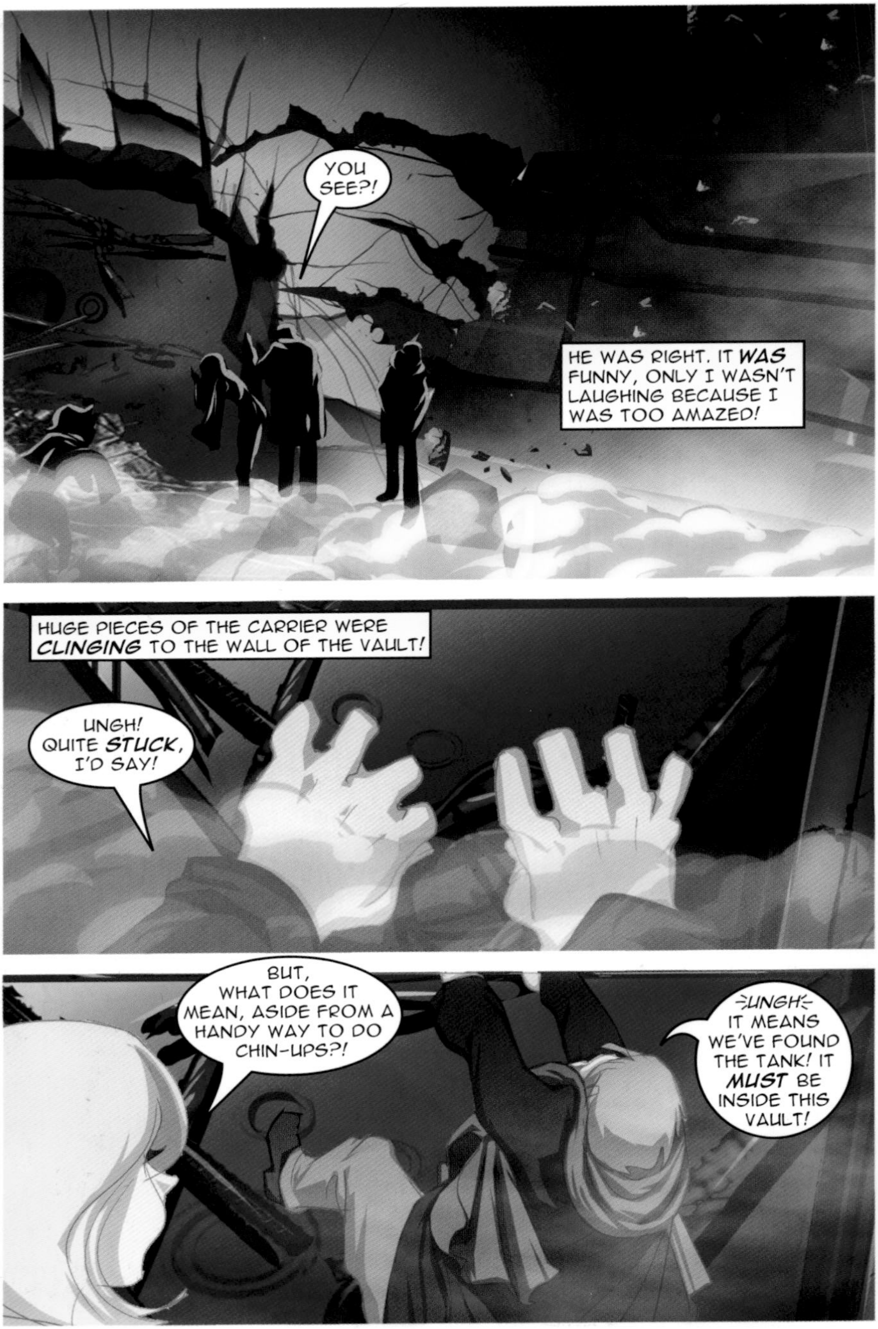
YOU SEE?!
HE WAS RIGHT. IT WAS FUNNY, ONLY I WASN'T LAUGHING BECAUSE I WAS TOO AMAZED!
HUGE PIECES OF THE CARRIER WERE CLINGING TO THE WALL OF THE VAULT!
UNGH! QUITE STUCK, I'D SAY!
BUT, WHAT DOES IT MEAN, ASIDE FROM A HANDY WAY TO DO CHIN-UPS?!
UNGH IT MEANS WE'VE FOUND THE TANK! IT MUST BE INSIDE THIS VAULT!

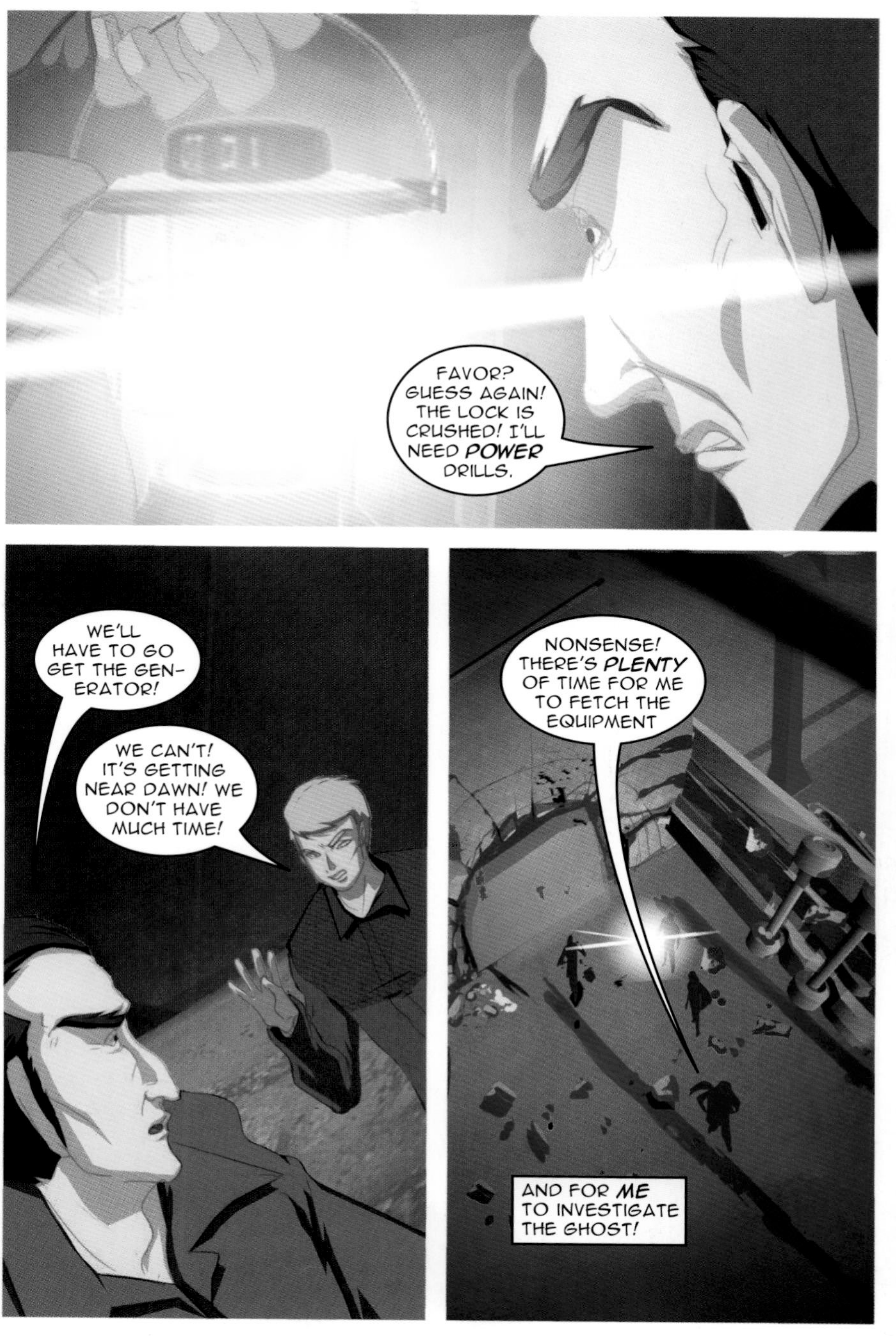
FAVOR? GUESS AGAIN! THE LOCK IS CRUSHED! I'LL NEED *POWER* DRILLS.
WE'LL HAVE TO GO GET THE GEN-ERATOR!
WE CAN'T! IT'S GETTING NEAR DAWN! WE DON'T HAVE MUCH TIME!
NONSENSE! THERE'S *PLENTY* OF TIME FOR ME TO FETCH THE EQUIPMENT
AND FOR *ME* TO INVESTIGATE THE GHOST!

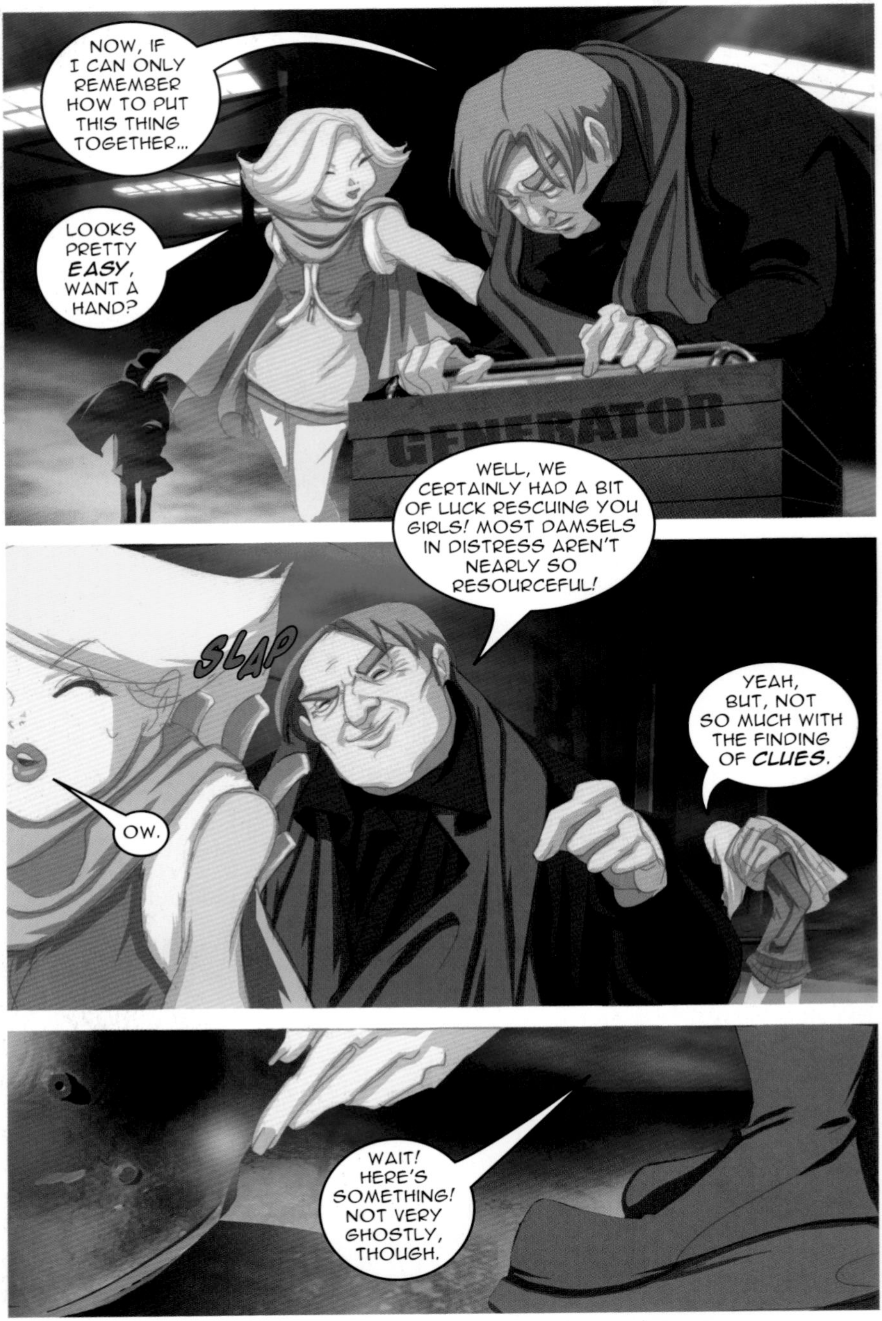
NOW, IF I CAN ONLY REMEMBER HOW TO PUT THIS THING TOGETHER...
LOOKS PRETTY *EASY*, WANT A HAND?
GENERATOR
WELL, WE CERTAINLY HAD A BIT OF LUCK RESCUING YOU GIRLS! MOST DAMSELS IN DISTRESS AREN'T NEARLY SO RESOURCEFUL!
SLAP
OW.
YEAH, BUT, NOT SO MUCH WITH THE FINDING OF *CLUES*.
WAIT! HERE'S SOMETHING! NOT VERY GHOSTLY, THOUGH.

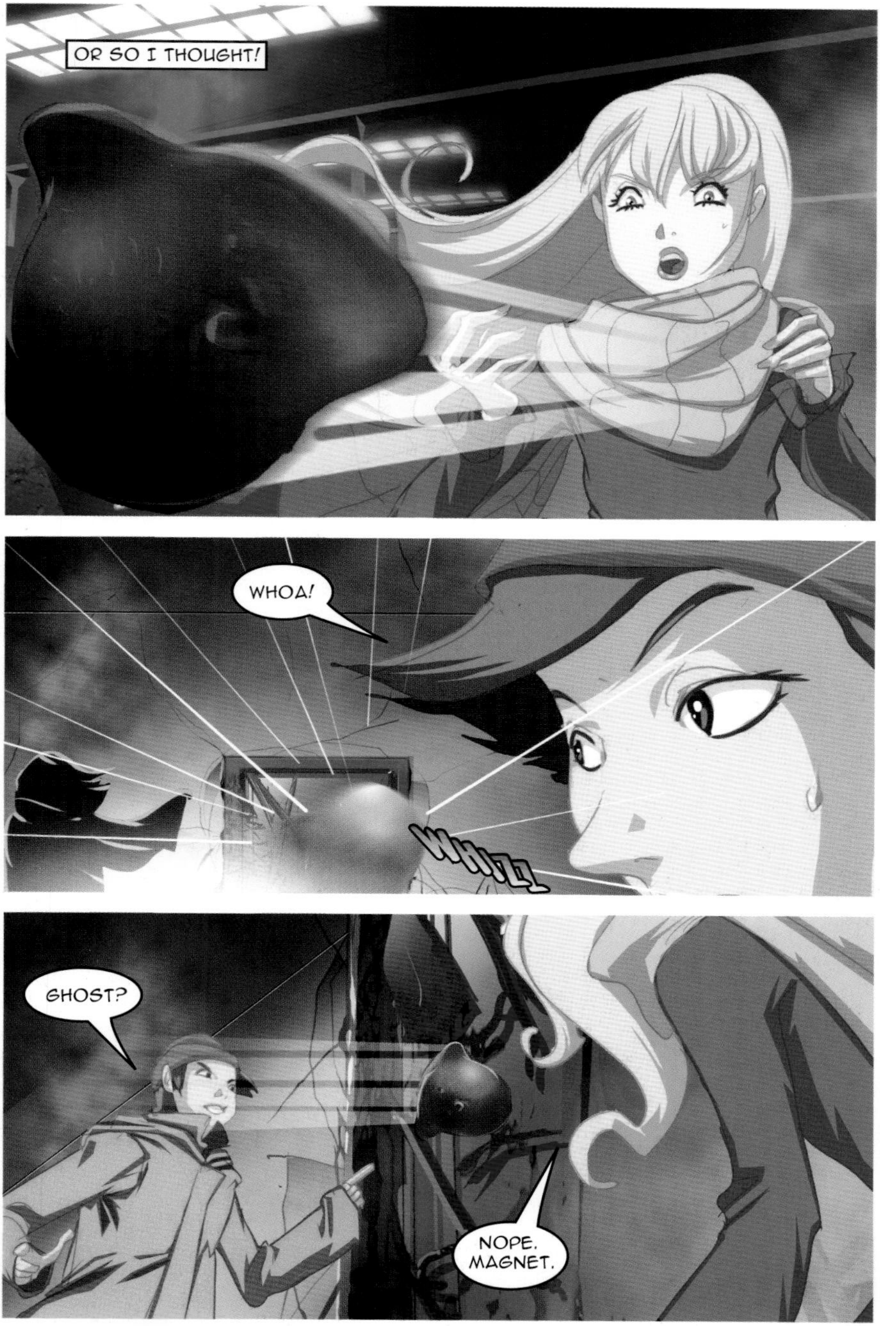
OR SO I THOUGHT!
WHOA!
WHIZZ
GHOST?
NOPE. MAGNET.

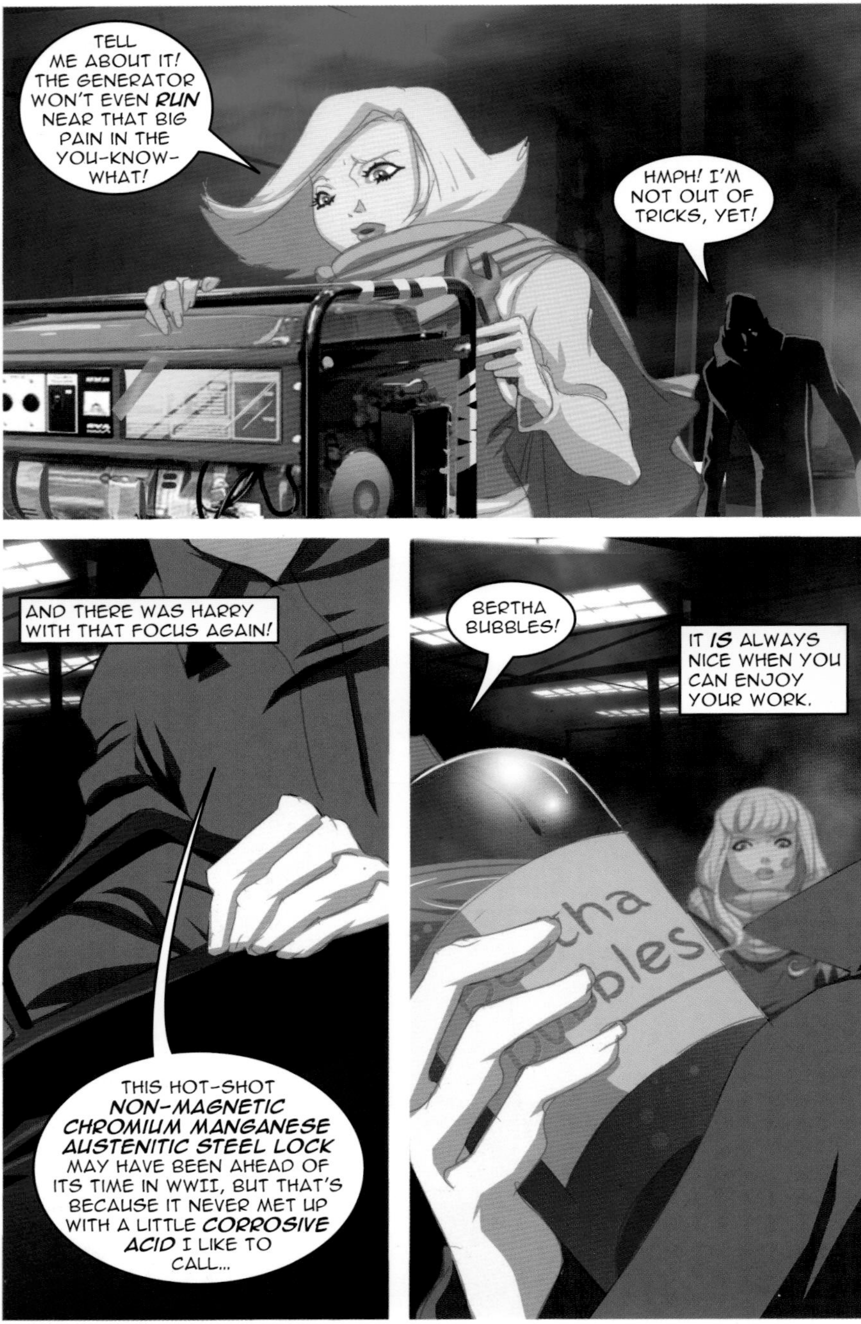
TELL ME ABOUT IT! THE GENERATOR WON'T EVEN RUN NEAR THAT BIG PAIN IN THE YOU-KNOW-WHAT!
HMPH! I'M NOT OUT OF TRICKS, YET!
AND THERE WAS HARRY WITH THAT FOCUS AGAIN!
THIS HOT-SHOT NON-MAGNETIC CHROMIUM MANGANESE AUSTENITIC STEEL LOCK MAY HAVE BEEN AHEAD OF ITS TIME IN WWII, BUT THAT'S BECAUSE IT NEVER MET UP WITH A LITTLE CORROSIVE ACID I LIKE TO CALL...
BERTHA BUBBLES!
IT IS ALWAYS NICE WHEN YOU CAN ENJOY YOUR WORK.

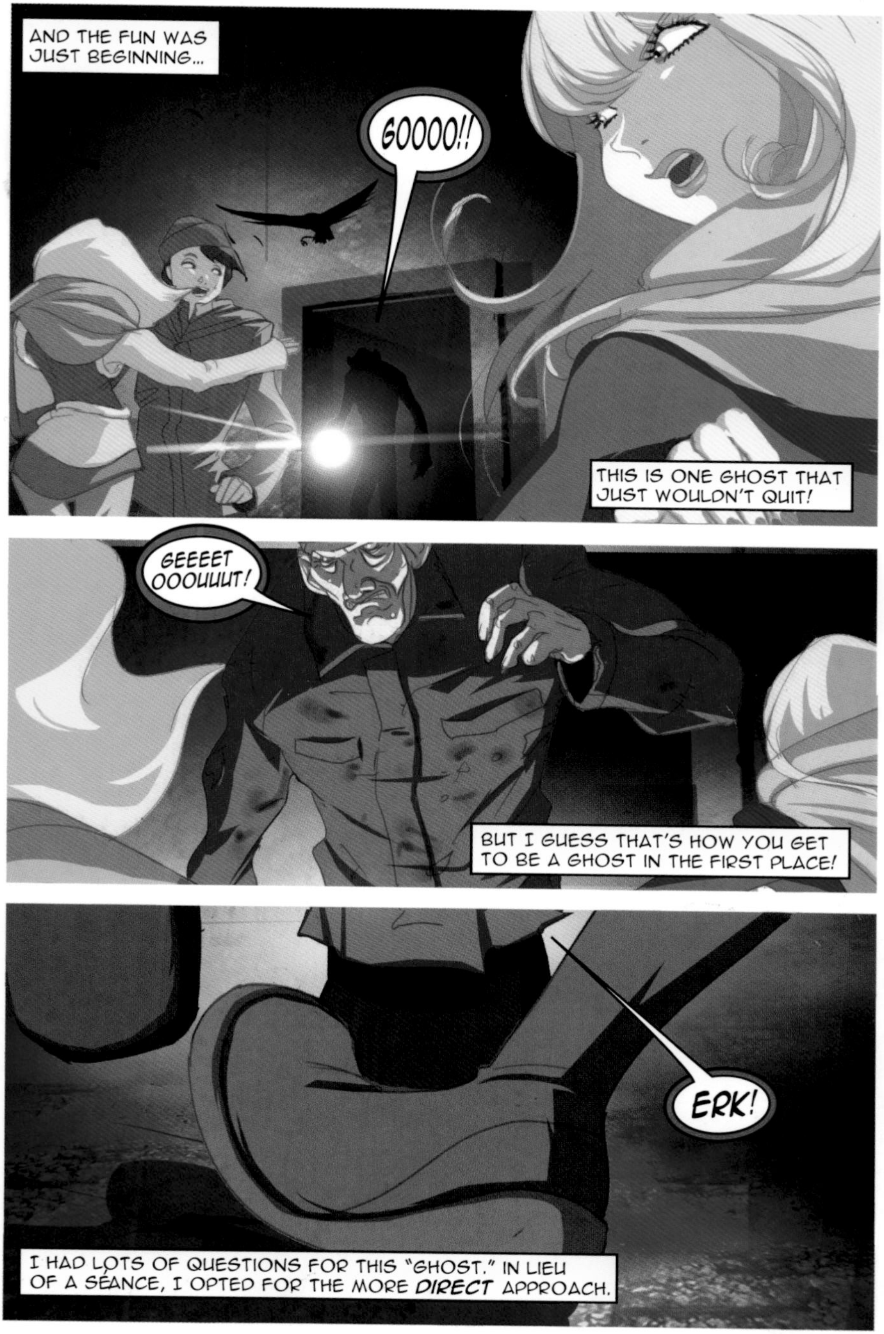
AND THE FUN WAS JUST BEGINNING...
GOOOO!!
THIS IS ONE GHOST THAT JUST WOULDN'T QUIT!
GEEEET OOOUUUT!
BUT I GUESS THAT'S HOW YOU GET TO BE A GHOST IN THE FIRST PLACE!
ERK!
I HAD LOTS OF QUESTIONS FOR THIS "GHOST." IN LIEU OF A SÉANCE, I OPTED FOR THE MORE *DIRECT* APPROACH.

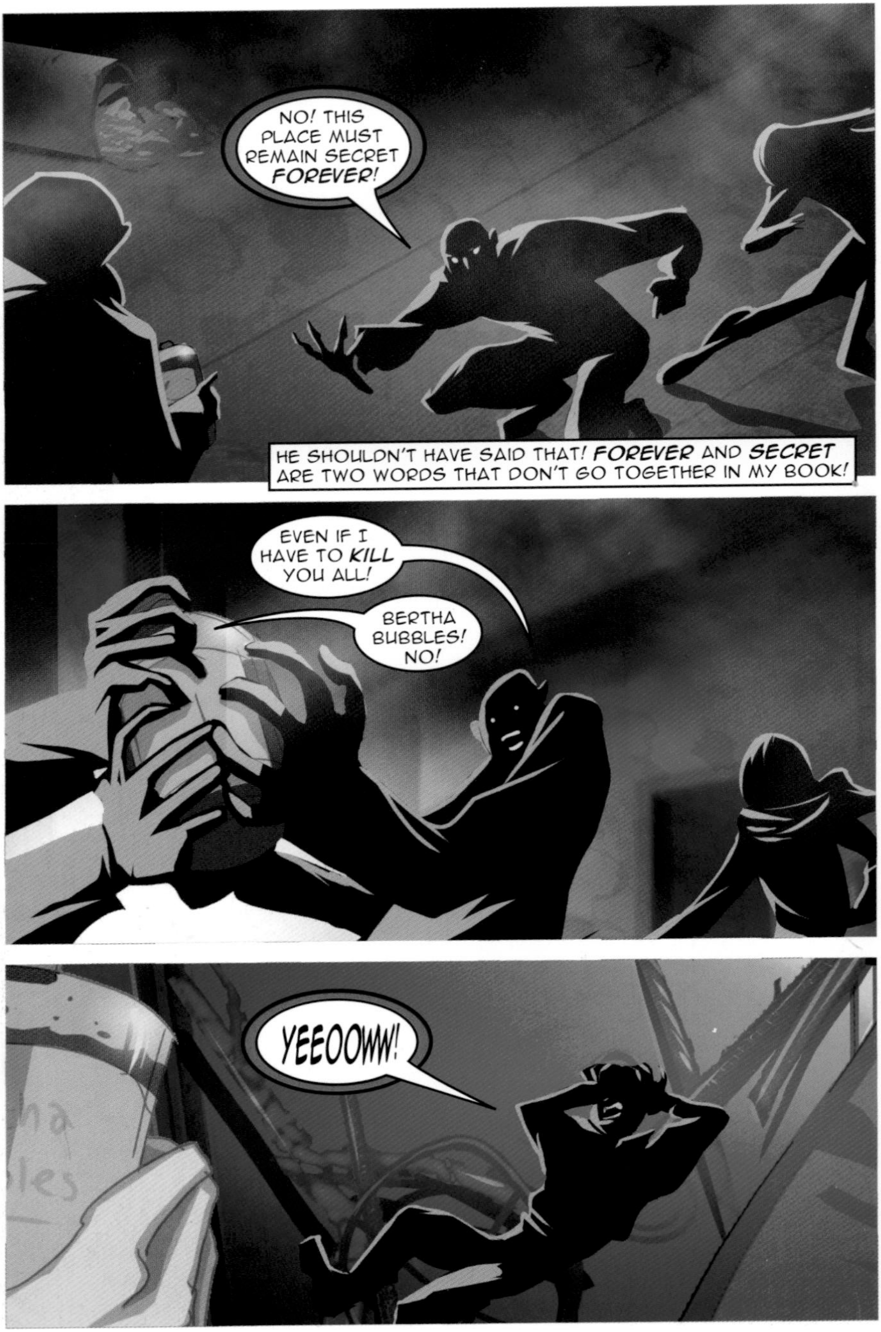
NO! THIS PLACE MUST REMAIN SECRET *FOREVER*!
HE SHOULDN'T HAVE SAID THAT! *FOREVER* AND *SECRET* ARE TWO WORDS THAT DON'T GO TOGETHER IN MY BOOK!
EVEN IF I HAVE TO *KILL* YOU ALL!
BERTHA BUBBLES! NO!
YEEOOWW!

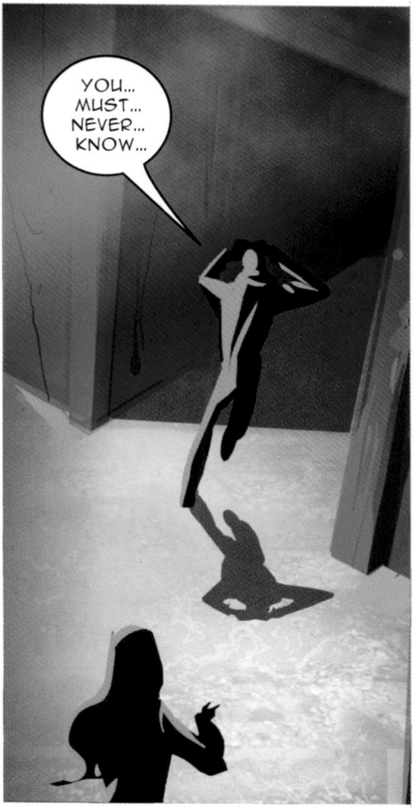
YOU... MUST... NEVER... KNOW...

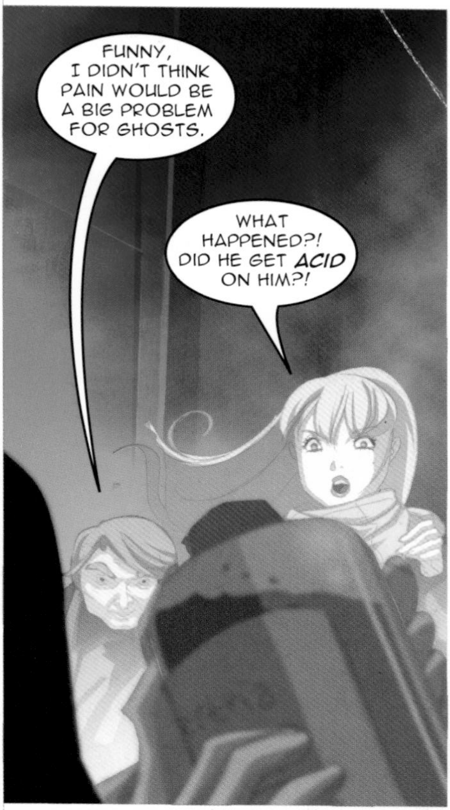
FUNNY, I DIDN'T THINK PAIN WOULD BE A BIG PROBLEM FOR GHOSTS.
WHAT HAPPENED?! DID HE GET ACID ON HIM?!

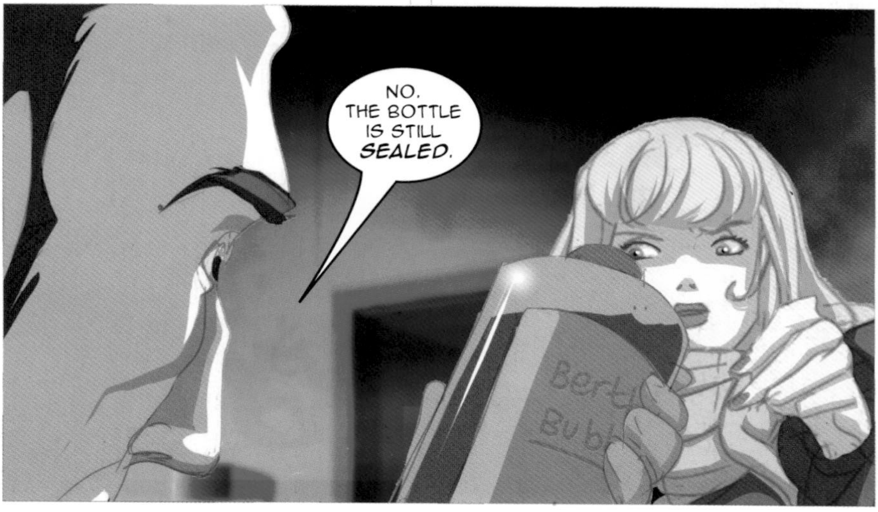
NO. THE BOTTLE IS STILL SEALED.

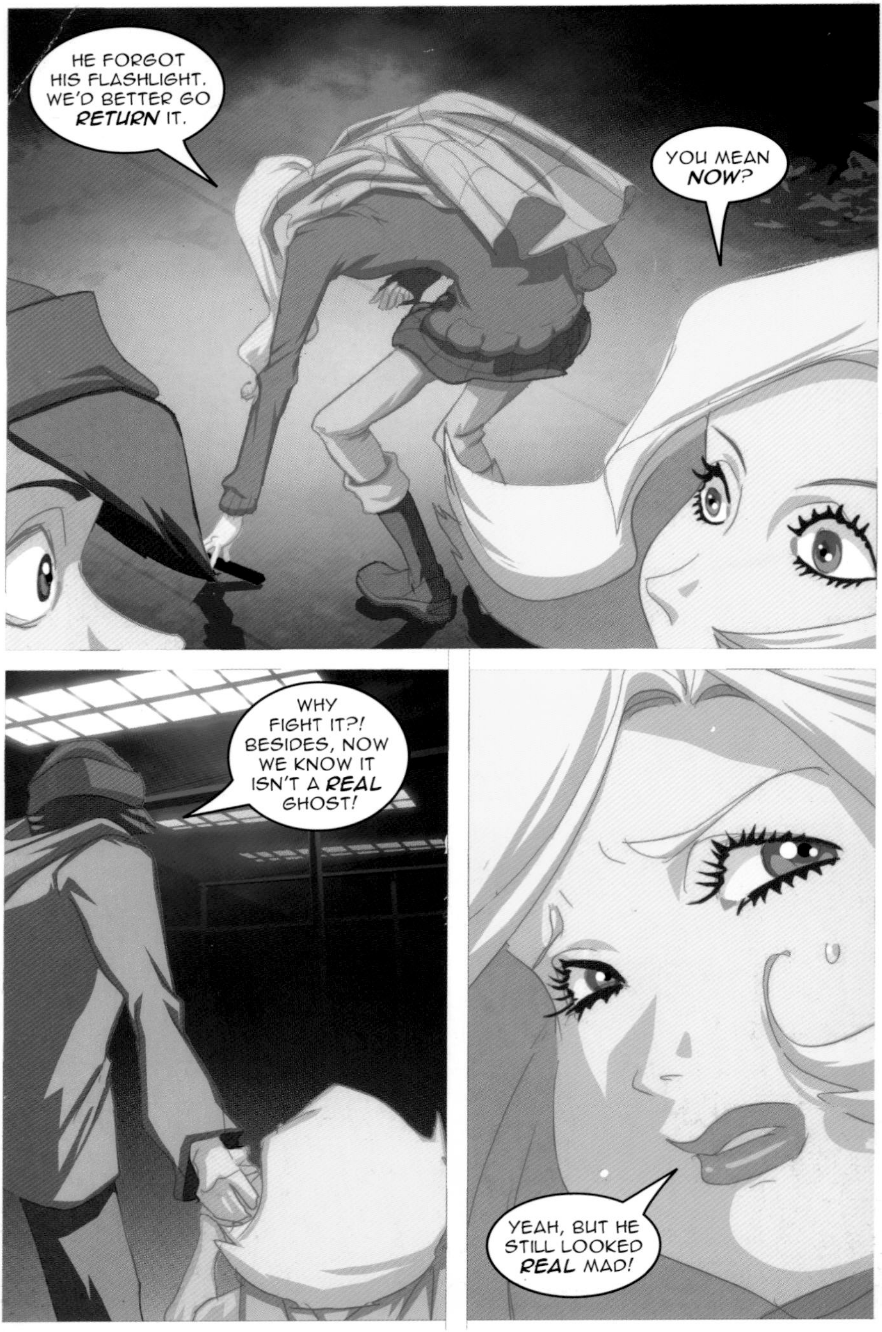
HE FORGOT HIS FLASHLIGHT. WE'D BETTER GO RETURN IT.
YOU MEAN NOW?
WHY FIGHT IT?! BESIDES, NOW WE KNOW IT ISN'T A REAL GHOST!
YEAH, BUT HE STILL LOOKED REAL MAD!

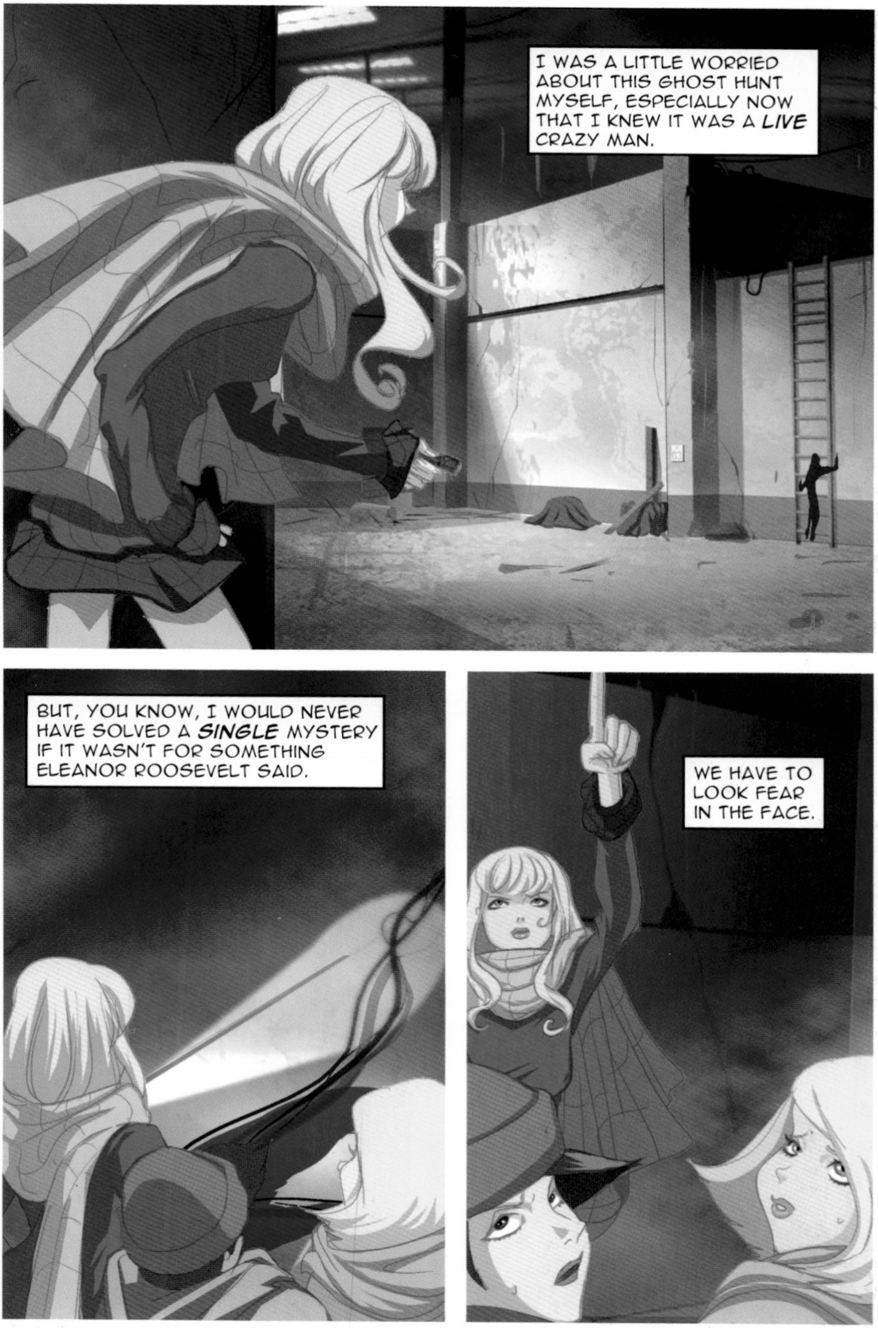
I WAS A LITTLE WORRIED ABOUT THIS GHOST HUNT MYSELF, ESPECIALLY NOW THAT I KNEW IT WAS A *LIVE* CRAZY MAN.
BUT, YOU KNOW, I WOULD NEVER HAVE SOLVED A *SINGLE* MYSTERY IF IT WASN'T FOR SOMETHING ELEANOR ROOSEVELT SAID.
WE HAVE TO LOOK FEAR IN THE FACE.

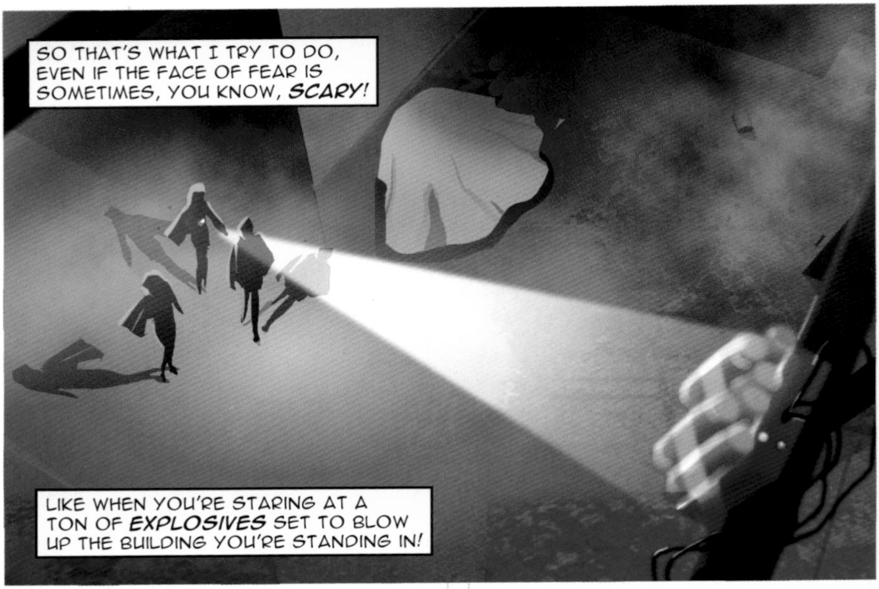
SO THAT'S WHAT I TRY TO DO, EVEN IF THE FACE OF FEAR IS SOMETIMES, YOU KNOW, SCARY!
LIKE WHEN YOU'RE STARING AT A TON OF EXPLOSIVES SET TO BLOW UP THE BUILDING YOU'RE STANDING IN!
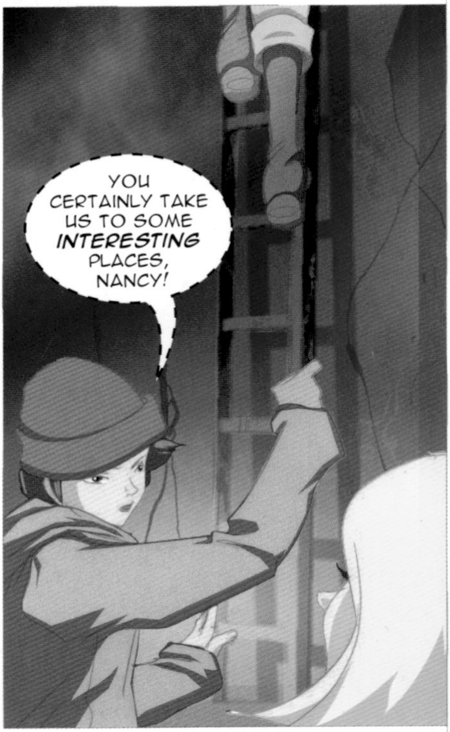
YOU CERTAINLY TAKE US TO SOME INTERESTING PLACES, NANCY!
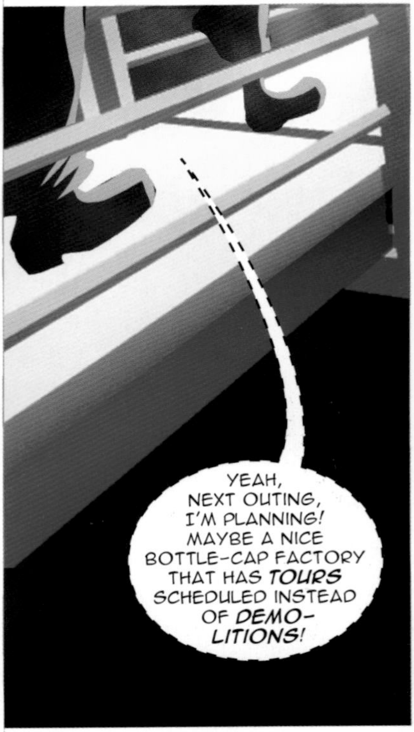
YEAH, NEXT OUTING, I'M PLANNING! MAYBE A NICE BOTTLE-CAP FACTORY THAT HAS TOURS SCHEDULED INSTEAD OF DEMO-LITIONS!

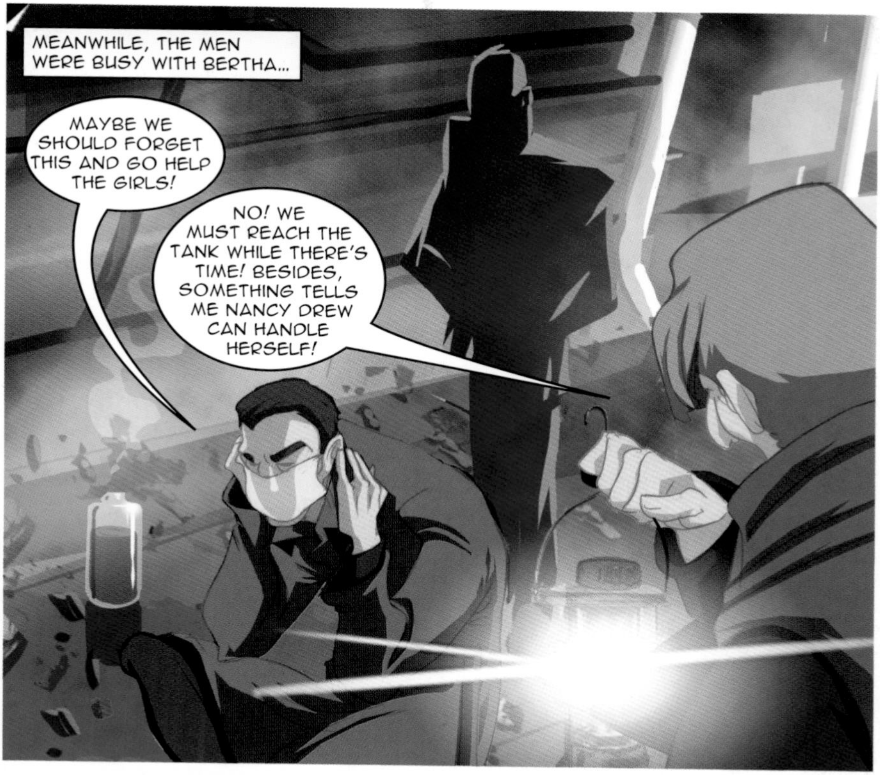
MEANWHILE, THE MEN WERE BUSY WITH BERTHA...
MAYBE WE SHOULD FORGET THIS AND GO HELP THE GIRLS!
NO! WE MUST REACH THE TANK WHILE THERE'S TIME! BESIDES, SOMETHING TELLS ME NANCY DREW CAN HANDLE HERSELF!

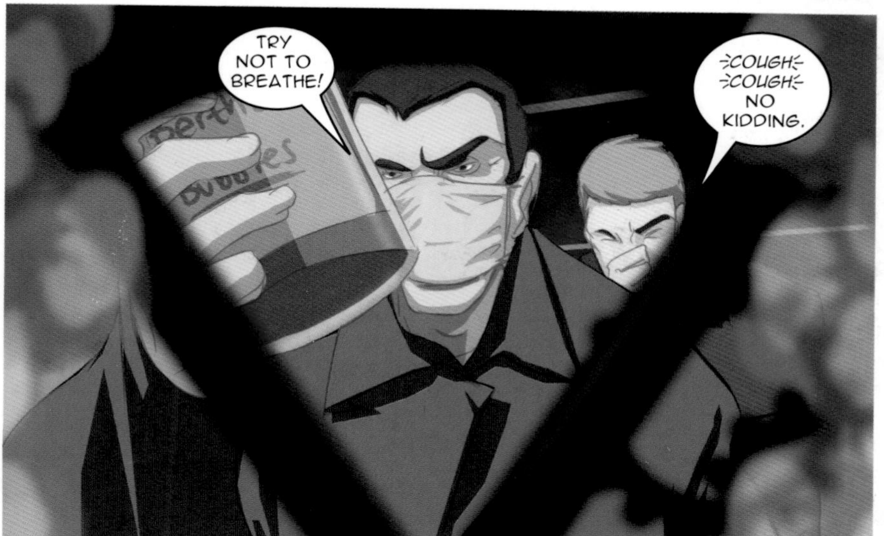
TRY NOT TO BREATHE!
COUGH COUGH NO KIDDING.

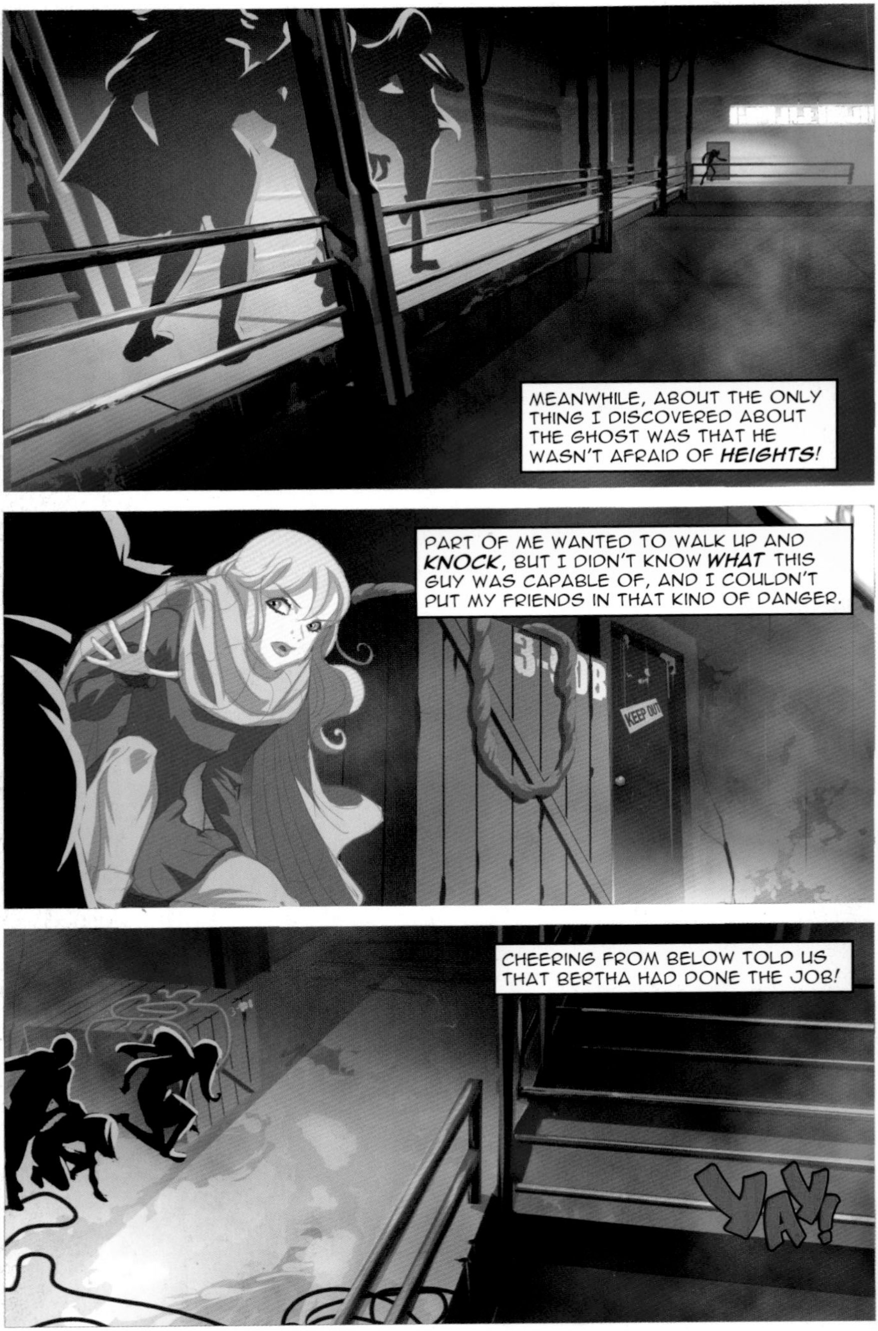
MEANWHILE, ABOUT THE ONLY THING I DISCOVERED ABOUT THE GHOST WAS THAT HE WASN'T AFRAID OF ***HEIGHTS***!
PART OF ME WANTED TO WALK UP AND ***KNOCK***, BUT I DIDN'T KNOW ***WHAT*** THIS GUY WAS CAPABLE OF, AND I COULDN'T PUT MY FRIENDS IN THAT KIND OF DANGER.
KEEP OUT
CHEERING FROM BELOW TOLD US THAT BERTHA HAD DONE THE JOB!
YAY!

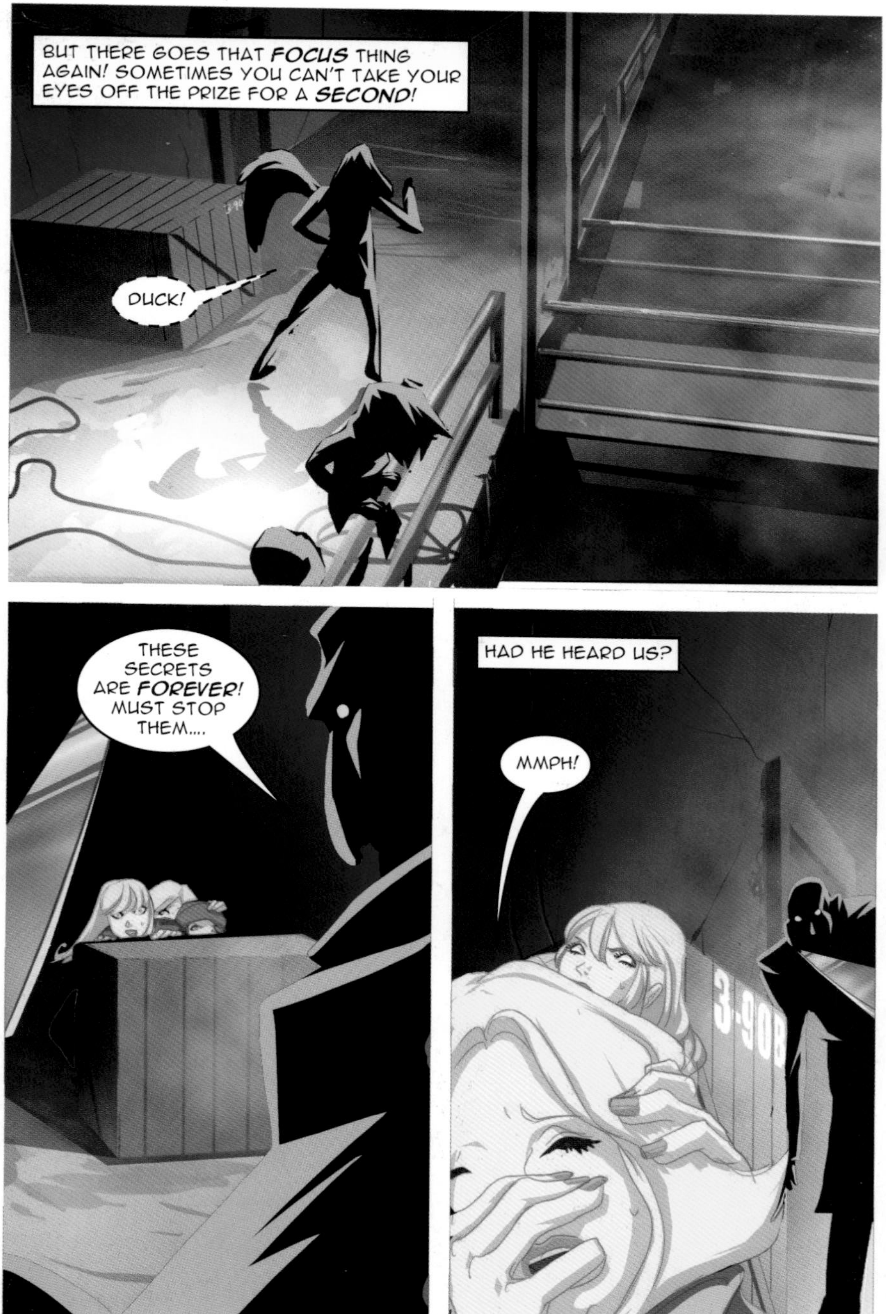

BUT THERE GOES THAT FOCUS THING AGAIN! SOMETIMES YOU CAN'T TAKE YOUR EYES OFF THE PRIZE FOR A SECOND!
DUCK!
3-90
THESE SECRETS ARE FOREVER! MUST STOP THEM....
HAD HE HEARD US?
MMPH!
3-908

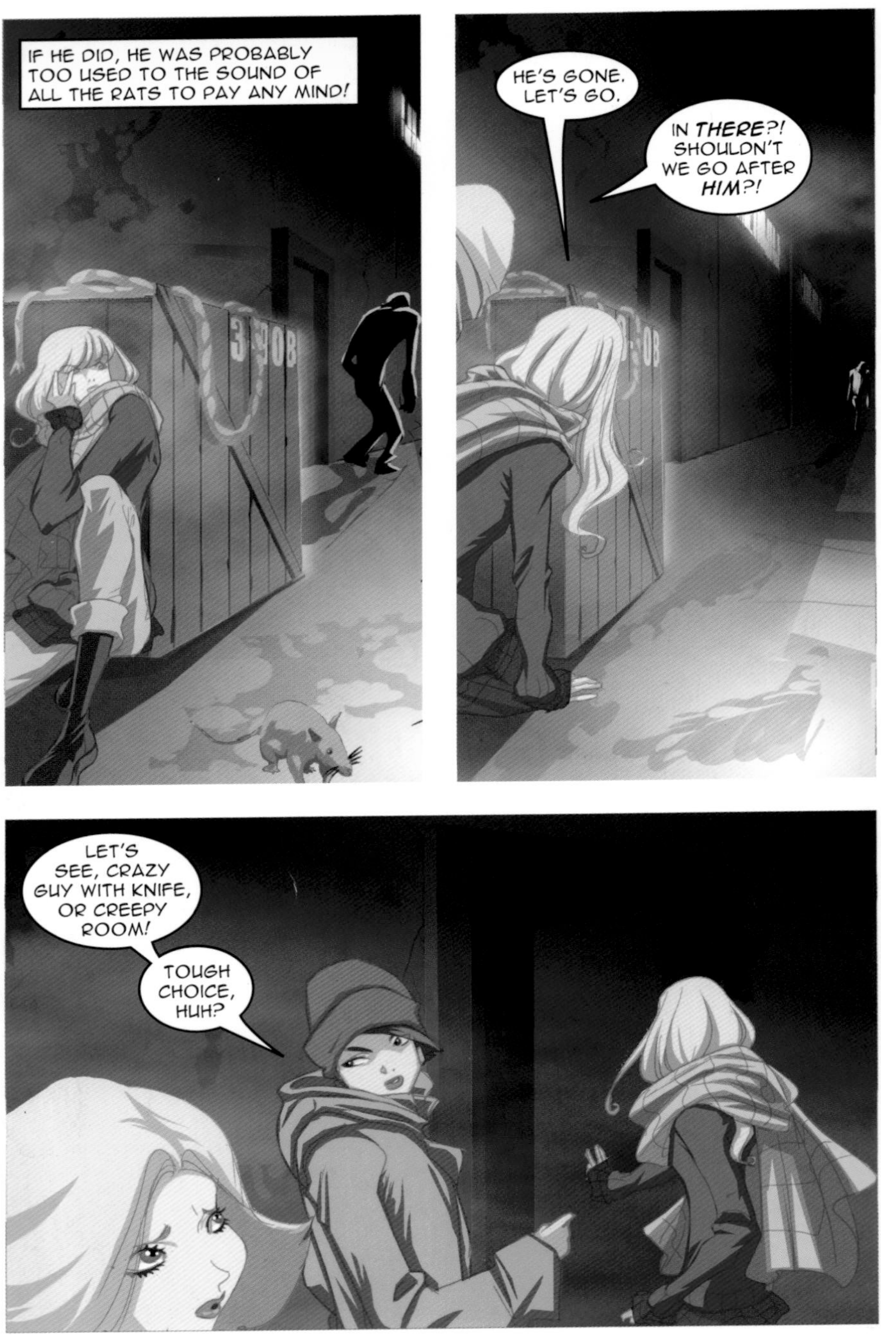
IF HE DID, HE WAS PROBABLY TOO USED TO THE SOUND OF ALL THE RATS TO PAY ANY MIND!
HE'S GONE. LET'S GO.
IN THERE?! SHOULDN'T WE GO AFTER HIM?!
LET'S SEE, CRAZY GUY WITH KNIFE, OR CREEPY ROOM!
TOUGH CHOICE, HUH?

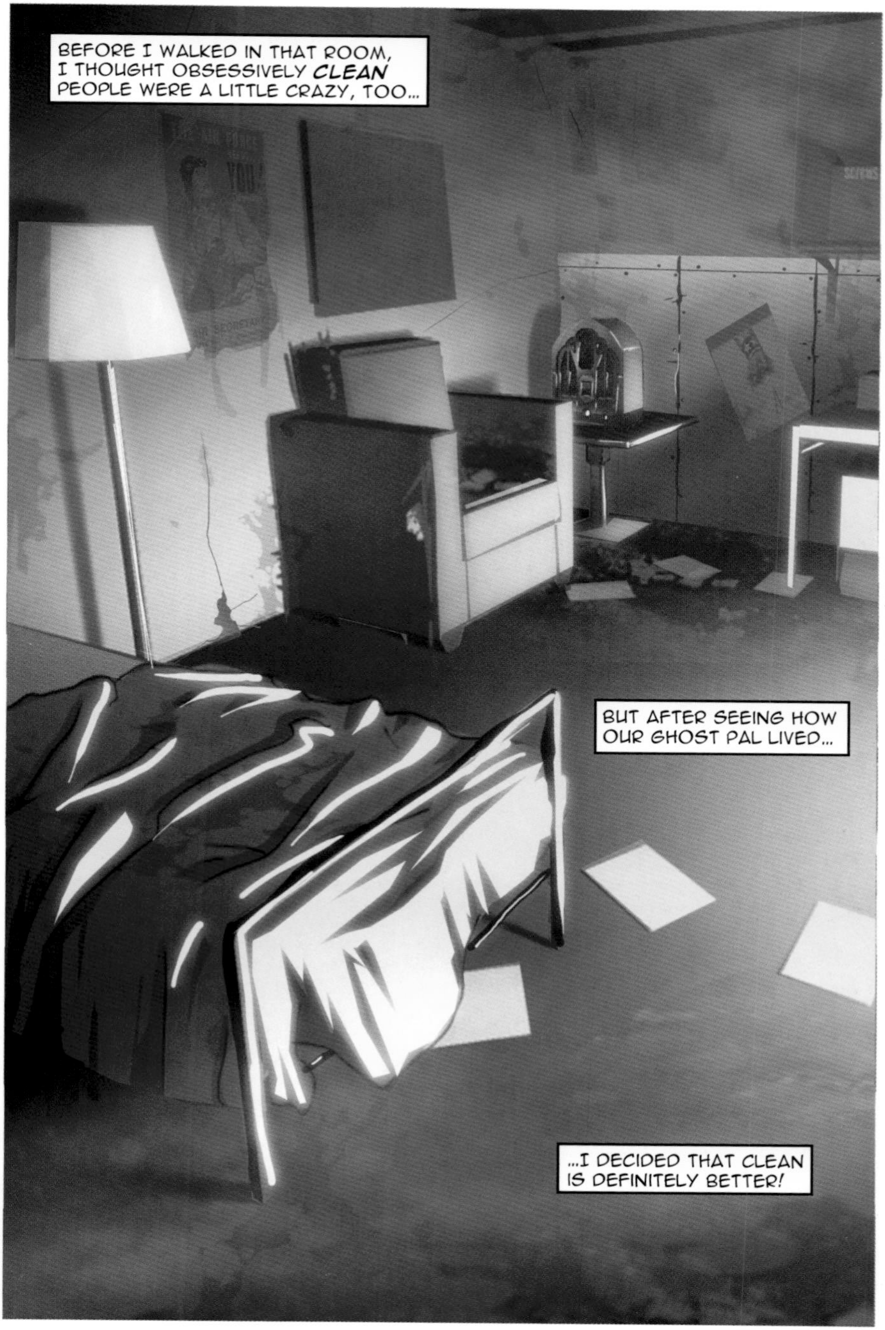
BEFORE I WALKED IN THAT ROOM, I THOUGHT OBSESSIVELY CLEAN PEOPLE WERE A LITTLE CRAZY, TOO...
BUT AFTER SEEING HOW OUR GHOST PAL LIVED...
...I DECIDED THAT CLEAN IS DEFINITELY BETTER!

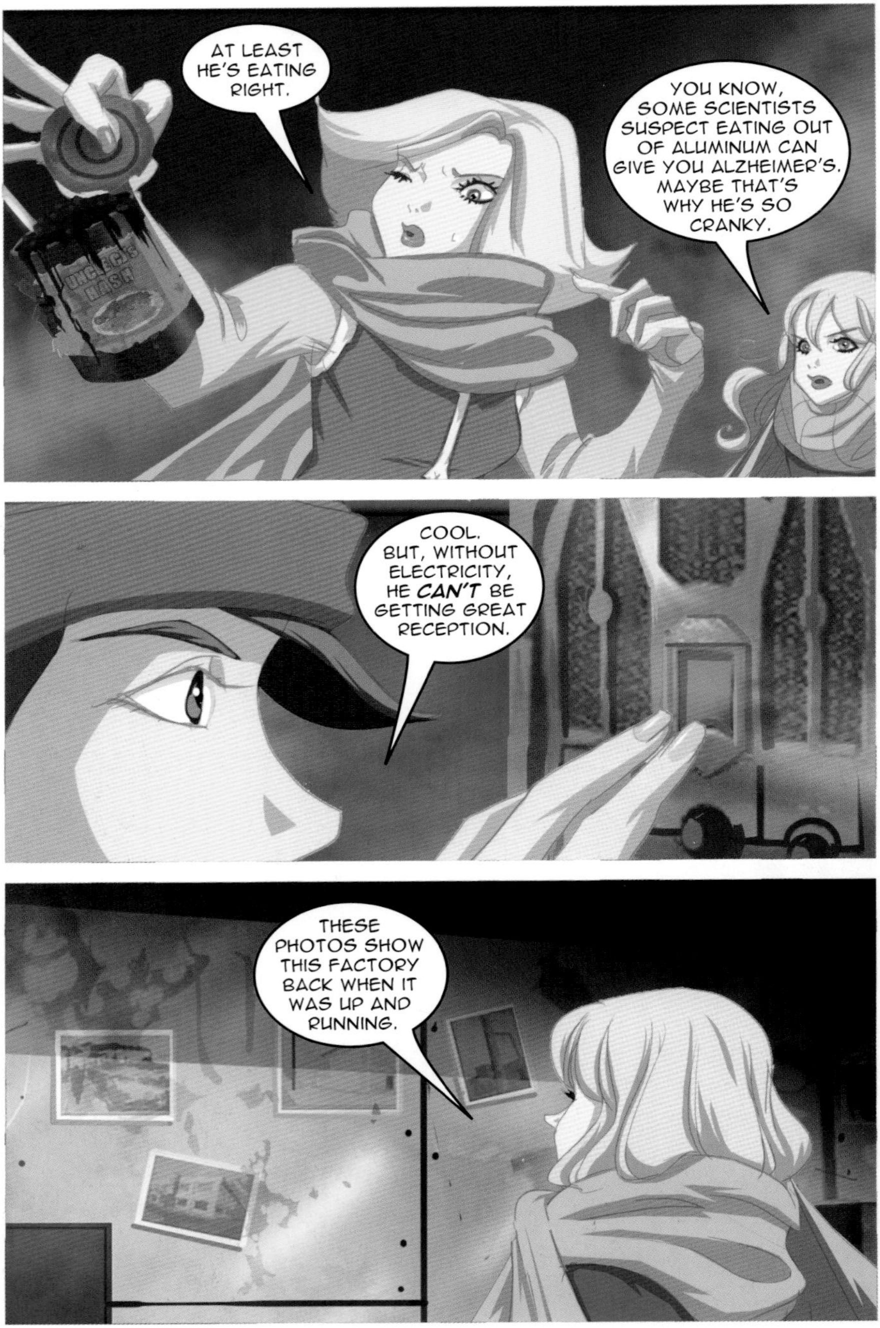
AT LEAST HE'S EATING RIGHT.
YOU KNOW, SOME SCIENTISTS SUSPECT EATING OUT OF ALUMINUM CAN GIVE YOU ALZHEIMER'S. MAYBE THAT'S WHY HE'S SO CRANKY.
COOL. BUT, WITHOUT ELECTRICITY, HE *CAN'T* BE GETTING GREAT RECEPTION.
THESE PHOTOS SHOW THIS FACTORY BACK WHEN IT WAS UP AND RUNNING.

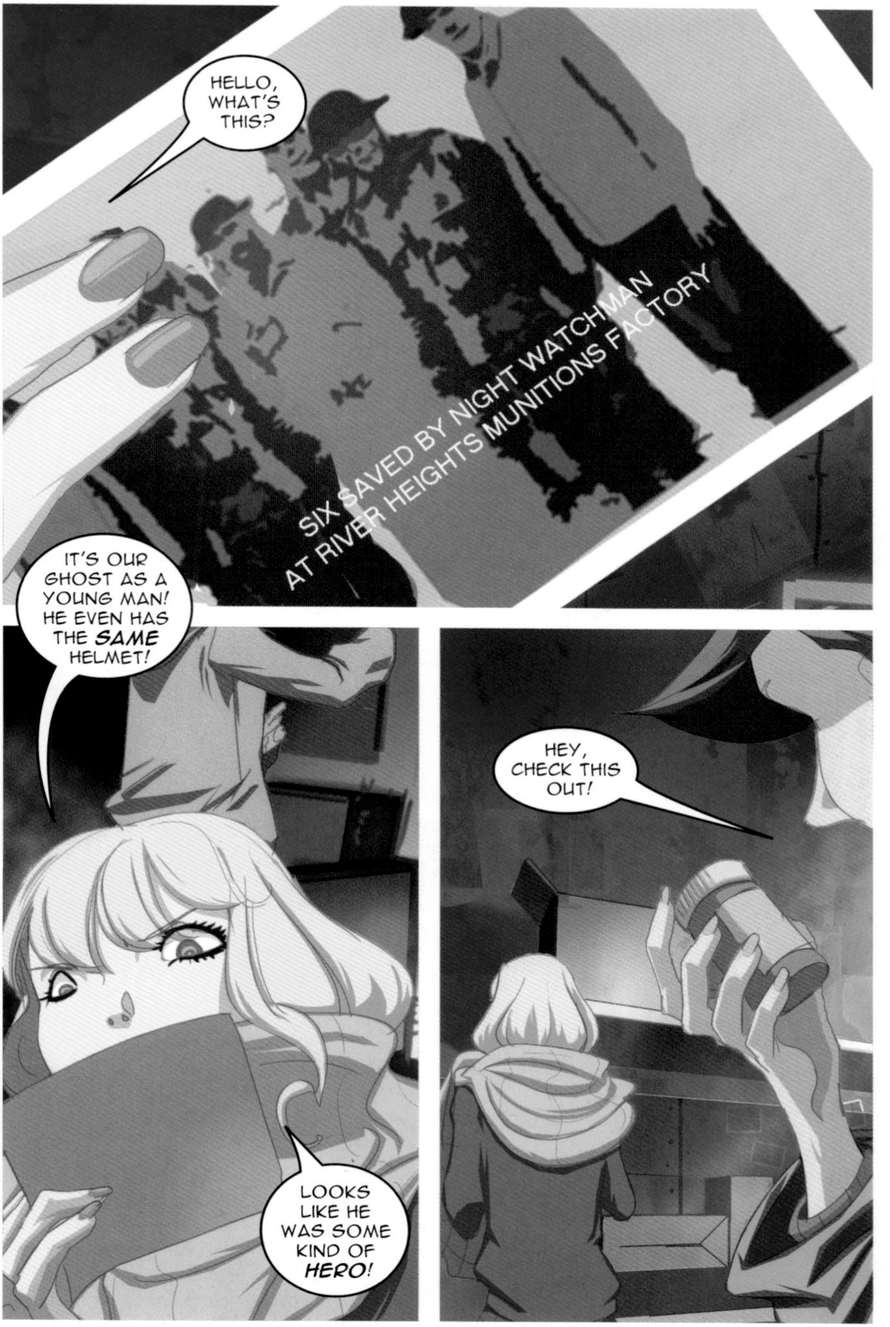
HELLO, WHAT'S THIS?
SIX SAVED BY NIGHT WATCHMAN AT RIVER HEIGHTS MUNITIONS FACTORY
IT'S OUR GHOST AS A YOUNG MAN! HE EVEN HAS THE SAME HELMET!
LOOKS LIKE HE WAS SOME KIND OF HERO!
HEY, CHECK THIS OUT!

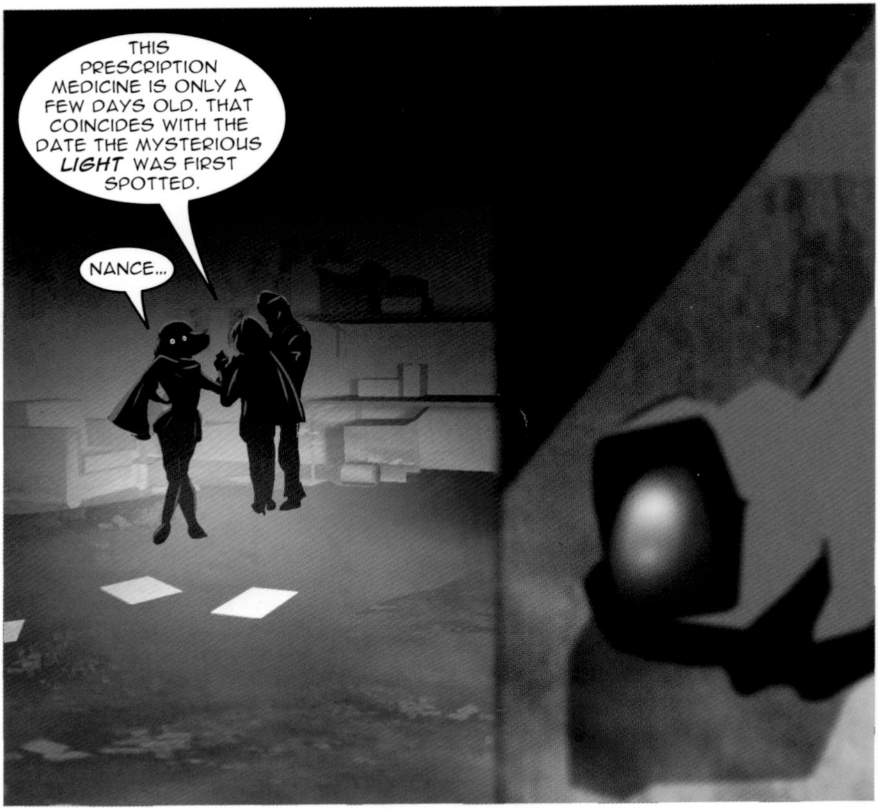
THIS PRESCRIPTION MEDICINE IS ONLY A FEW DAYS OLD. THAT COINCIDES WITH THE DATE THE MYSTERIOUS LIGHT WAS FIRST SPOTTED.
NANCE...

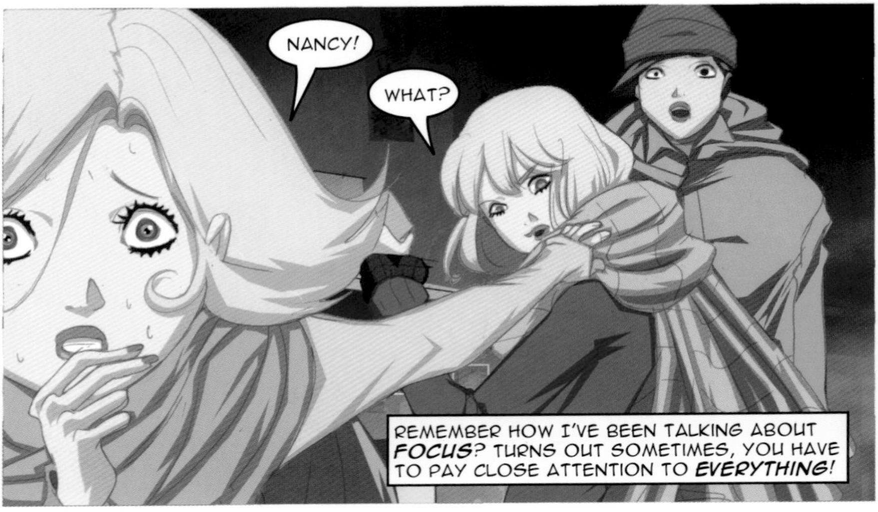
NANCY!
WHAT?
REMEMBER HOW I'VE BEEN TALKING ABOUT FOCUS? TURNS OUT SOMETIMES, YOU HAVE TO PAY CLOSE ATTENTION TO EVERYTHING!

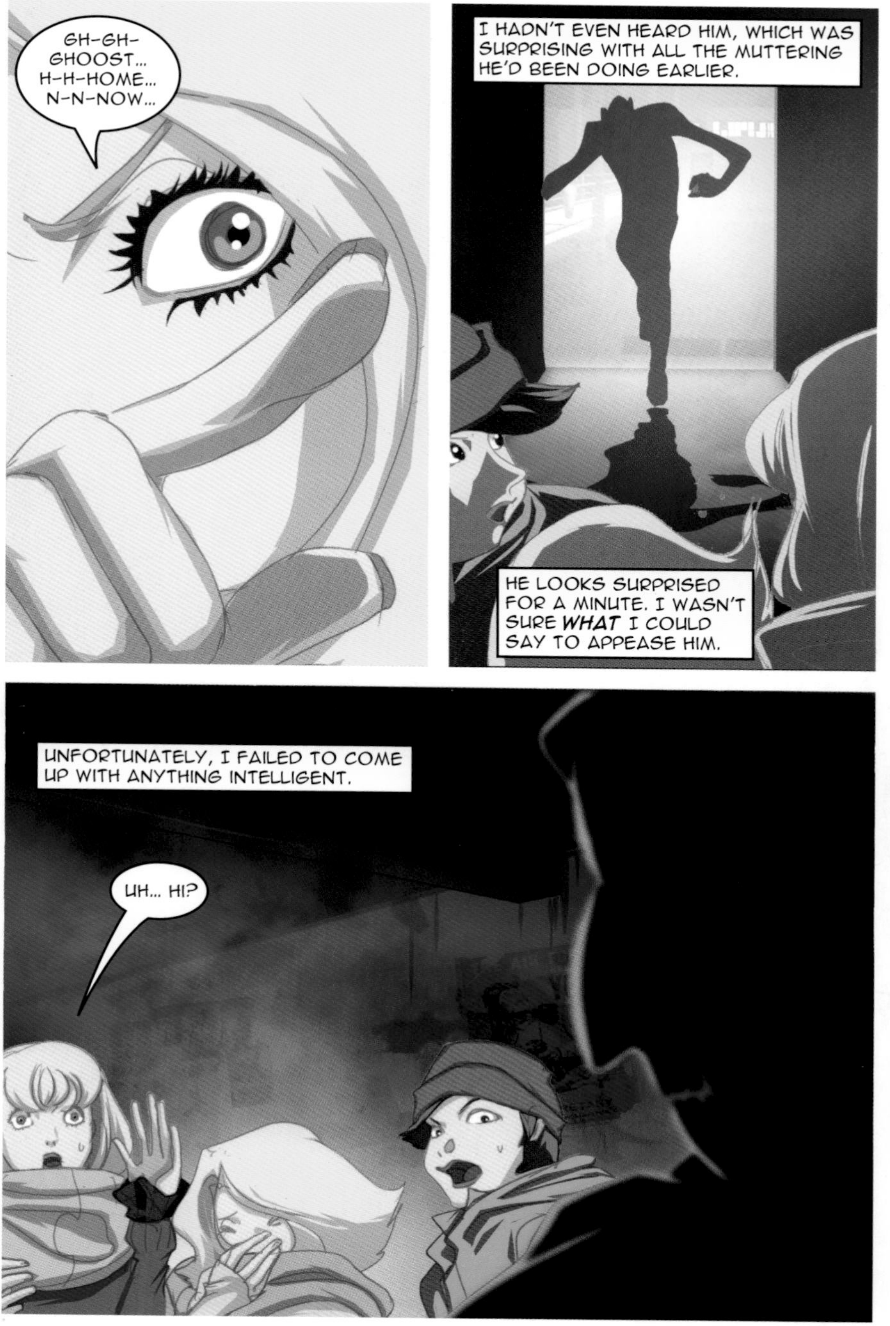
GH-GH-GHOOST... H-H-HOME... N-N-NOW...
I HADN'T EVEN HEARD HIM, WHICH WAS SURPRISING WITH ALL THE MUTTERING HE'D BEEN DOING EARLIER.
HE LOOKS SURPRISED FOR A MINUTE. I WASN'T SURE ***WHAT*** I COULD SAY TO APPEASE HIM.
UNFORTUNATELY, I FAILED TO COME UP WITH ANYTHING INTELLIGENT.
UH... HI?

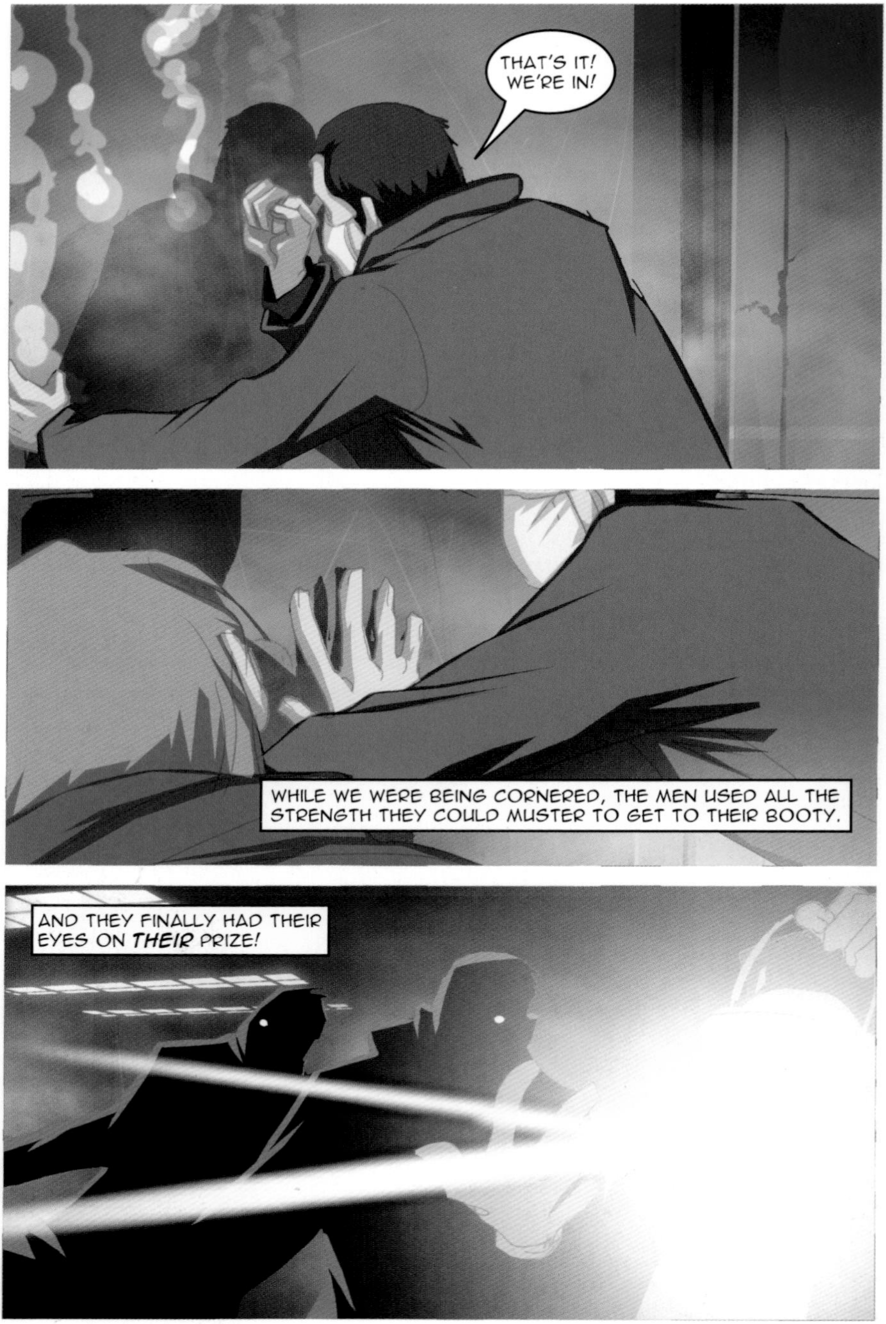
THAT'S IT! WE'RE IN!
WHILE WE WERE BEING CORNERED, THE MEN USED ALL THE STRENGTH THEY COULD MUSTER TO GET TO THEIR BOOTY.
AND THEY FINALLY HAD THEIR EYES ON *THEIR* PRIZE!

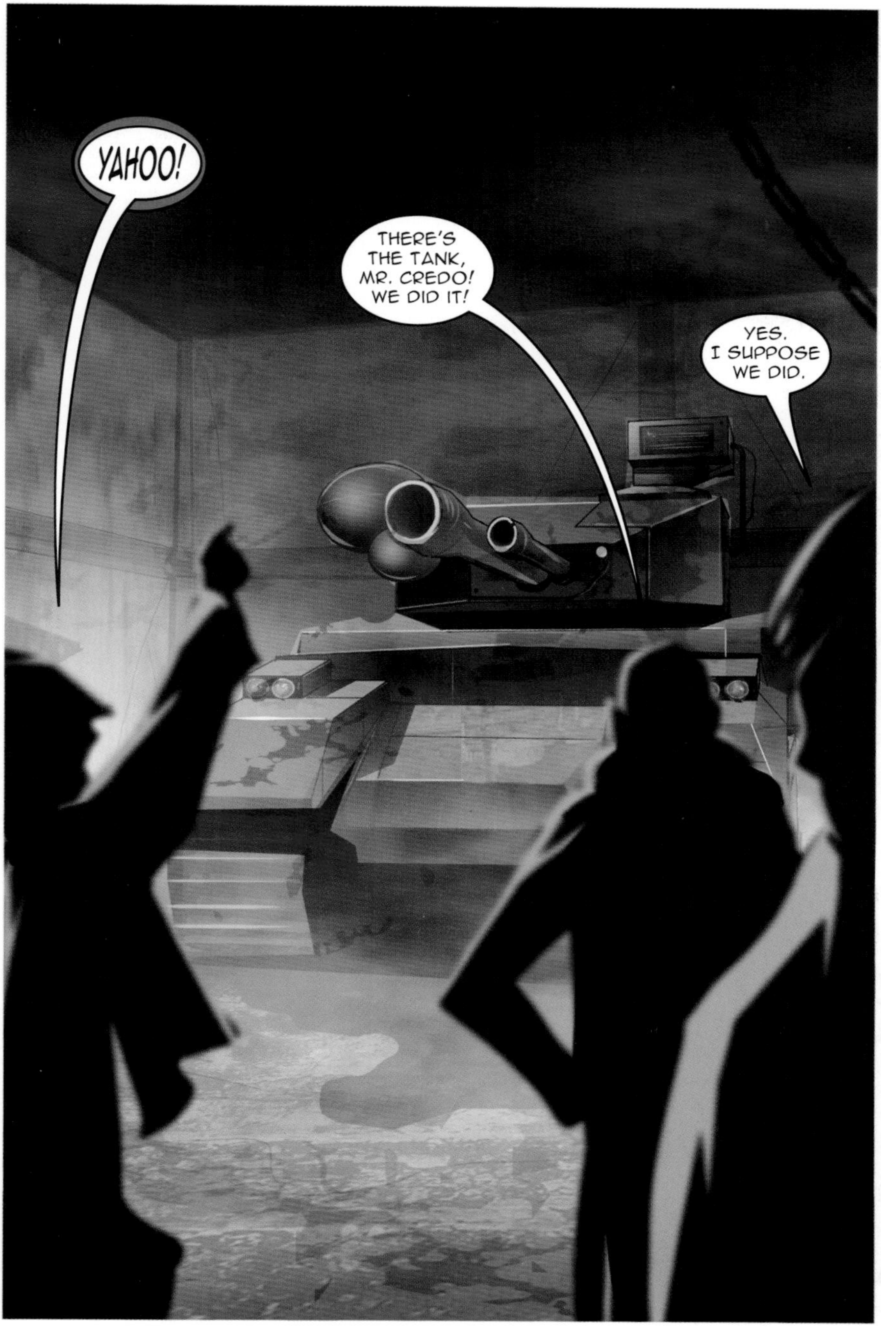
YAHOO!
THERE'S THE TANK, MR. CREDO! WE DID IT!
YES. I SUPPOSE WE DID.

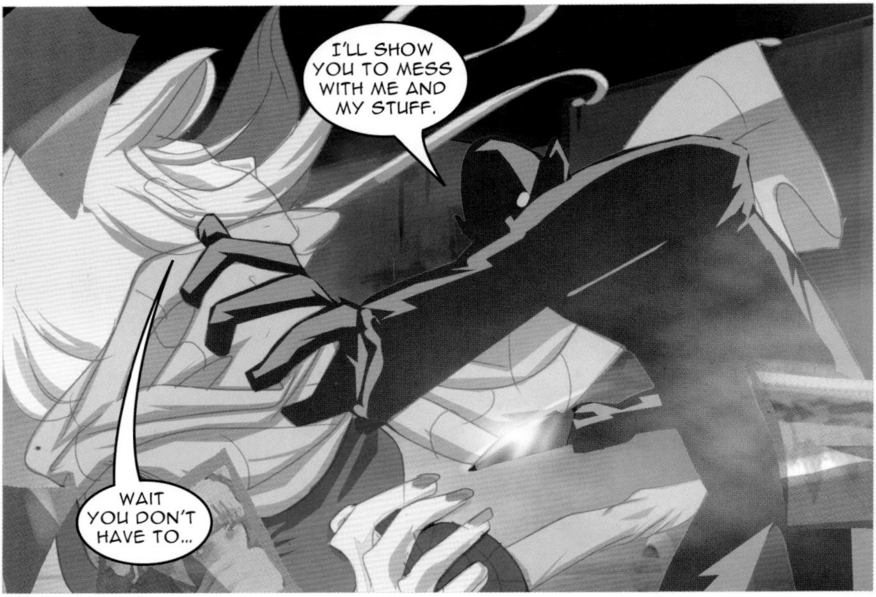
I'LL SHOW YOU TO MESS WITH ME AND MY STUFF.
WAIT YOU DON'T HAVE TO...

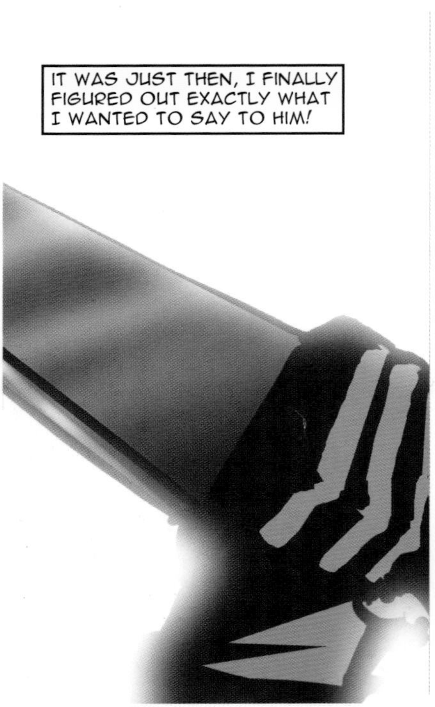
IT WAS JUST THEN, I FINALLY FIGURED OUT EXACTLY WHAT I WANTED TO SAY TO HIM!

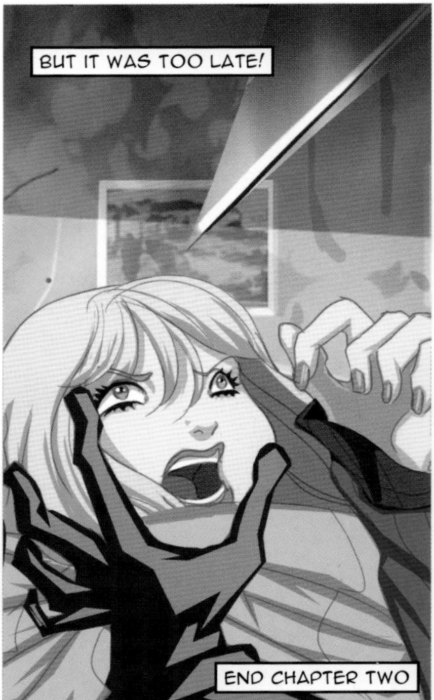
BUT IT WAS TOO LATE!
END CHAPTER TWO

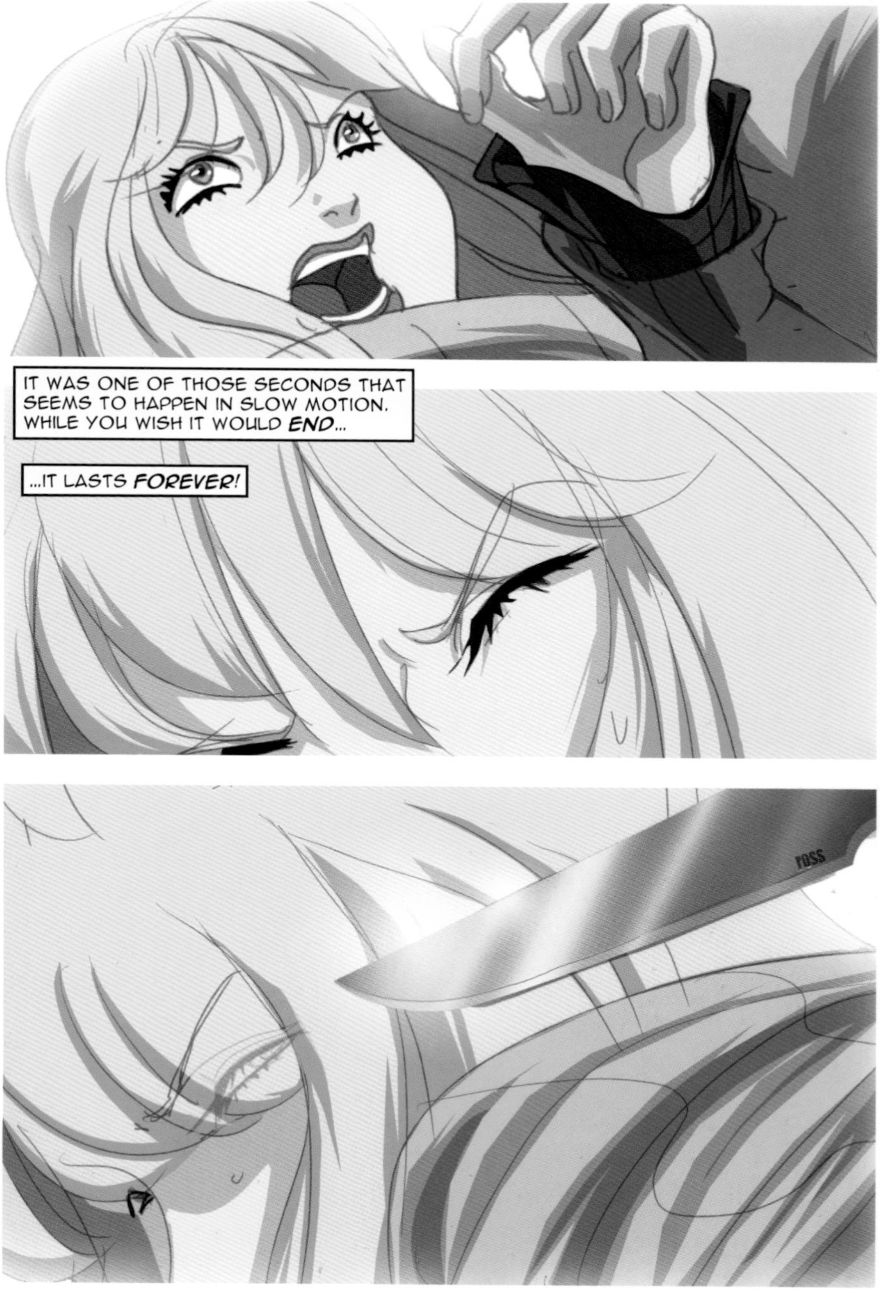
IT WAS ONE OF THOSE SECONDS THAT SEEMS TO HAPPEN IN SLOW MOTION. WHILE YOU WISH IT WOULD *END*...
...IT LASTS *FOREVER*!
ross

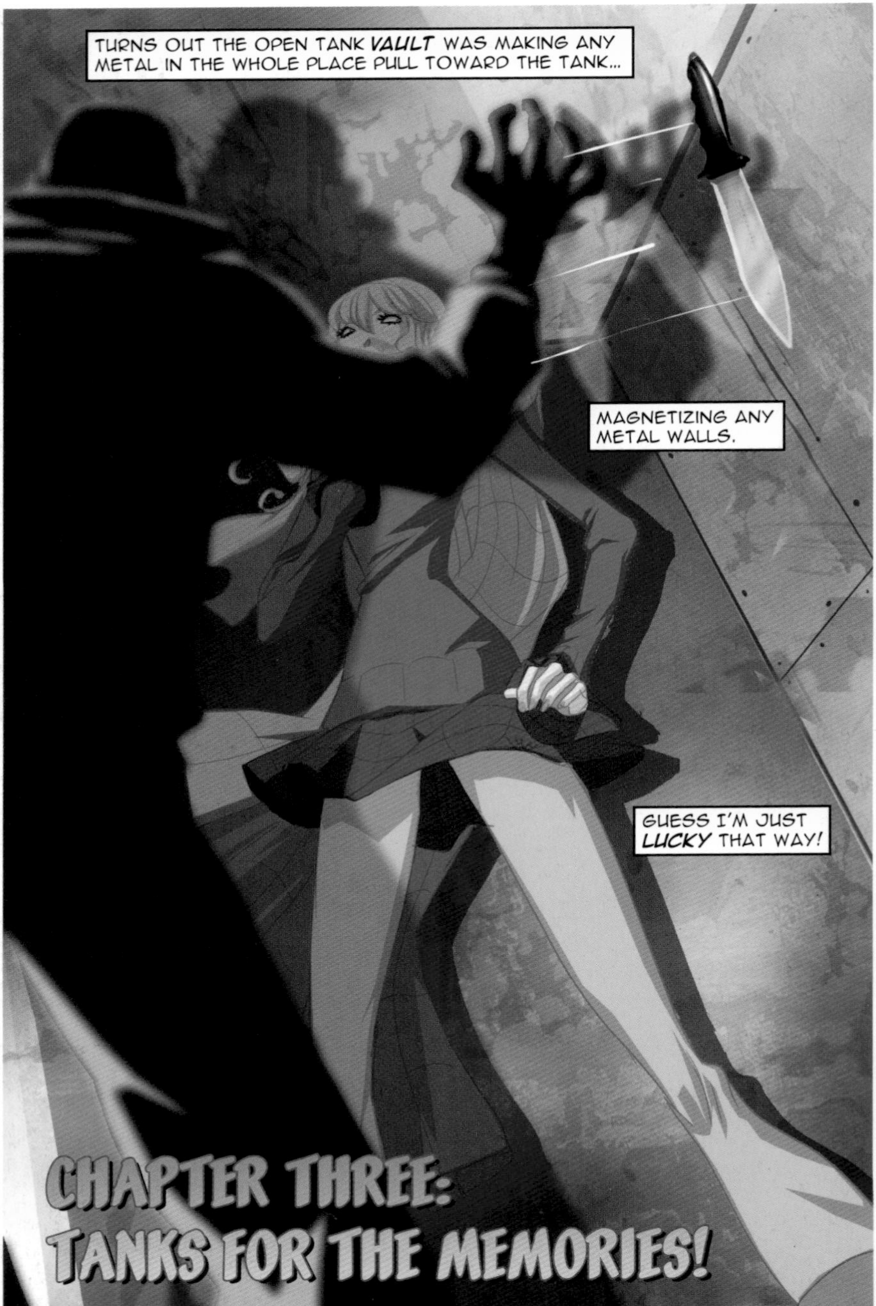
TURNS OUT THE OPEN TANK VAULT WAS MAKING ANY METAL IN THE WHOLE PLACE PULL TOWARD THE TANK...
MAGNETIZING ANY METAL WALLS.
GUESS I'M JUST LUCKY THAT WAY!
CHAPTER THREE: TANKS FOR THE MEMORIES!

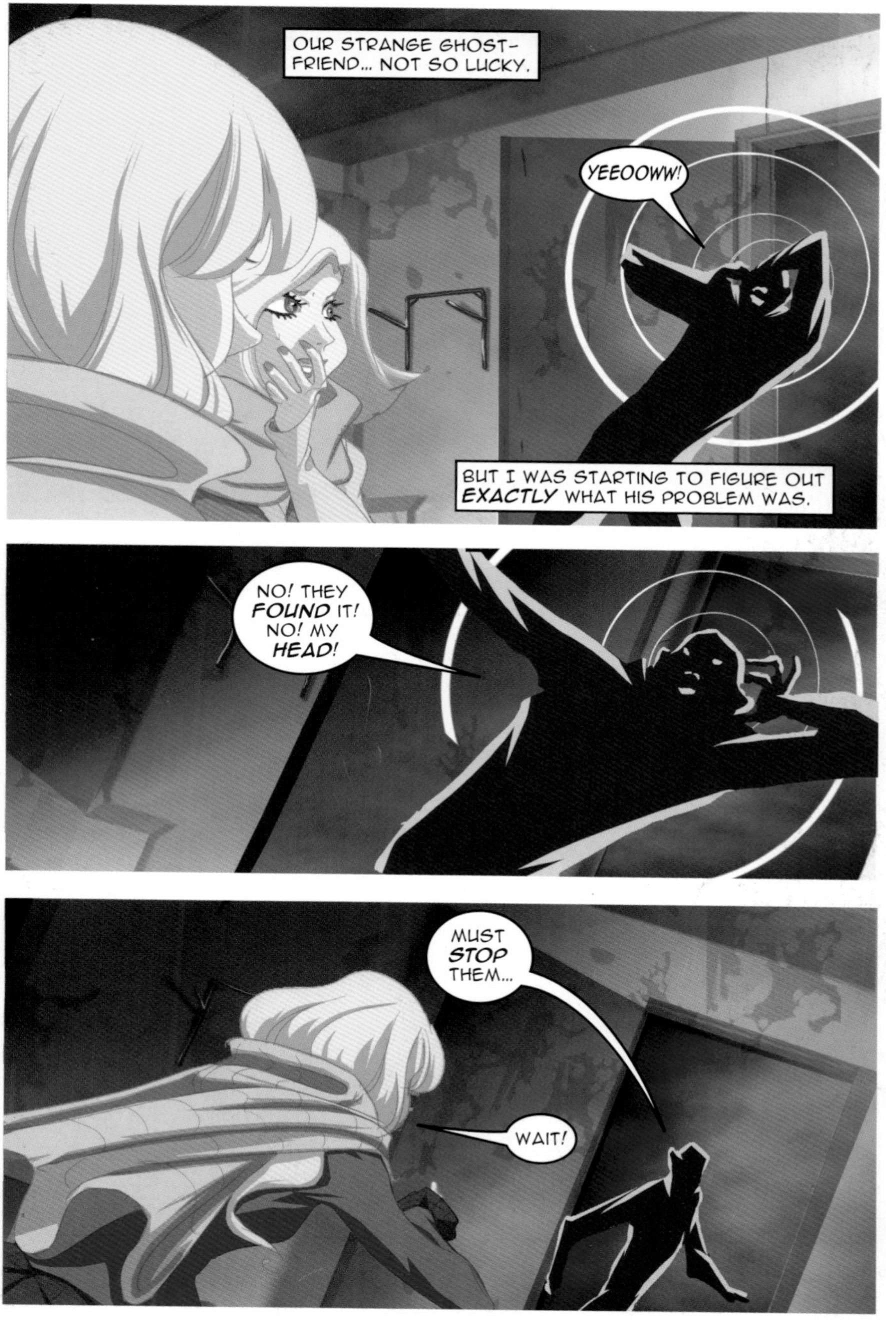
OUR STRANGE GHOST-FRIEND... NOT SO LUCKY.
YEEOOWW!
BUT I WAS STARTING TO FIGURE OUT EXACTLY WHAT HIS PROBLEM WAS.
NO! THEY FOUND IT! NO! MY HEAD!
MUST STOP THEM...
WAIT!

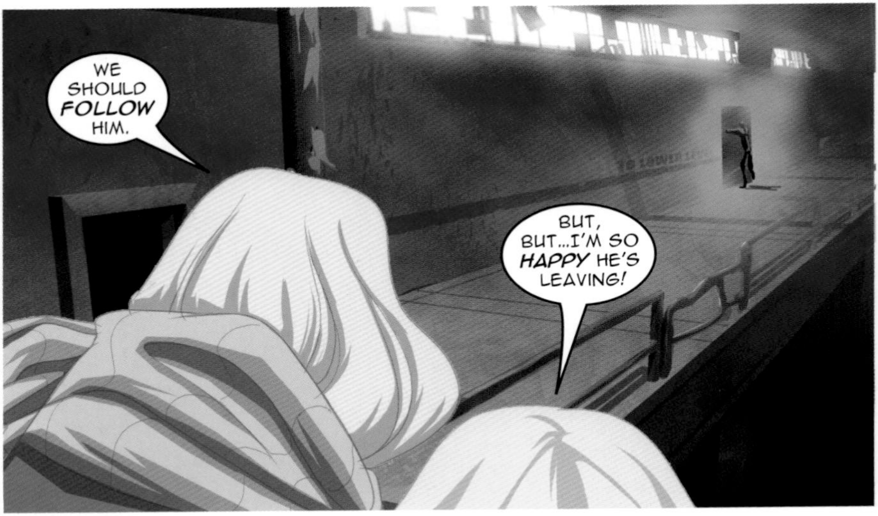
WE SHOULD FOLLOW HIM.
BUT, BUT...I'M SO HAPPY HE'S LEAVING!

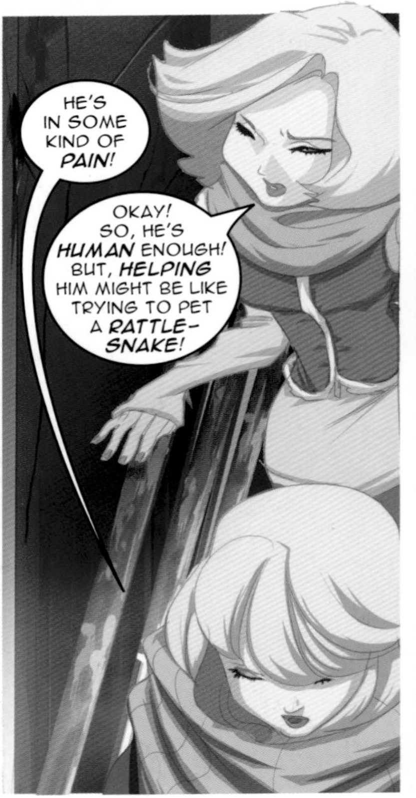
HE'S IN SOME KIND OF PAIN!
OKAY! SO, HE'S HUMAN ENOUGH! BUT, HELPING HIM MIGHT BE LIKE TRYING TO PET A RATTLE-SNAKE!

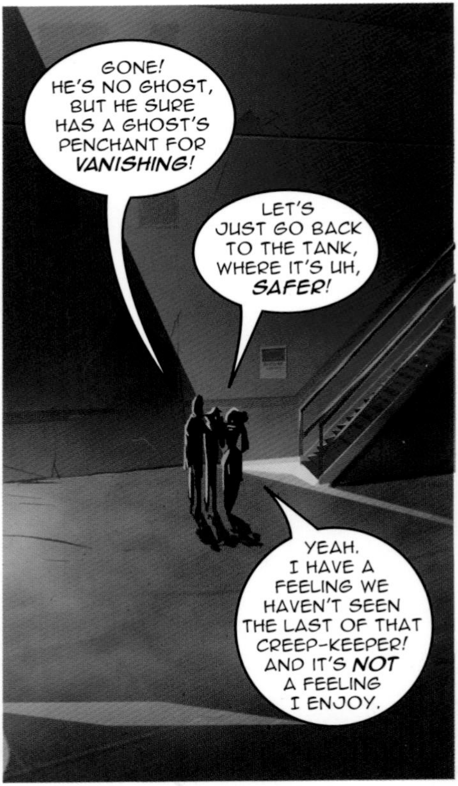
GONE! HE'S NO GHOST, BUT HE SURE HAS A GHOST'S PENCHANT FOR VANISHING!
LET'S JUST GO BACK TO THE TANK, WHERE IT'S UH, SAFER!
YEAH. I HAVE A FEELING WE HAVEN'T SEEN THE LAST OF THAT CREEP-KEEPER! AND IT'S NOT A FEELING I ENJOY.

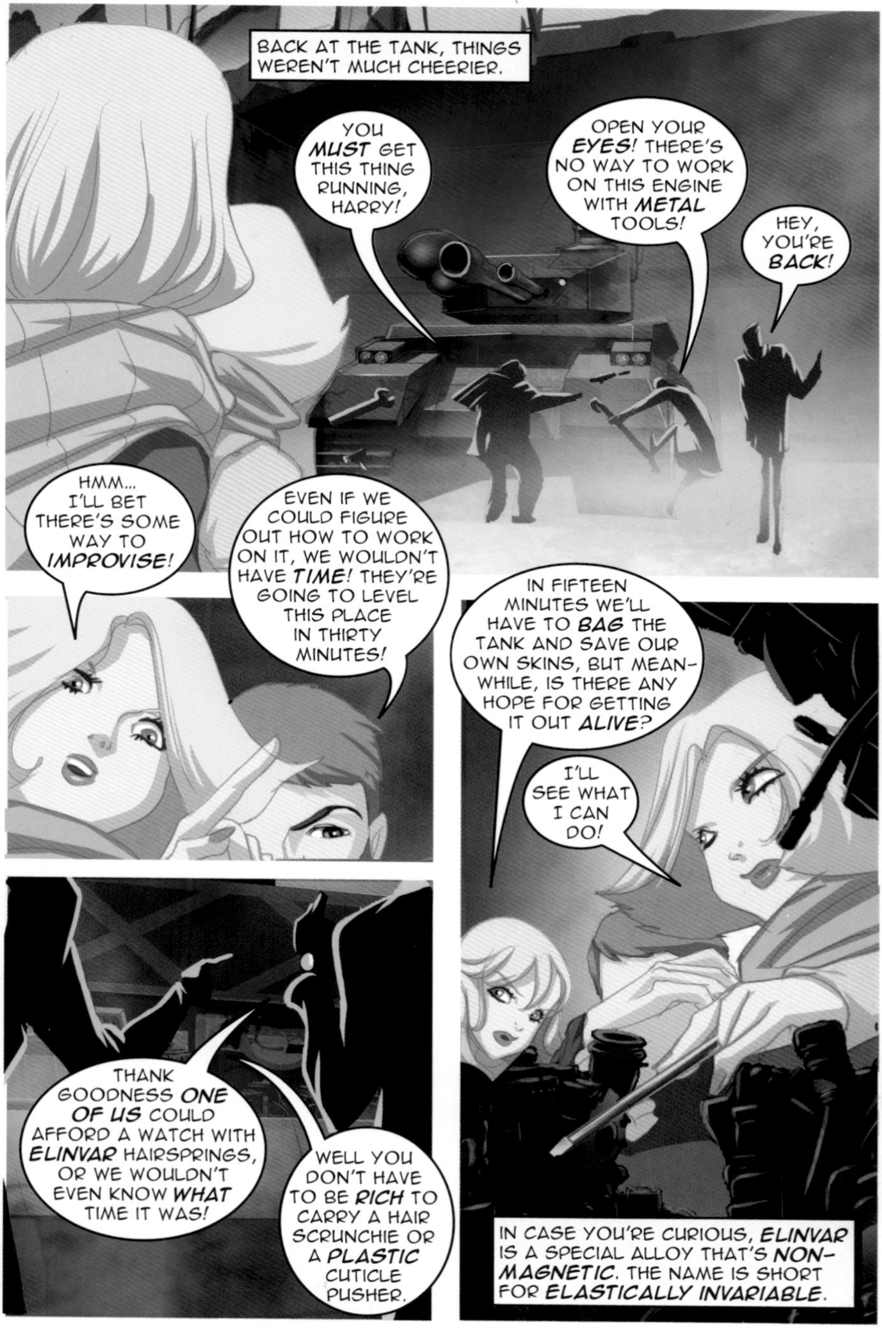
BACK AT THE TANK, THINGS WEREN'T MUCH CHEERIER.
YOU MUST GET THIS THING RUNNING, HARRY!
OPEN YOUR EYES! THERE'S NO WAY TO WORK ON THIS ENGINE WITH METAL TOOLS!
HEY, YOU'RE BACK!
HMM... I'LL BET THERE'S SOME WAY TO IMPROVISE!
EVEN IF WE COULD FIGURE OUT HOW TO WORK ON IT, WE WOULDN'T HAVE TIME! THEY'RE GOING TO LEVEL THIS PLACE IN THIRTY MINUTES!
IN FIFTEEN MINUTES WE'LL HAVE TO BAG THE TANK AND SAVE OUR OWN SKINS, BUT MEAN-WHILE, IS THERE ANY HOPE FOR GETTING IT OUT ALIVE?
I'LL SEE WHAT I CAN DO!
THANK GOODNESS ONE OF US COULD AFFORD A WATCH WITH ELINVAR HAIRSPRINGS, OR WE WOULDN'T EVEN KNOW WHAT TIME IT WAS!
WELL YOU DON'T HAVE TO BE RICH TO CARRY A HAIR SCRUNCHIE OR A PLASTIC CUTICLE PUSHER.
IN CASE YOU'RE CURIOUS, ELINVAR IS A SPECIAL ALLOY THAT'S NON-MAGNETIC. THE NAME IS SHORT FOR ELASTICALLY INVARIABLE.

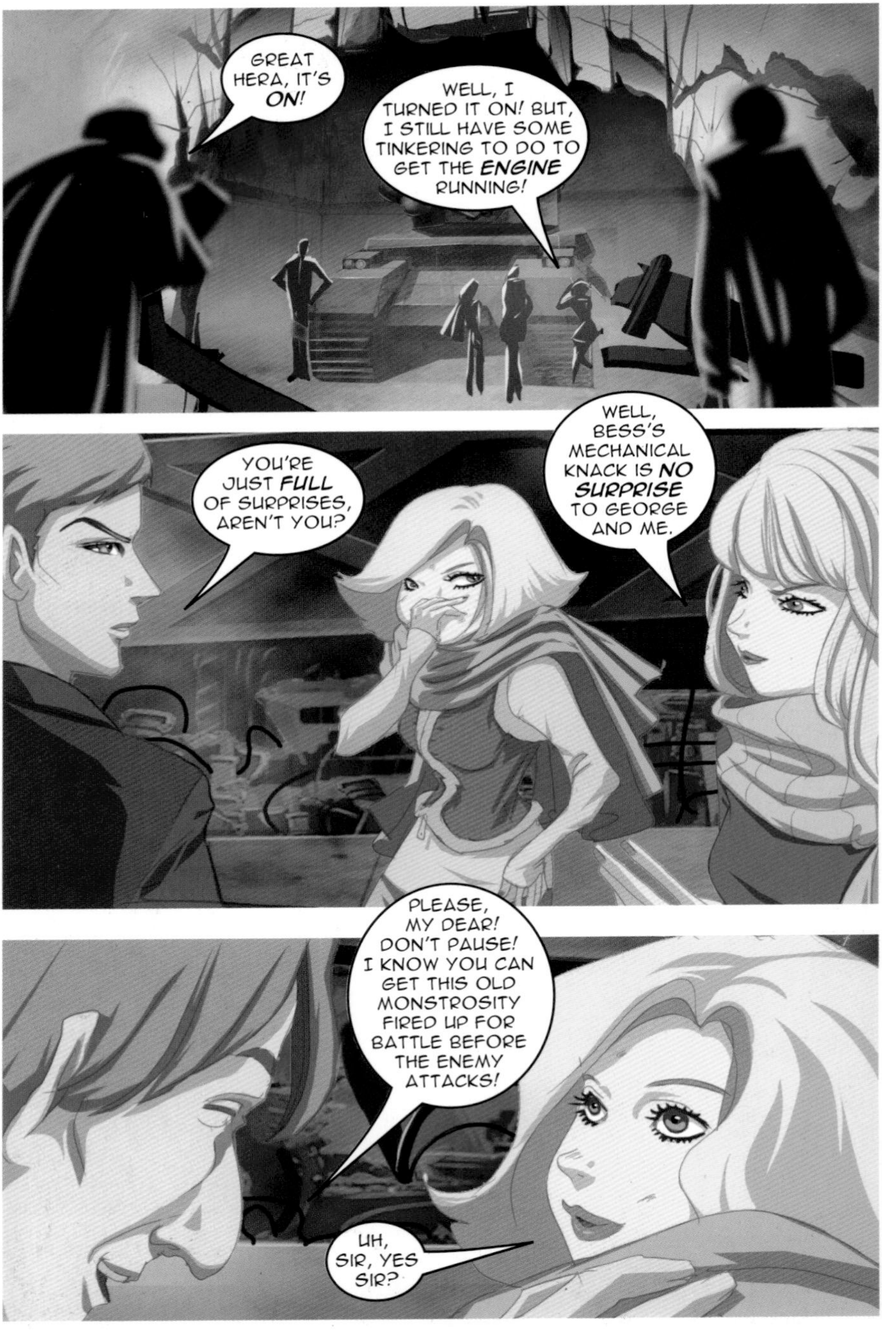
GREAT HERA, IT'S ON!
WELL, I TURNED IT ON! BUT, I STILL HAVE SOME TINKERING TO DO TO GET THE ENGINE RUNNING!
YOU'RE JUST FULL OF SURPRISES, AREN'T YOU?
WELL, BESS'S MECHANICAL KNACK IS NO SURPRISE TO GEORGE AND ME.
PLEASE, MY DEAR! DON'T PAUSE! I KNOW YOU CAN GET THIS OLD MONSTROSITY FIRED UP FOR BATTLE BEFORE THE ENEMY ATTACKS!
UH, SIR, YES SIR?

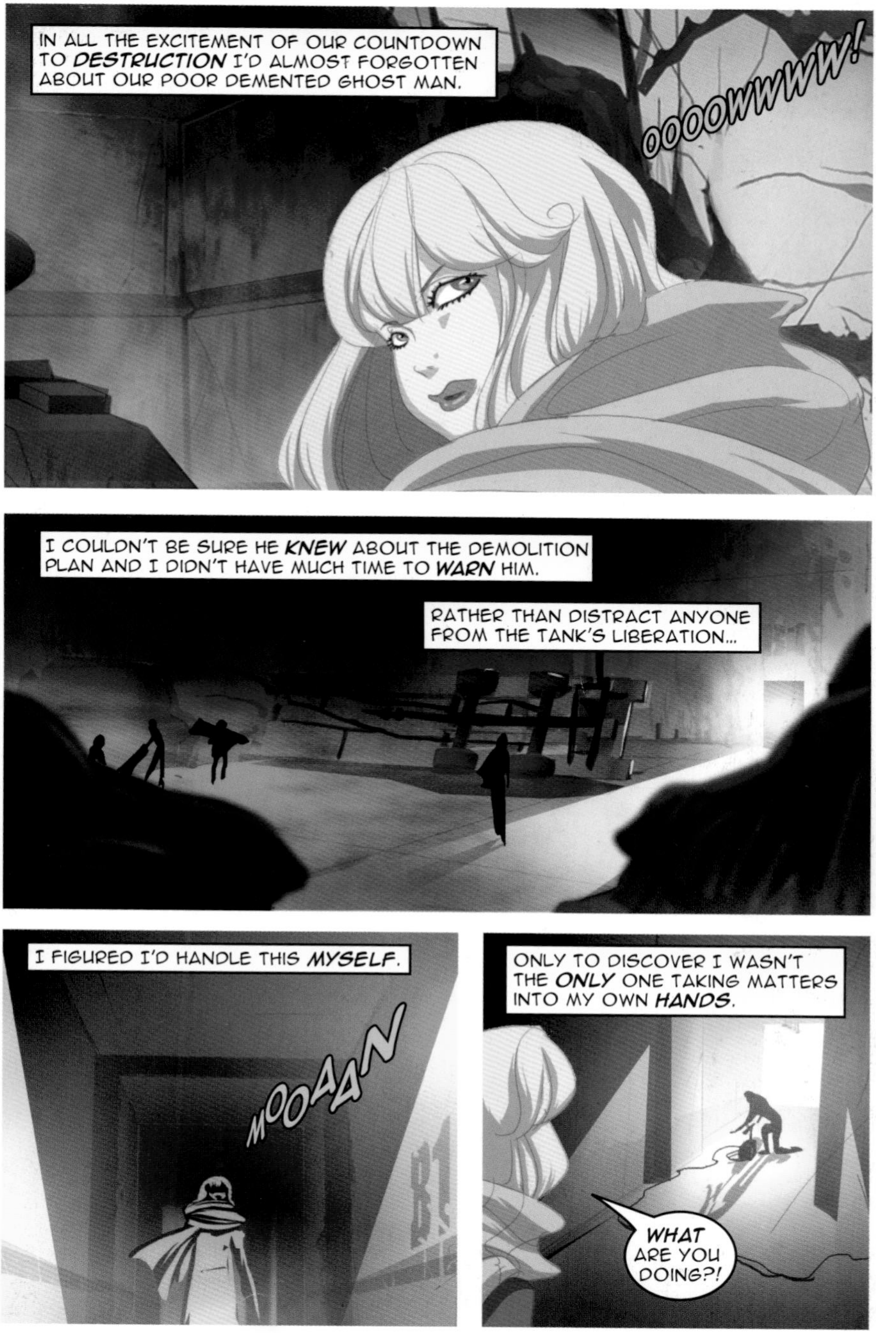
IN ALL THE EXCITEMENT OF OUR COUNTDOWN TO DESTRUCTION I'D ALMOST FORGOTTEN ABOUT OUR POOR DEMENTED GHOST MAN.
OOOOWWWW!
I COULDN'T BE SURE HE KNEW ABOUT THE DEMOLITION PLAN AND I DIDN'T HAVE MUCH TIME TO WARN HIM.
RATHER THAN DISTRACT ANYONE FROM THE TANK'S LIBERATION...
I FIGURED I'D HANDLE THIS MYSELF.
MOOAAN
ONLY TO DISCOVER I WASN'T THE ONLY ONE TAKING MATTERS INTO MY OWN HANDS.
WHAT ARE YOU DOING?!

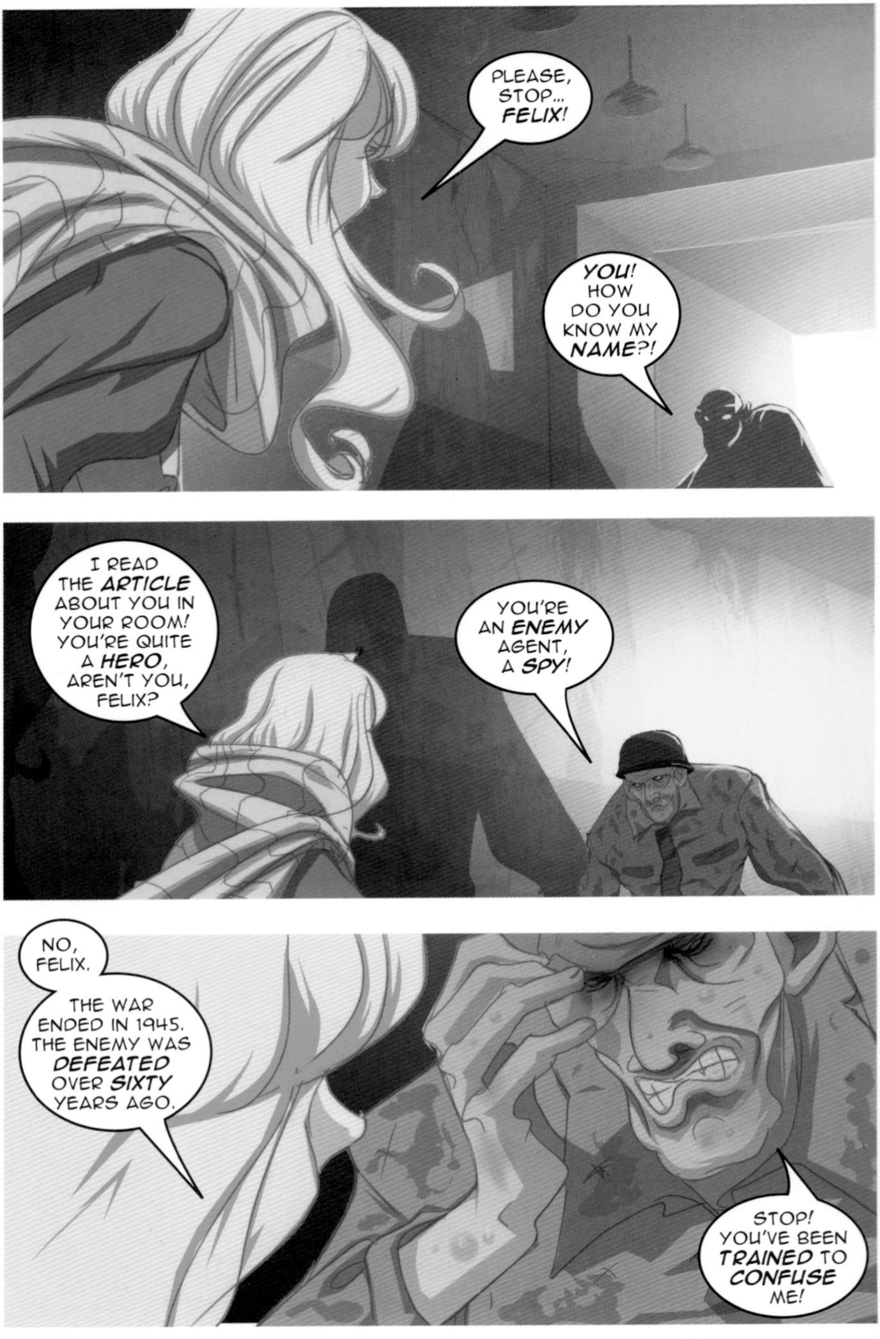
PLEASE, STOP... FELIX!
YOU! HOW DO YOU KNOW MY NAME?!
I READ THE ARTICLE ABOUT YOU IN YOUR ROOM! YOU'RE QUITE A HERO, AREN'T YOU, FELIX?
YOU'RE AN ENEMY AGENT, A SPY!
NO, FELIX.
THE WAR ENDED IN 1945. THE ENEMY WAS DEFEATED OVER SIXTY YEARS AGO.
STOP! YOU'VE BEEN TRAINED TO CONFUSE ME!

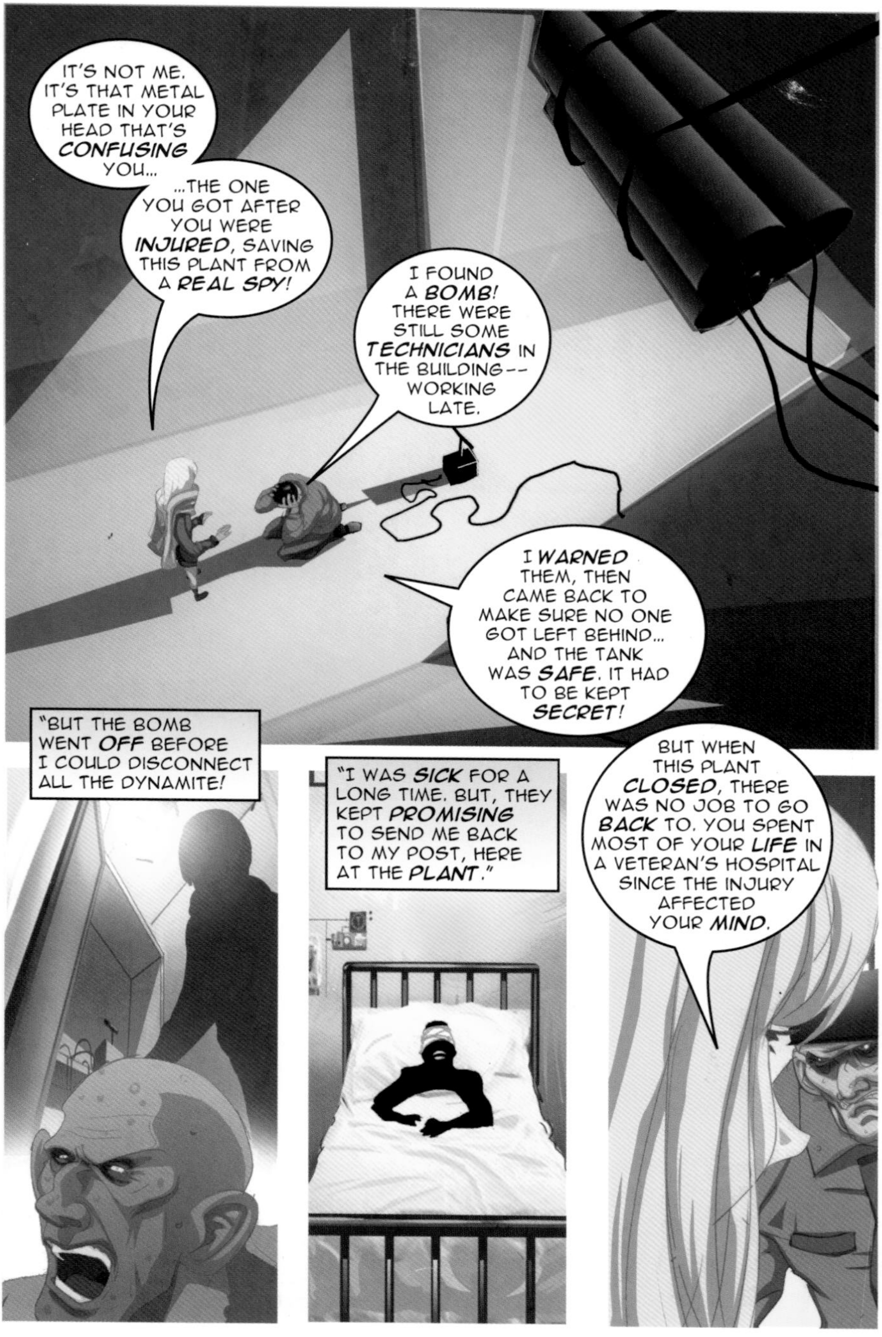

IT'S NOT ME. IT'S THAT METAL PLATE IN YOUR HEAD THAT'S CONFUSING YOU...
...THE ONE YOU GOT AFTER YOU WERE INJURED, SAVING THIS PLANT FROM A REAL SPY!
I FOUND A BOMB! THERE WERE STILL SOME TECHNICIANS IN THE BUILDING-- WORKING LATE.
I WARNED THEM, THEN CAME BACK TO MAKE SURE NO ONE GOT LEFT BEHIND... AND THE TANK WAS SAFE. IT HAD TO BE KEPT SECRET!
"BUT THE BOMB WENT OFF BEFORE I COULD DISCONNECT ALL THE DYNAMITE!
"I WAS SICK FOR A LONG TIME. BUT, THEY KEPT PROMISING TO SEND ME BACK TO MY POST, HERE AT THE PLANT."
BUT WHEN THIS PLANT CLOSED, THERE WAS NO JOB TO GO BACK TO. YOU SPENT MOST OF YOUR LIFE IN A VETERAN'S HOSPITAL SINCE THE INJURY AFFECTED YOUR MIND.

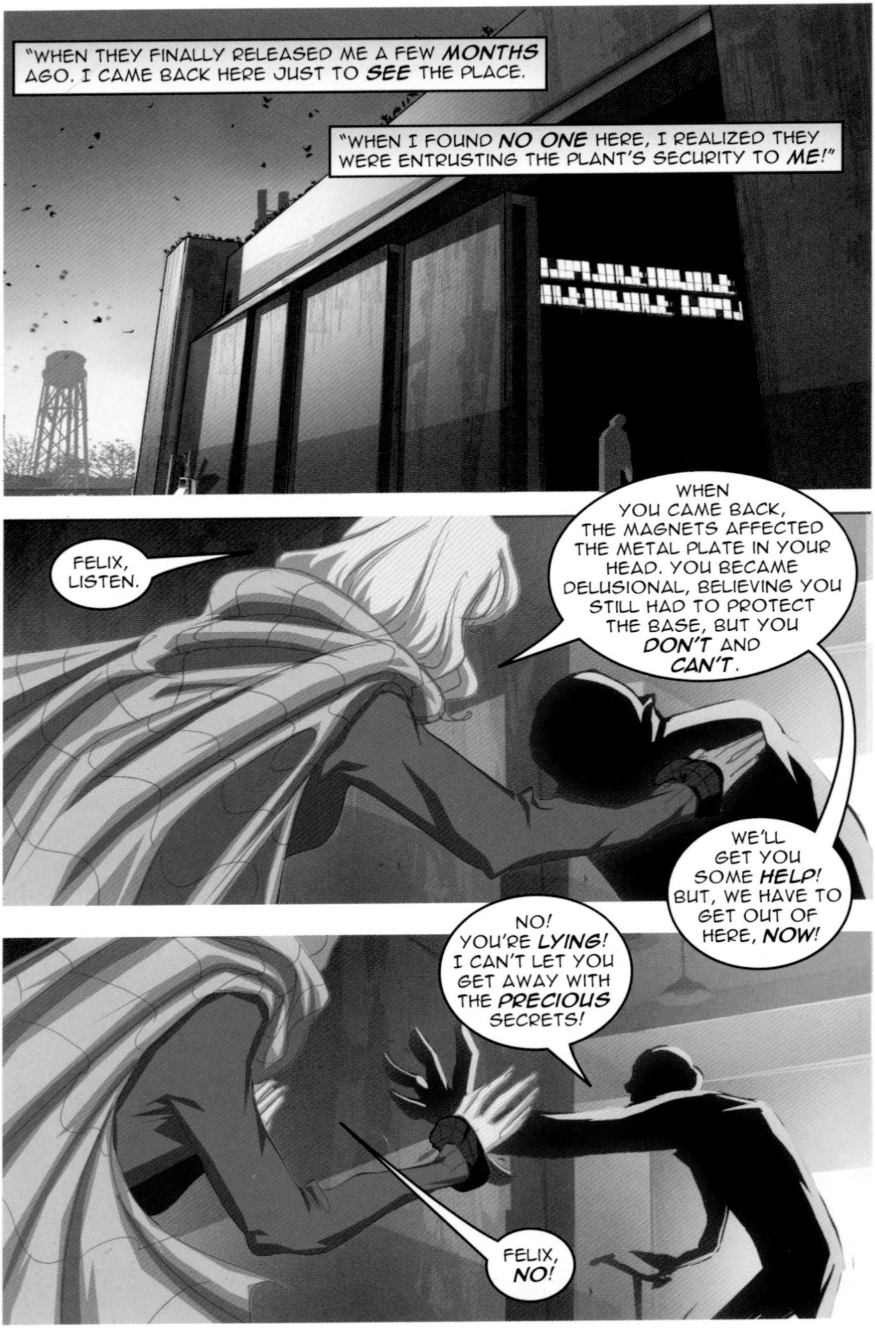
"WHEN THEY FINALLY RELEASED ME A FEW MONTHS AGO. I CAME BACK HERE JUST TO SEE THE PLACE.
"WHEN I FOUND NO ONE HERE, I REALIZED THEY WERE ENTRUSTING THE PLANT'S SECURITY TO ME!"
FELIX, LISTEN.
WHEN YOU CAME BACK, THE MAGNETS AFFECTED THE METAL PLATE IN YOUR HEAD. YOU BECAME DELUSIONAL, BELIEVING YOU STILL HAD TO PROTECT THE BASE, BUT YOU DON'T AND CAN'T.
WE'LL GET YOU SOME HELP! BUT, WE HAVE TO GET OUT OF HERE, NOW!
NO! YOU'RE LYING! I CAN'T LET YOU GET AWAY WITH THE PRECIOUS SECRETS!
FELIX, NO!

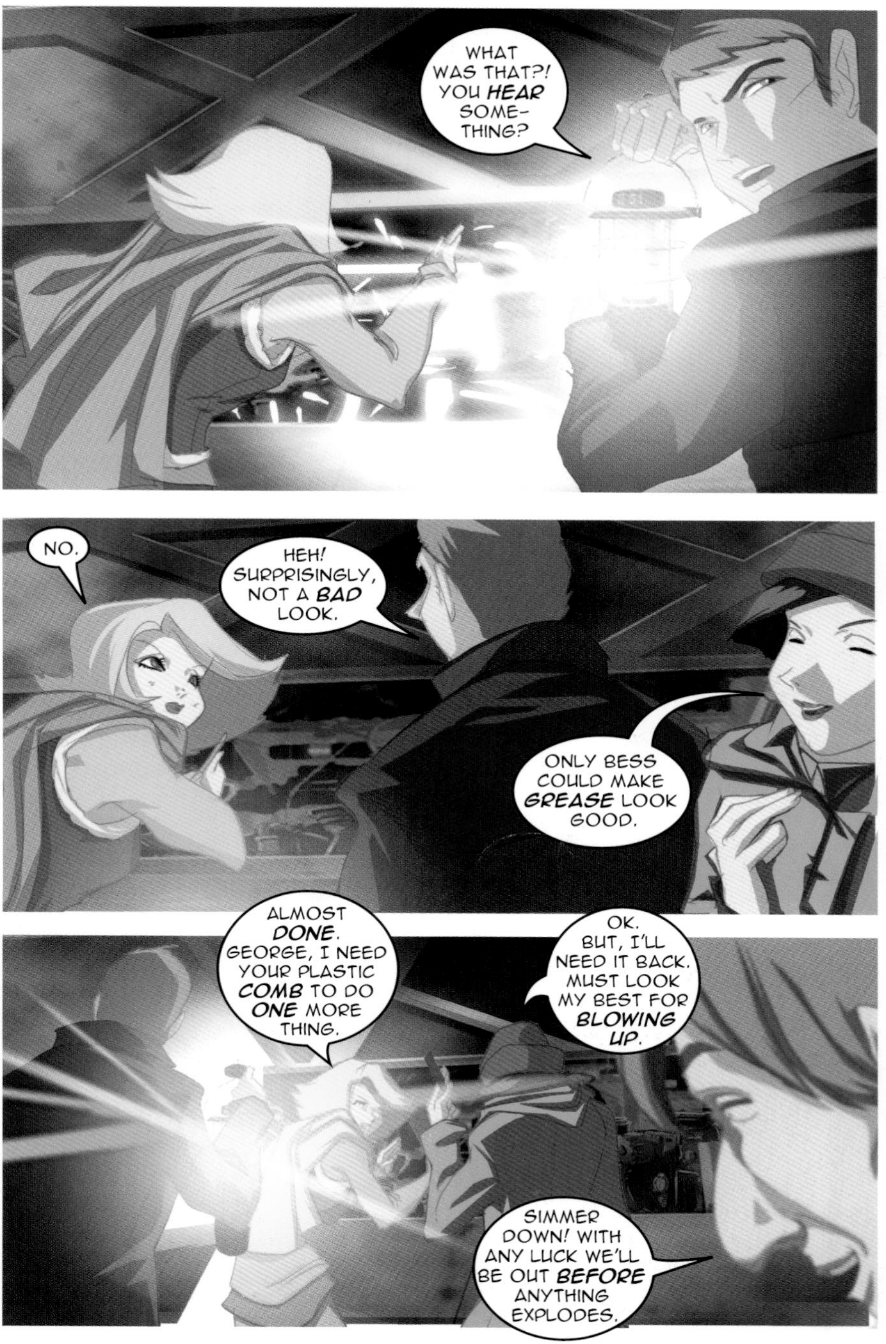
WHAT WAS THAT?! YOU HEAR SOME-THING?
NO.
HEH! SURPRISINGLY, NOT A BAD LOOK.
ONLY BESS COULD MAKE GREASE LOOK GOOD.
ALMOST DONE. GEORGE, I NEED YOUR PLASTIC COMB TO DO ONE MORE THING.
OK. BUT, I'LL NEED IT BACK. MUST LOOK MY BEST FOR BLOWING UP.
SIMMER DOWN! WITH ANY LUCK WE'LL BE OUT BEFORE ANYTHING EXPLODES.

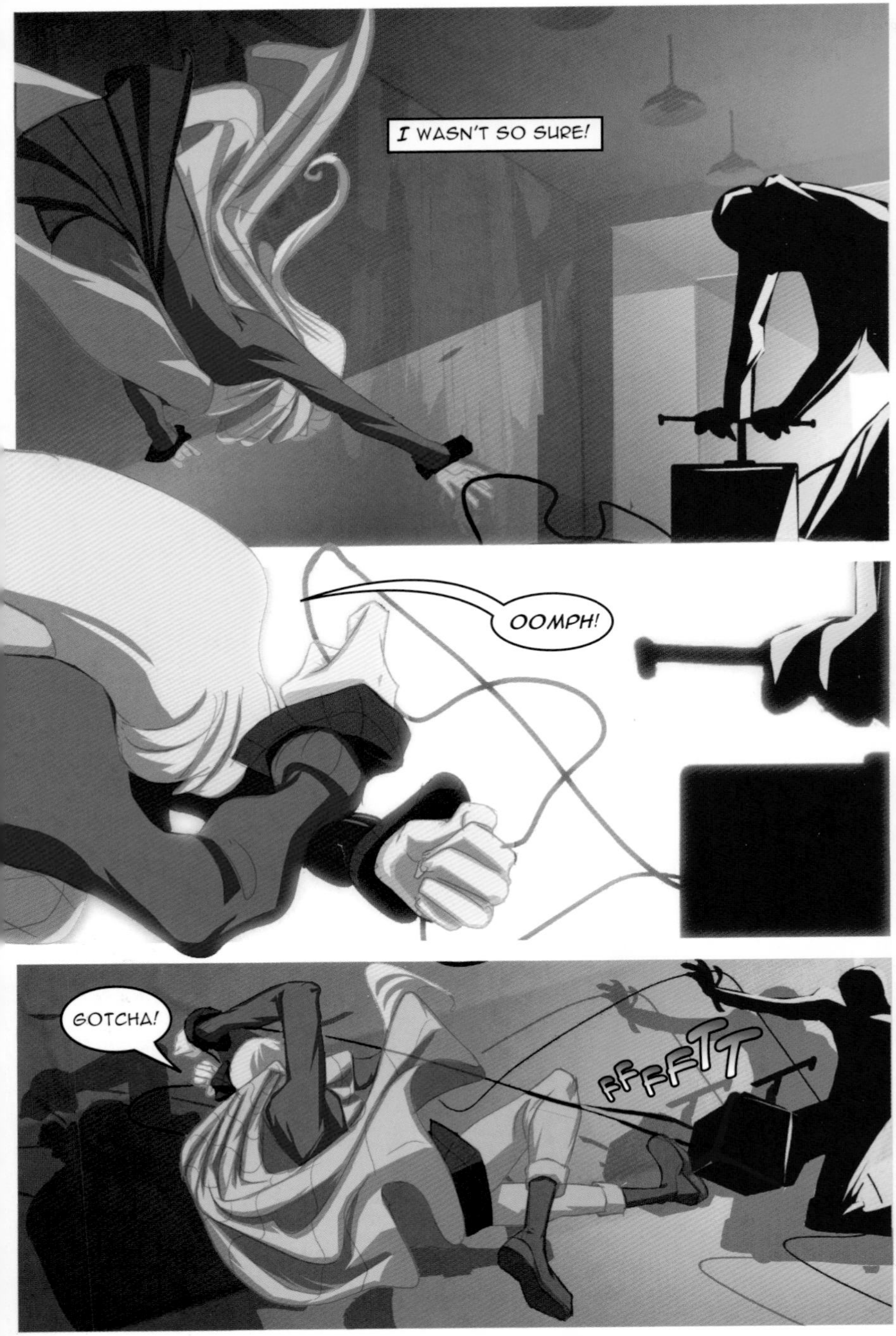
I WASN'T SO SURE!
OOMPH!
GOTCHA!
FFFFTT

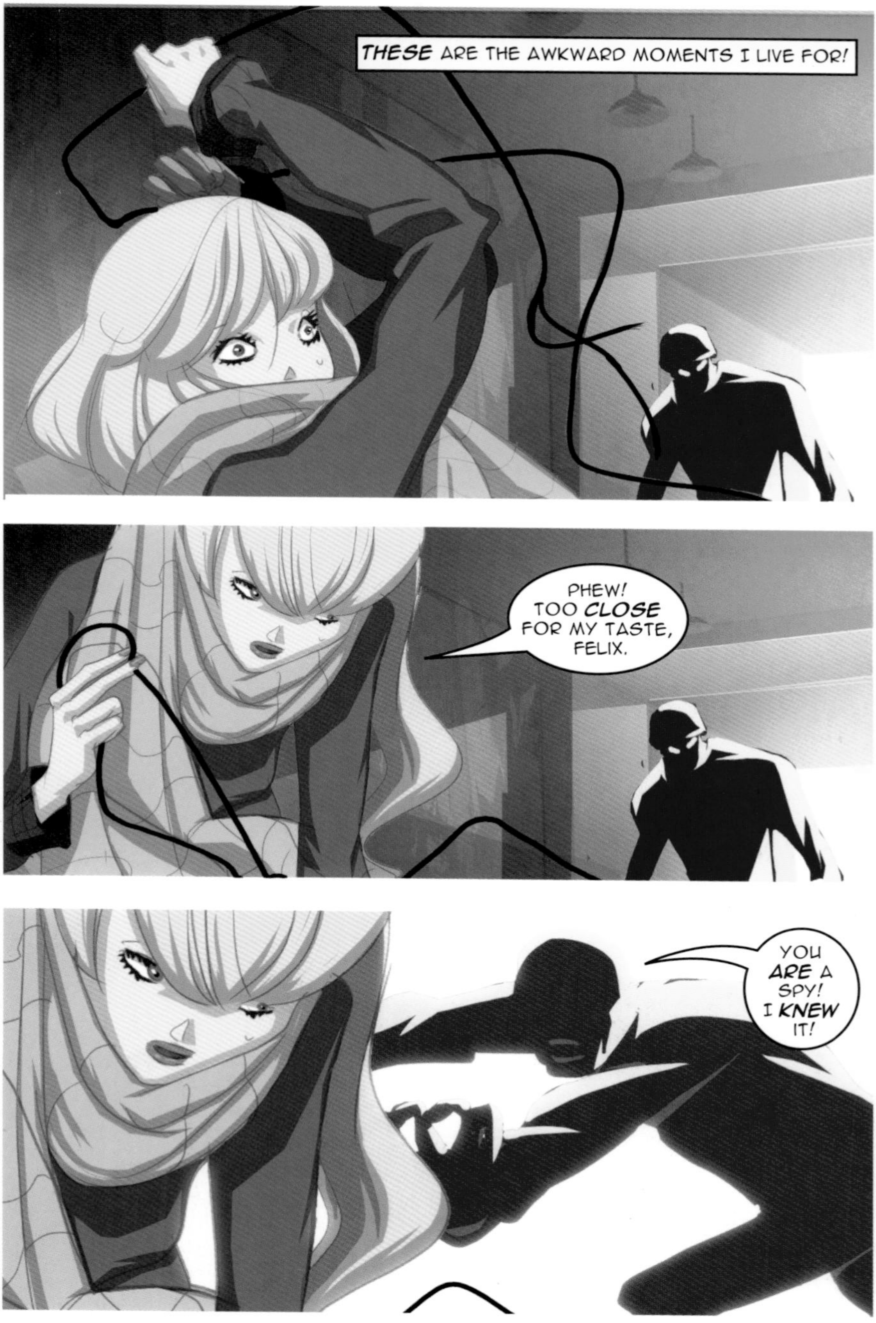
THESE ARE THE AWKWARD MOMENTS I LIVE FOR!
PHEW! TOO CLOSE FOR MY TASTE, FELIX.
YOU ARE A SPY! I KNEW IT!

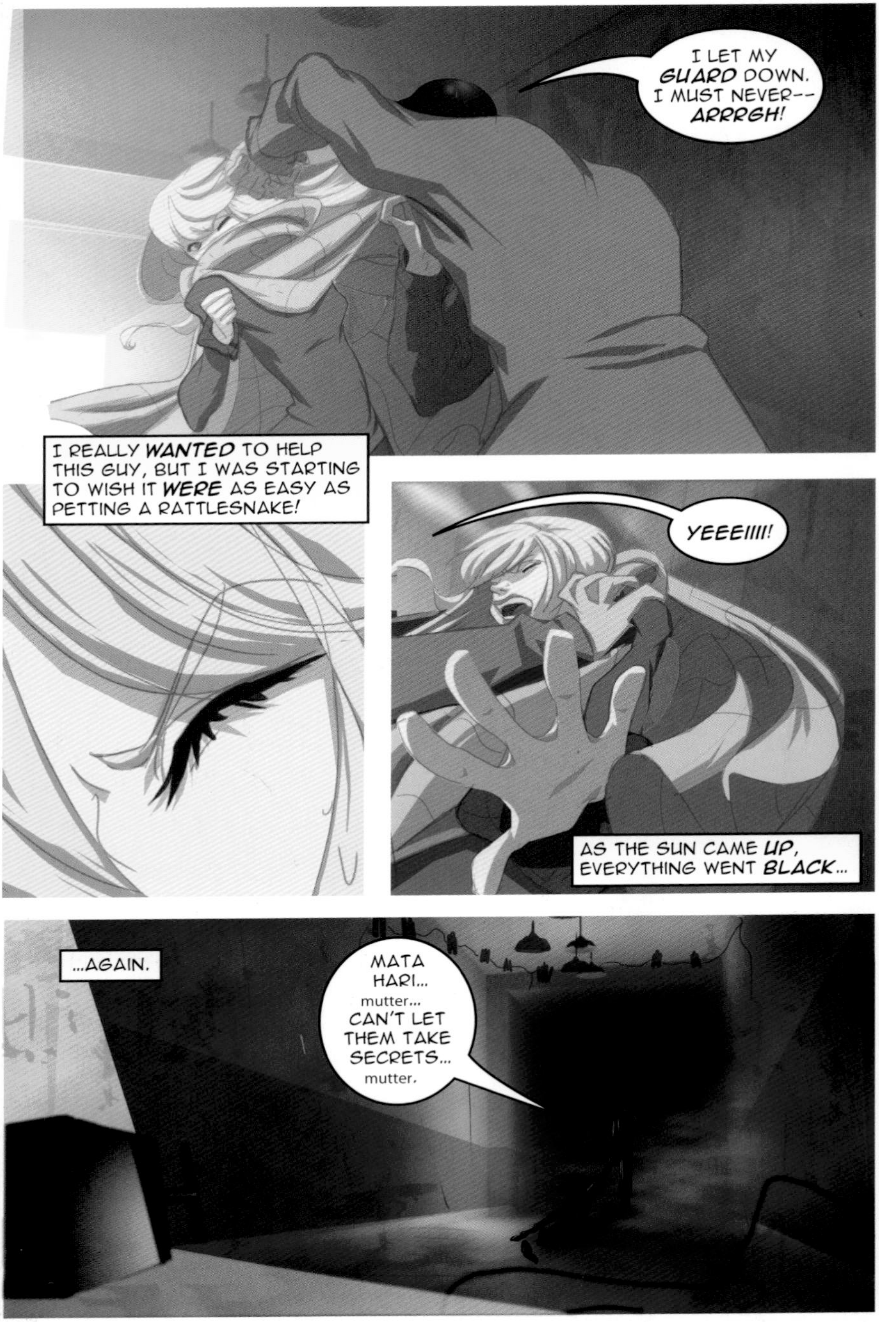

I LET MY GUARD DOWN. I MUST NEVER-- ARRRGH!
I REALLY WANTED TO HELP THIS GUY, BUT I WAS STARTING TO WISH IT WERE AS EASY AS PETTING A RATTLESNAKE!
YEEEIIII!
AS THE SUN CAME UP, EVERYTHING WENT BLACK...
...AGAIN.
MATA HARI... mutter... CAN'T LET THEM TAKE SECRETS... mutter.

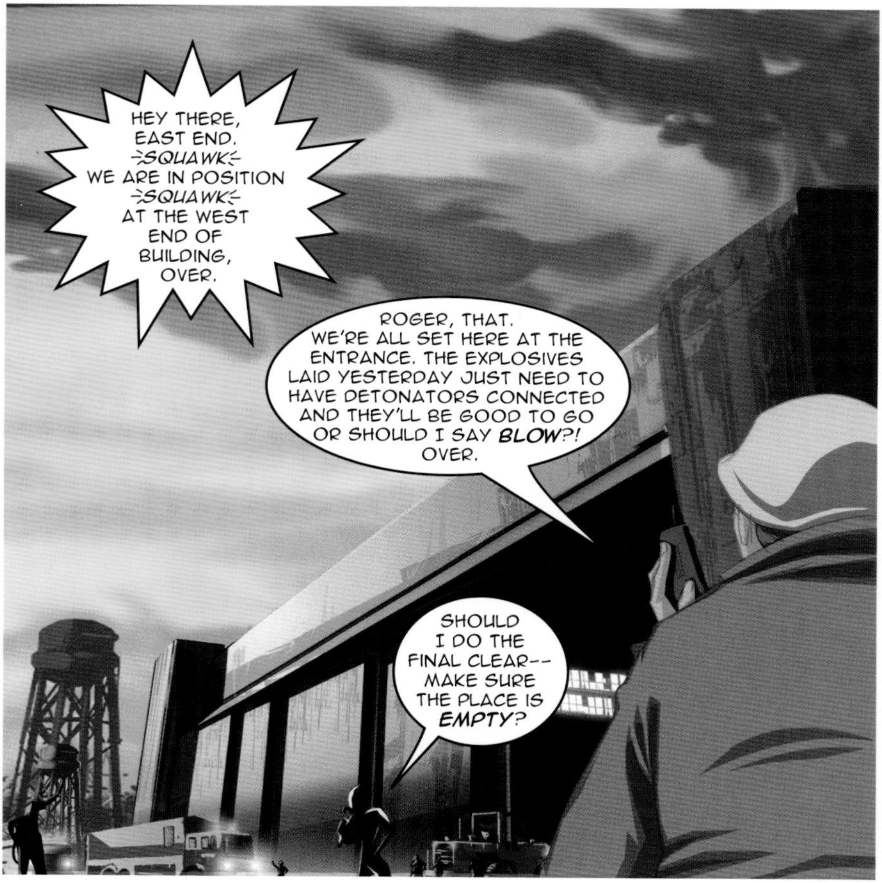
HEY THERE, EAST END. ~SQUAWK~ WE ARE IN POSITION ~SQUAWK~ AT THE WEST END OF BUILDING, OVER.
ROGER, THAT. WE'RE ALL SET HERE AT THE ENTRANCE. THE EXPLOSIVES LAID YESTERDAY JUST NEED TO HAVE DETONATORS CONNECTED AND THEY'LL BE GOOD TO GO OR SHOULD I SAY *BLOW*?! OVER.
SHOULD I DO THE FINAL CLEAR-- MAKE SURE THE PLACE IS *EMPTY*?

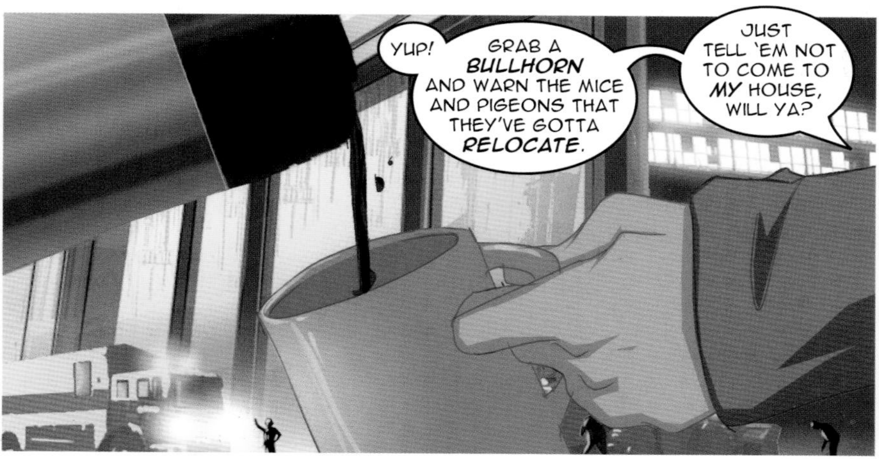
YUP!
GRAB A ***BULLHORN*** AND WARN THE MICE AND PIGEONS THAT THEY'VE GOTTA ***RELOCATE***.
JUST TELL 'EM NOT TO COME TO *MY* HOUSE, WILL YA?

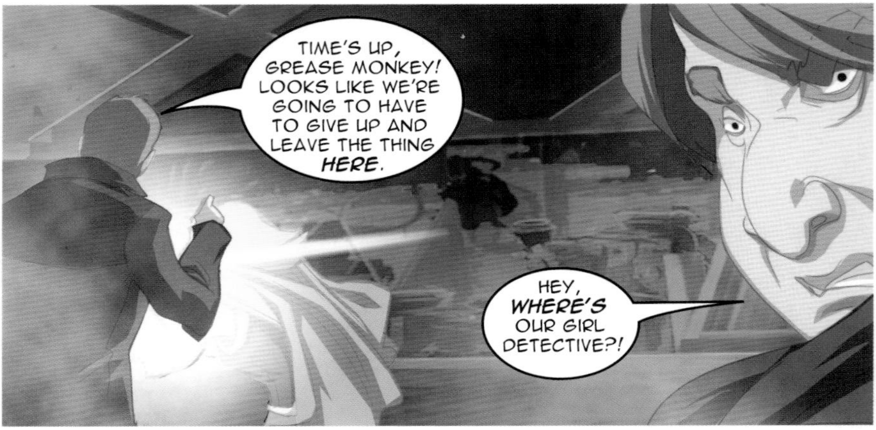
TIME'S UP, GREASE MONKEY! LOOKS LIKE WE'RE GOING TO HAVE TO GIVE UP AND LEAVE THE THING **HERE**.
HEY, **WHERE'S** OUR GIRL DETECTIVE?!

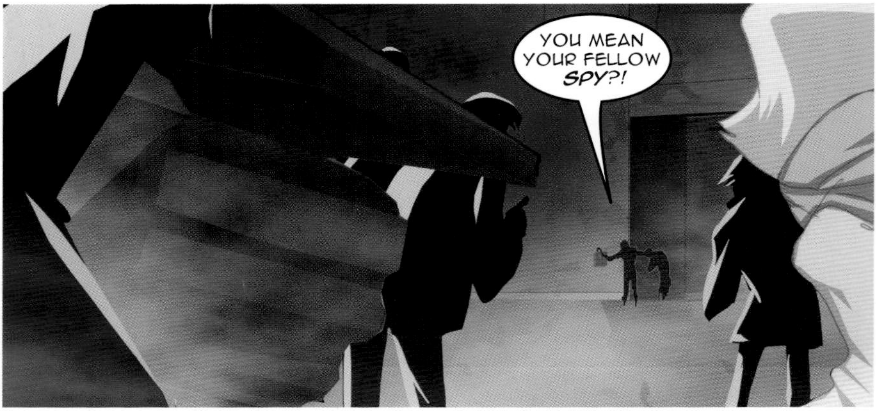
YOU MEAN YOUR FELLOW **SPY**?!

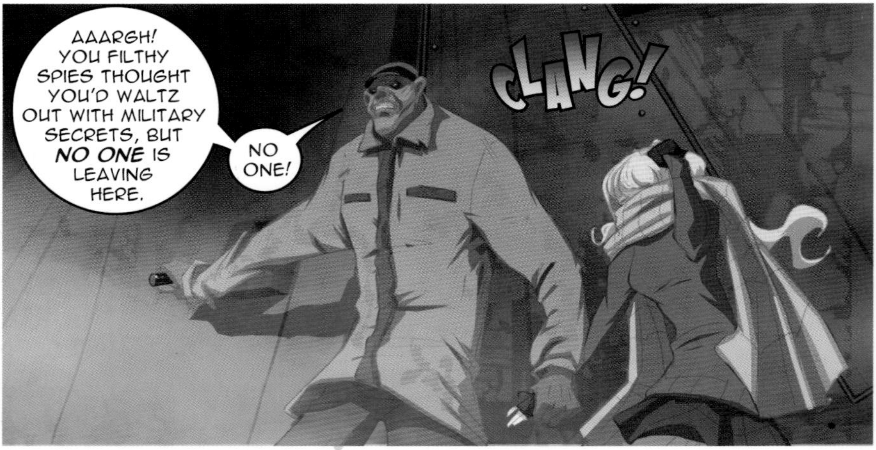
AAARGH! YOU FILTHY SPIES THOUGHT YOU'D WALTZ OUT WITH MILITARY SECRETS, BUT **NO ONE** IS LEAVING HERE.
NO ONE!
CLANG!

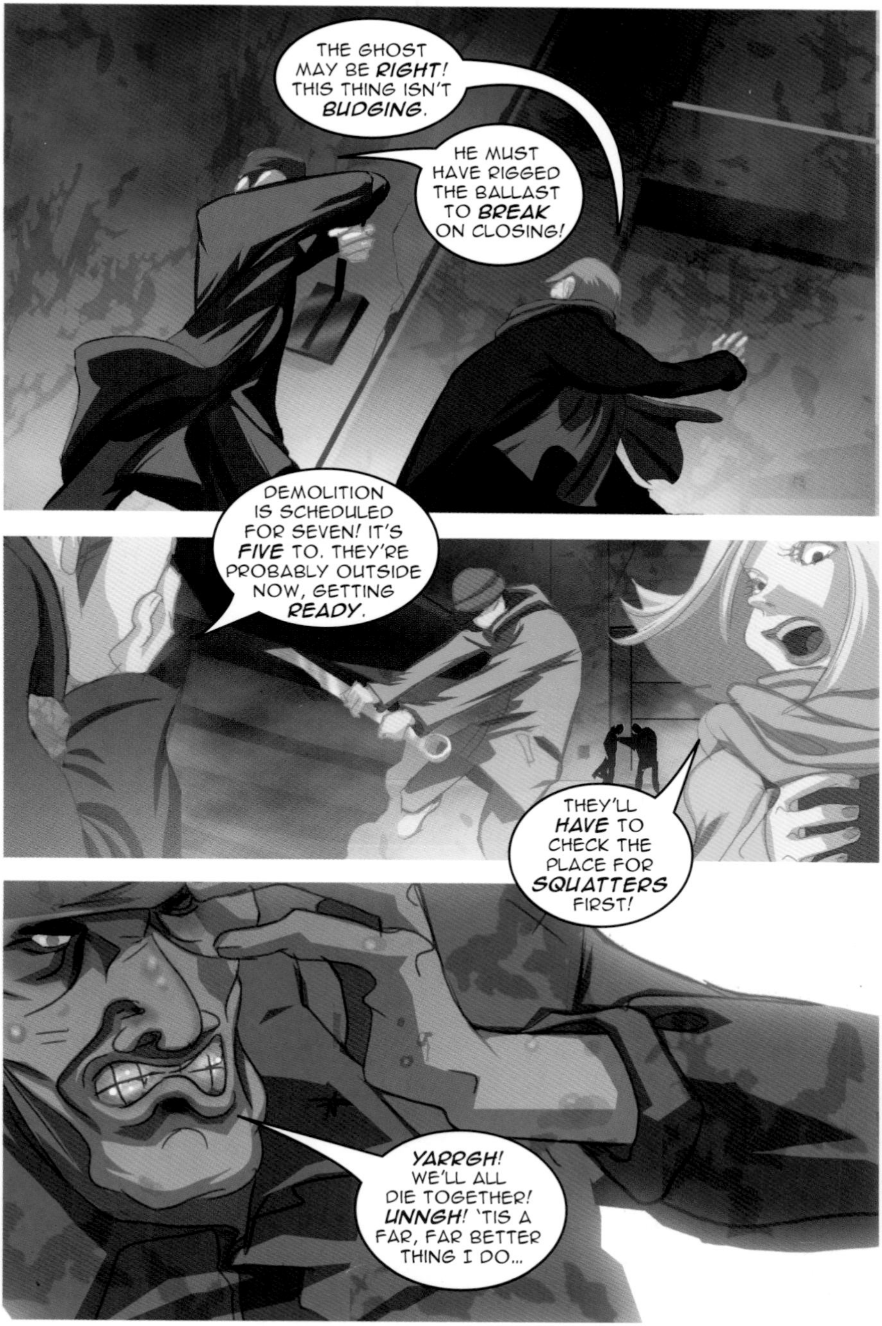
THE GHOST MAY BE RIGHT! THIS THING ISN'T BUDGING.
HE MUST HAVE RIGGED THE BALLAST TO BREAK ON CLOSING!
DEMOLITION IS SCHEDULED FOR SEVEN! IT'S FIVE TO. THEY'RE PROBABLY OUTSIDE NOW, GETTING READY.
THEY'LL HAVE TO CHECK THE PLACE FOR SQUATTERS FIRST!
YARRGH! WE'LL ALL DIE TOGETHER! UNNGH! 'TIS A FAR, FAR BETTER THING I DO...

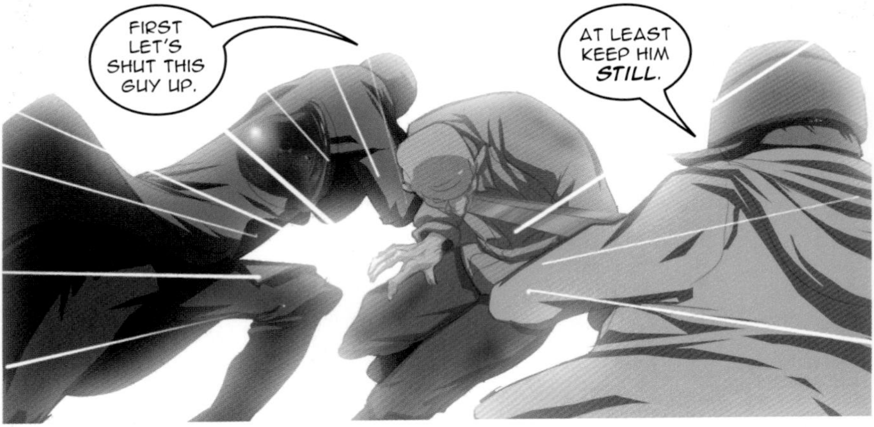
FIRST LET'S SHUT THIS GUY UP.
AT LEAST KEEP HIM STILL.

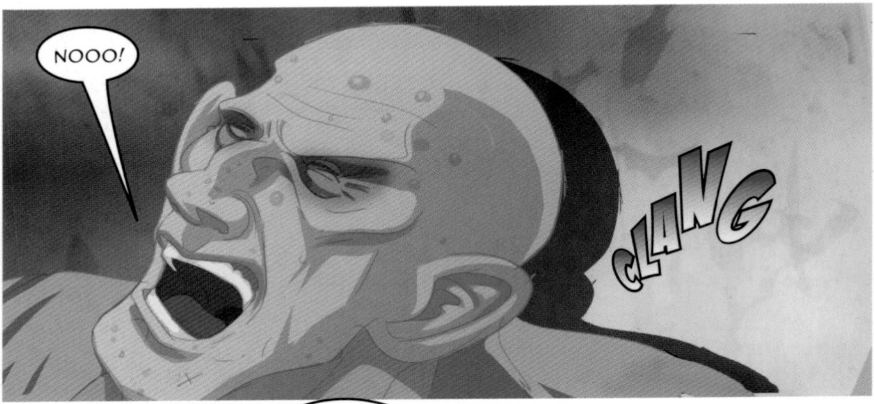
NOOO!
CLANG

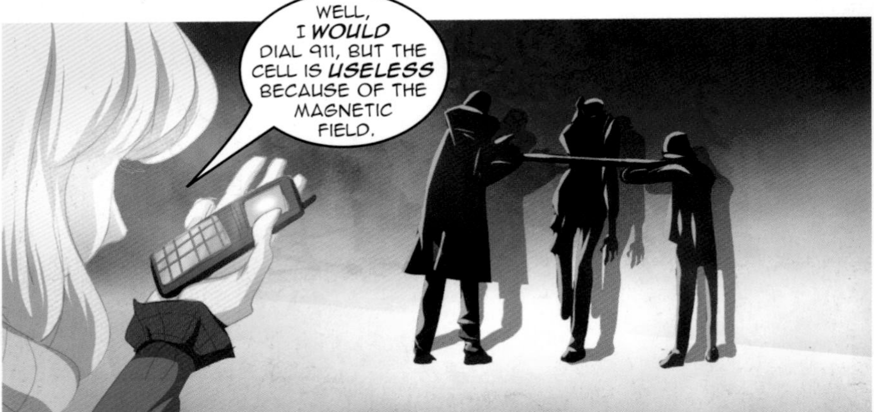
WELL, I WOULD DIAL 911, BUT THE CELL IS USELESS BECAUSE OF THE MAGNETIC FIELD.

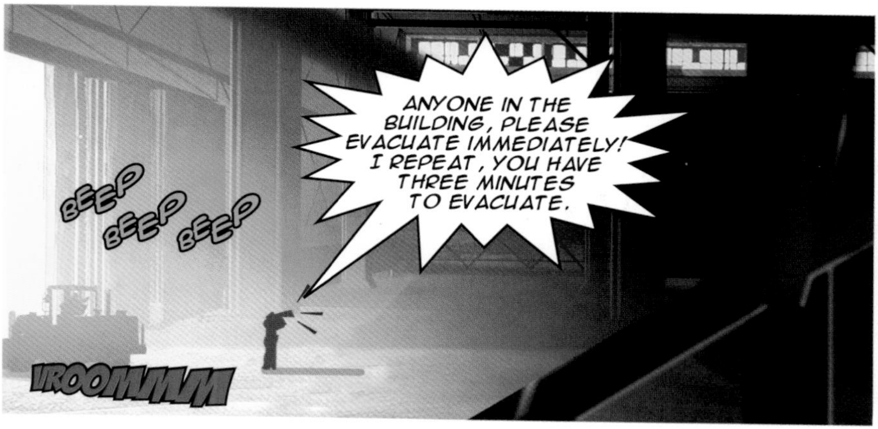
BEEP BEEP BEEP
ANYONE IN THE BUILDING, PLEASE EVACUATE IMMEDIATELY! I REPEAT, YOU HAVE THREE MINUTES TO EVACUATE.
VROOMMM

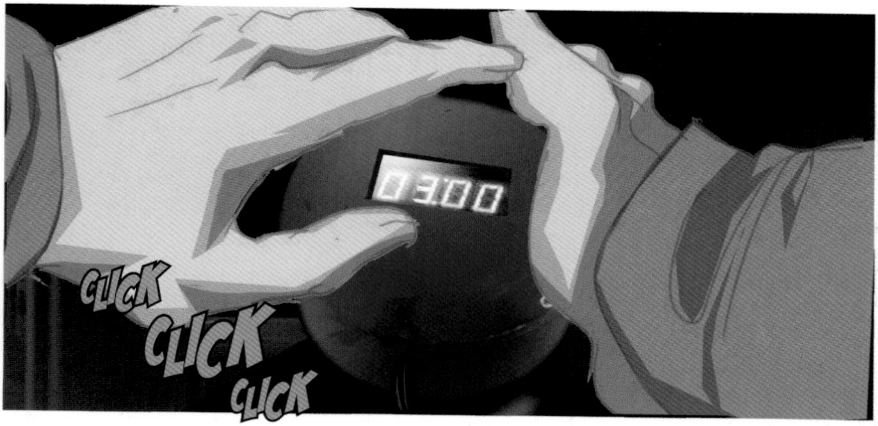
03:00
CLICK CLICK CLICK

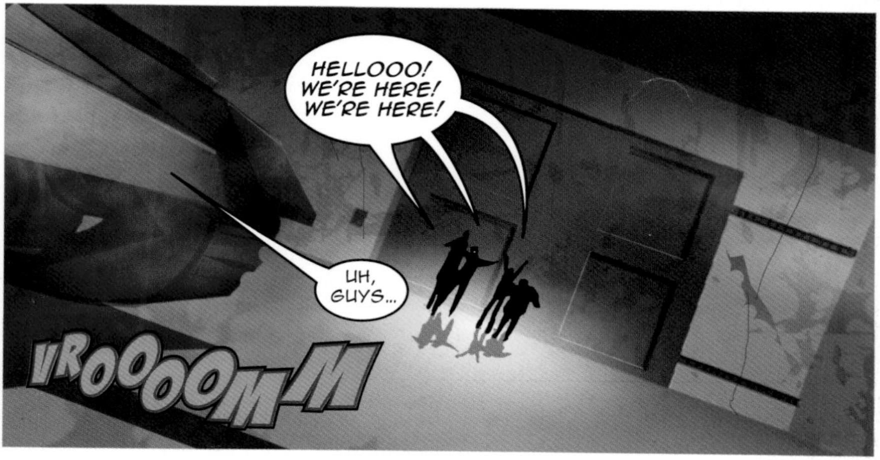
HELLOOO! WE'RE HERE! WE'RE HERE!
UH, GUYS...
VROOOOM-M

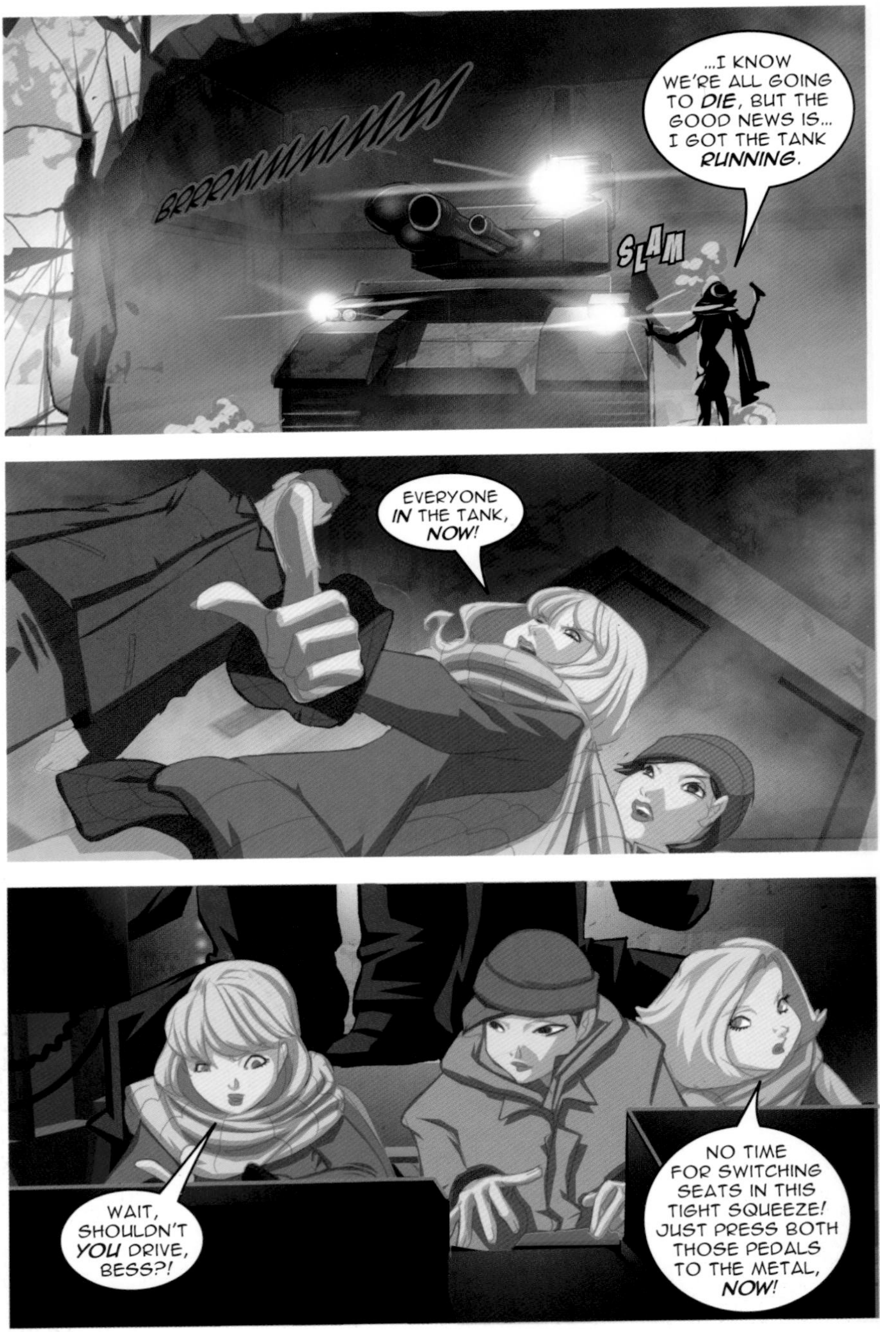

BRRRMMMMMMMMM
SLAM
...I KNOW WE'RE ALL GOING TO ***DIE***, BUT THE GOOD NEWS IS... I GOT THE TANK ***RUNNING***.
EVERYONE ***IN*** THE TANK, ***NOW***!
WAIT, SHOULDN'T ***YOU*** DRIVE, BESS?!
NO TIME FOR SWITCHING SEATS IN THIS TIGHT SQUEEZE! JUST PRESS BOTH THOSE PEDALS TO THE METAL, ***NOW***!

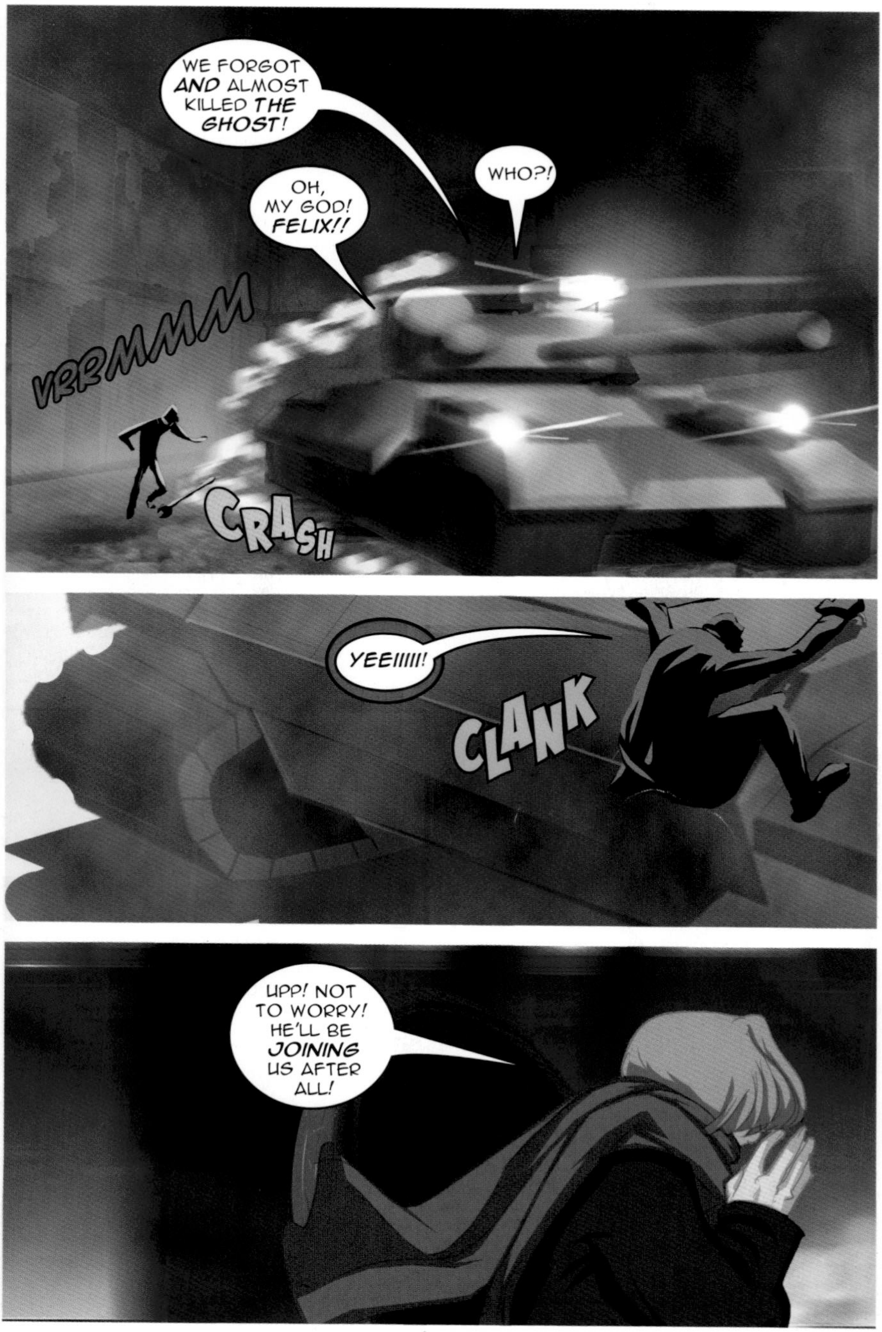
WE FORGOT AND ALMOST KILLED THE GHOST!
OH, MY GOD! FELIX!!
WHO?!
VRRMMMM
CRASH
YEEIIIIII!
CLANK
UPP! NOT TO WORRY! HE'LL BE JOINING US AFTER ALL!

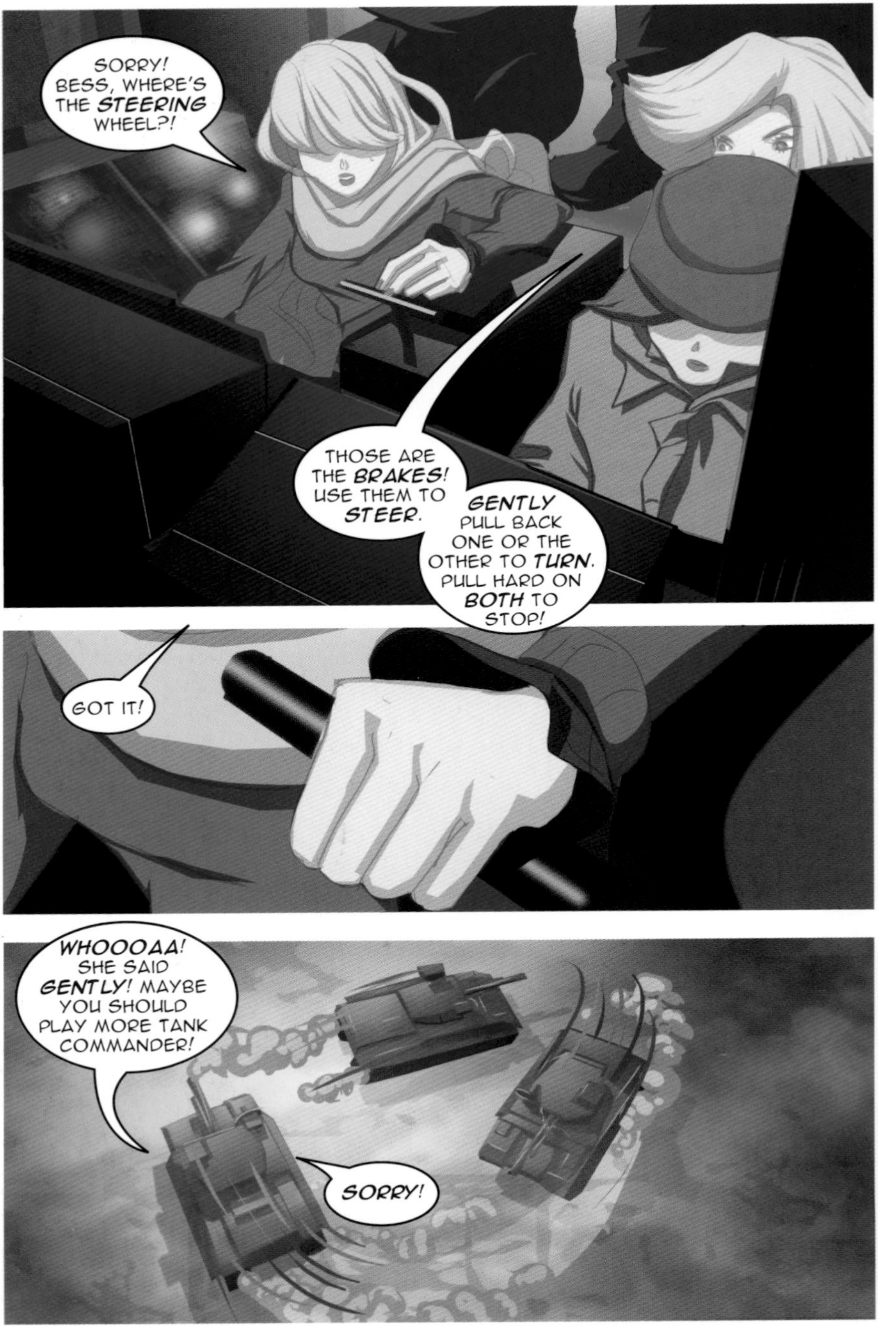
SORRY! BESS, WHERE'S THE STEERING WHEEL?!
THOSE ARE THE BRAKES! USE THEM TO STEER.
GENTLY PULL BACK ONE OR THE OTHER TO TURN. PULL HARD ON BOTH TO STOP!
GOT IT!
WHOOOAA! SHE SAID GENTLY! MAYBE YOU SHOULD PLAY MORE TANK COMMANDER!
SORRY!

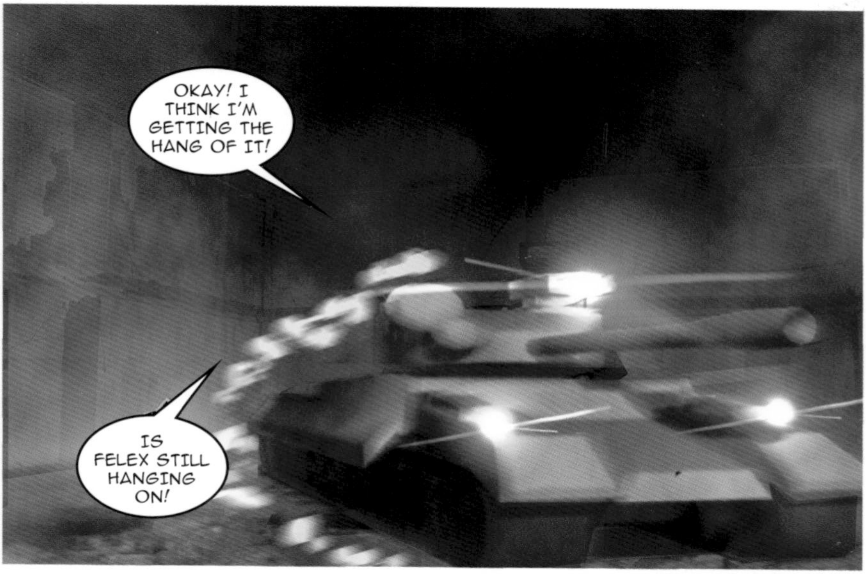
OKAY! I THINK I'M GETTING THE HANG OF IT!
IS FELEX STILL HANGING ON!

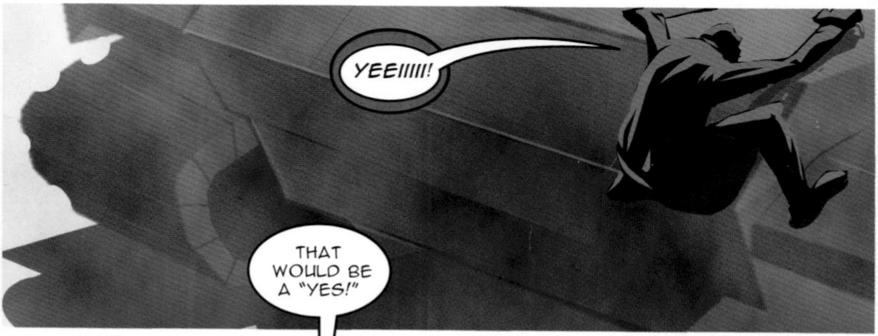
YEEIIIII!
THAT WOULD BE A "YES!"

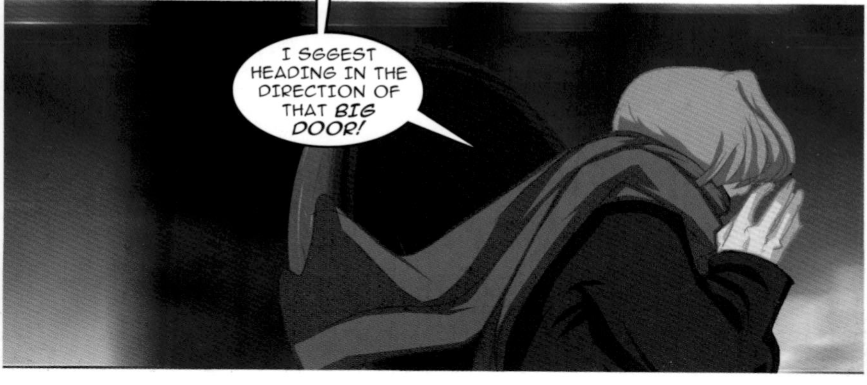
I SGGEST HEADING IN THE DIRECTION OF THAT *BIG DOOR!*

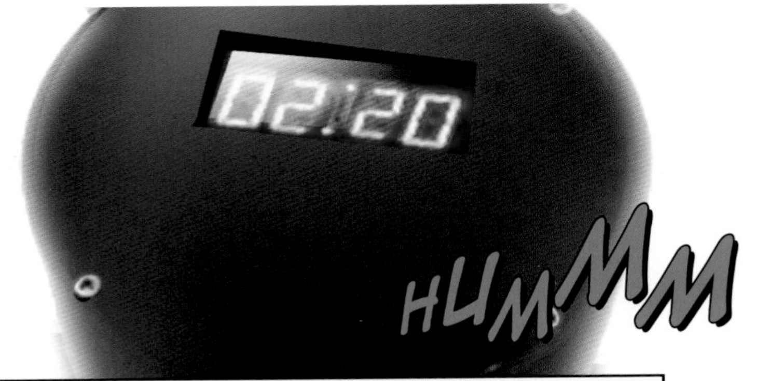
02:20
HUMMMM

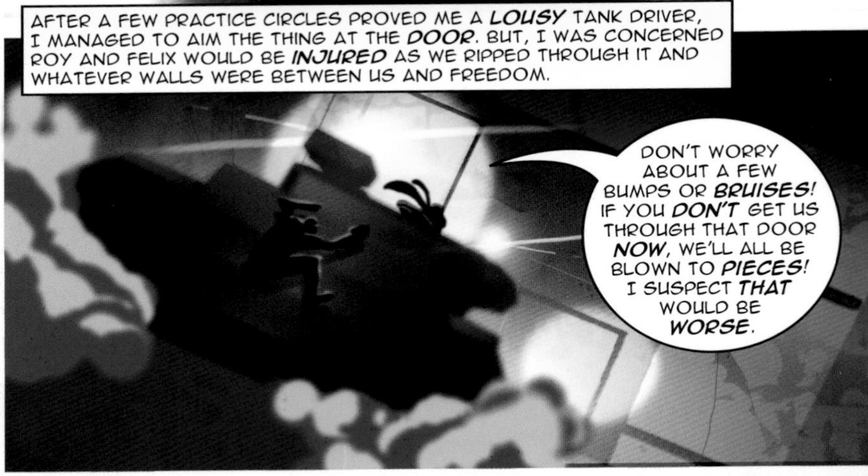
AFTER A FEW PRACTICE CIRCLES PROVED ME A *LOUSY* TANK DRIVER, I MANAGED TO AIM THE THING AT THE *DOOR*. BUT, I WAS CONCERNED ROY AND FELIX WOULD BE *INJURED* AS WE RIPPED THROUGH IT AND WHATEVER WALLS WERE BETWEEN US AND FREEDOM.
DON'T WORRY ABOUT A FEW BUMPS OR *BRUISES*! IF YOU *DON'T* GET US THROUGH THAT DOOR *NOW*, WE'LL ALL BE BLOWN TO *PIECES*! I SUSPECT *THAT* WOULD BE *WORSE*.

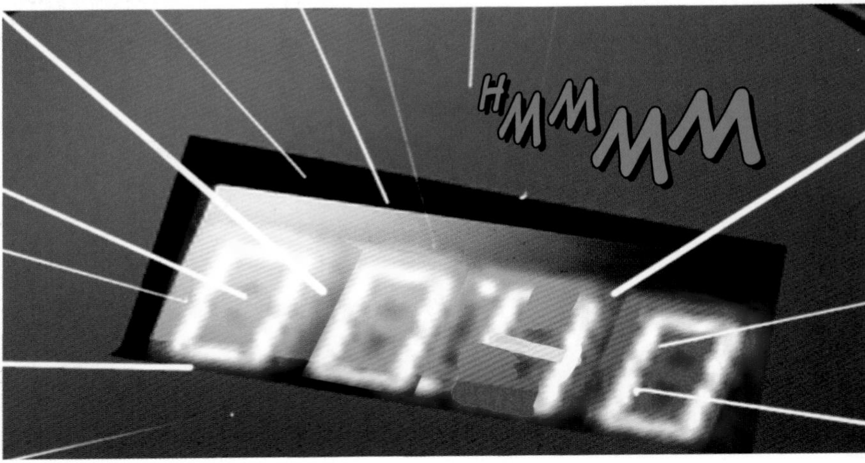
HMMMMM
00:40

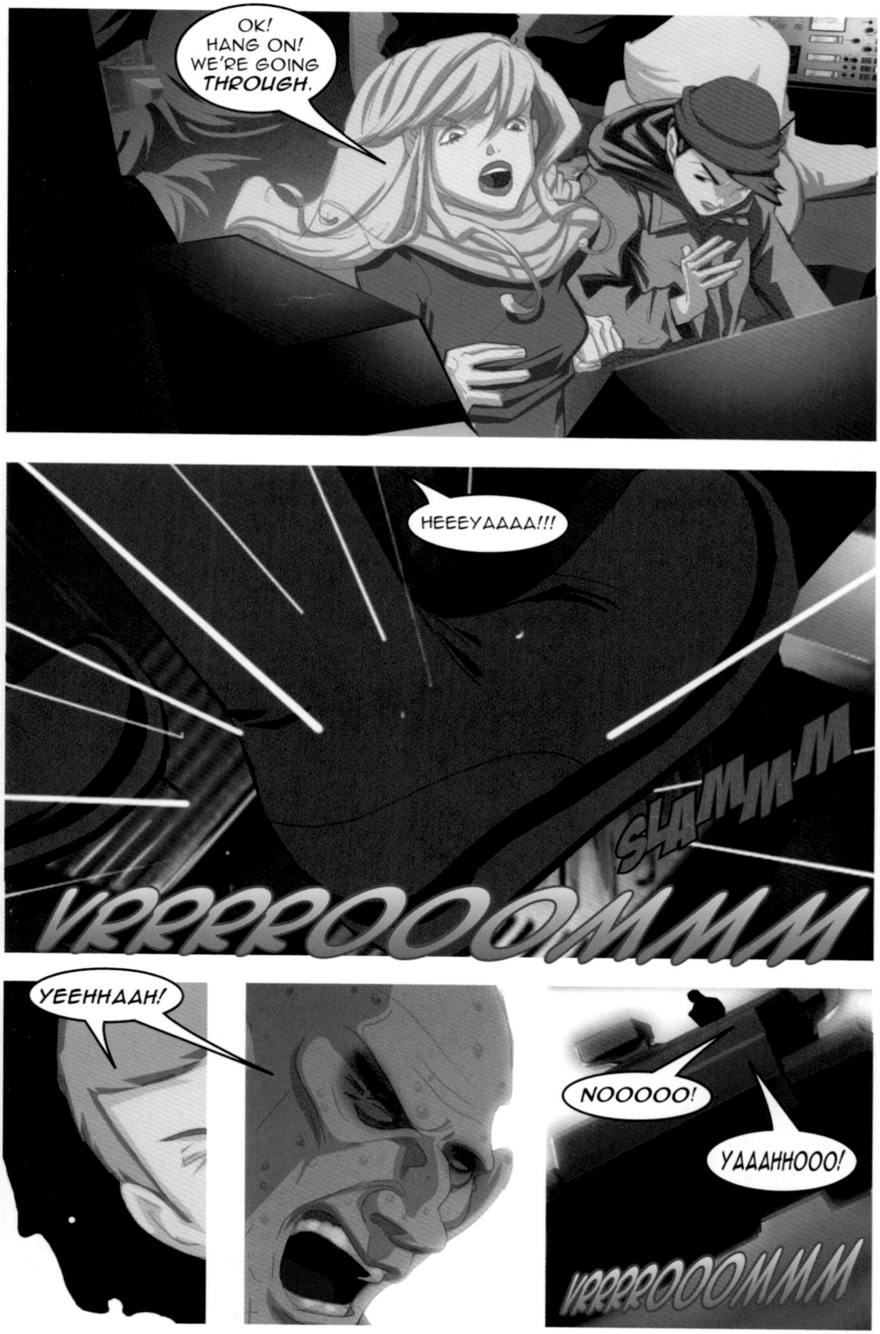
OK! HANG ON! WE'RE GOING THROUGH.
HEEEYAAAA!!!
SLAMMM
VRRRROOOOMMMM
YEEHHAAH!
NOOOOO!
YAAAHHOOO!
VRRRROOOOMMMM

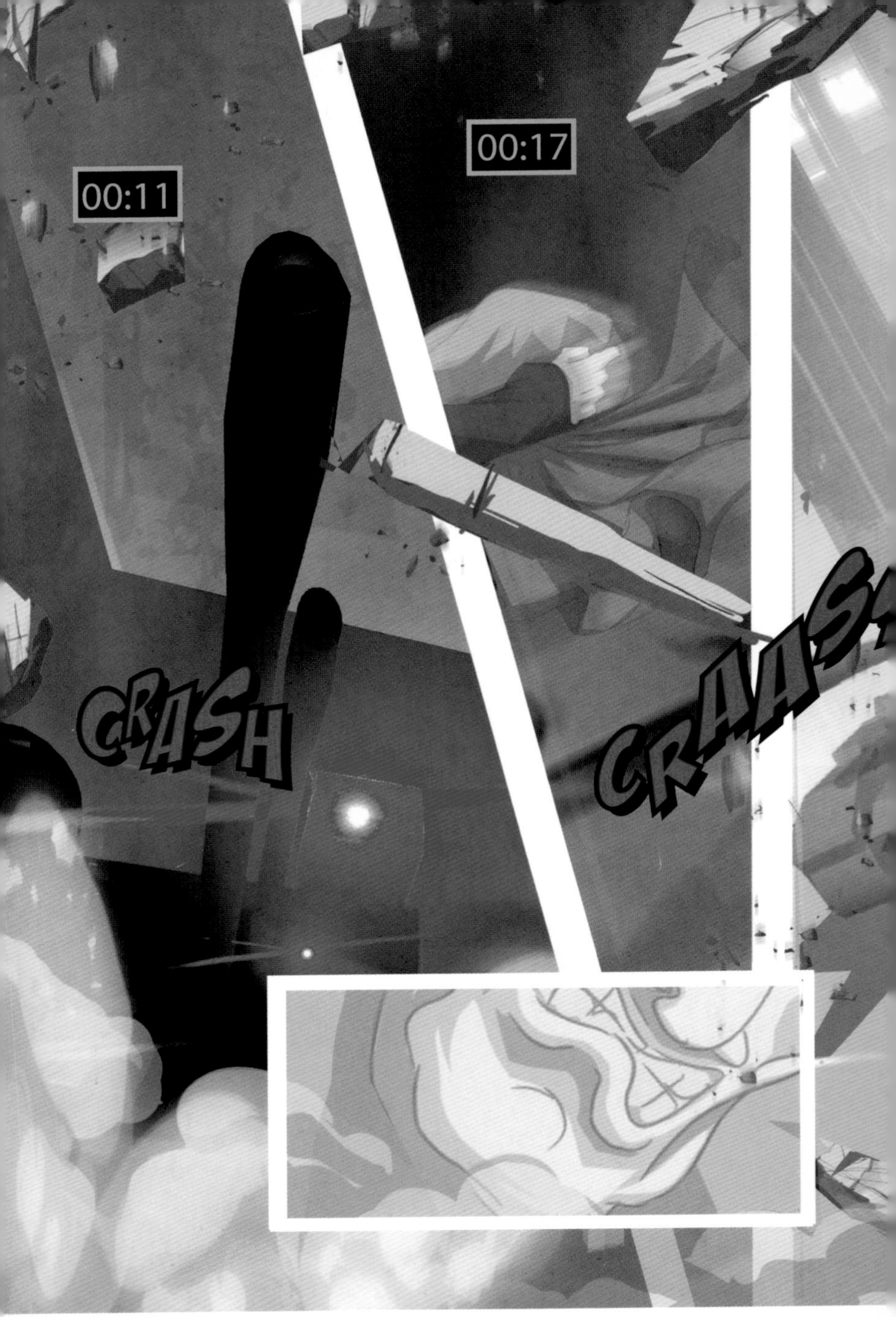

00:11
00:17
CRASH
CRAAS

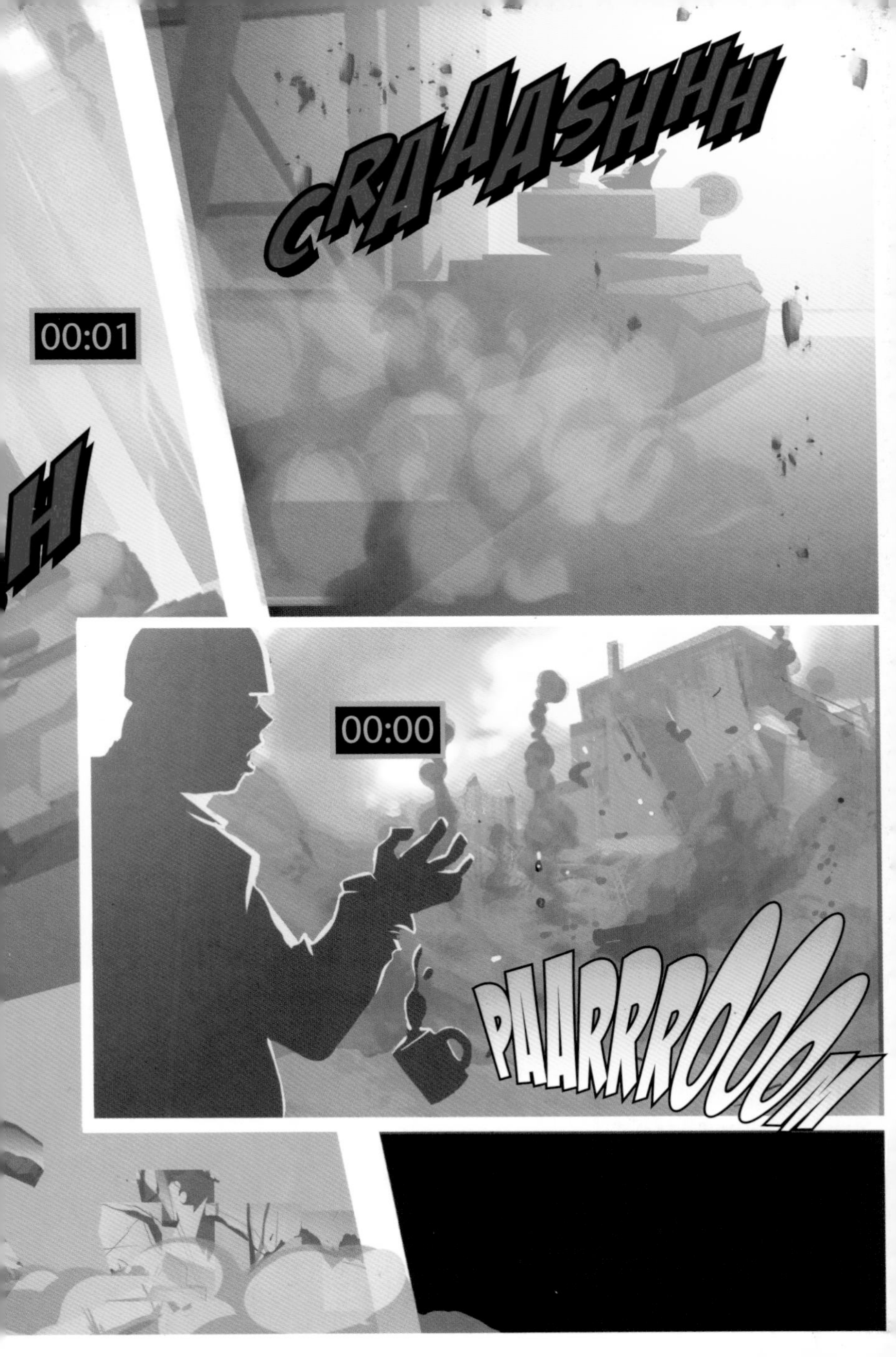
CRAAASHHH
00:01
00:00
PAARRROOOM

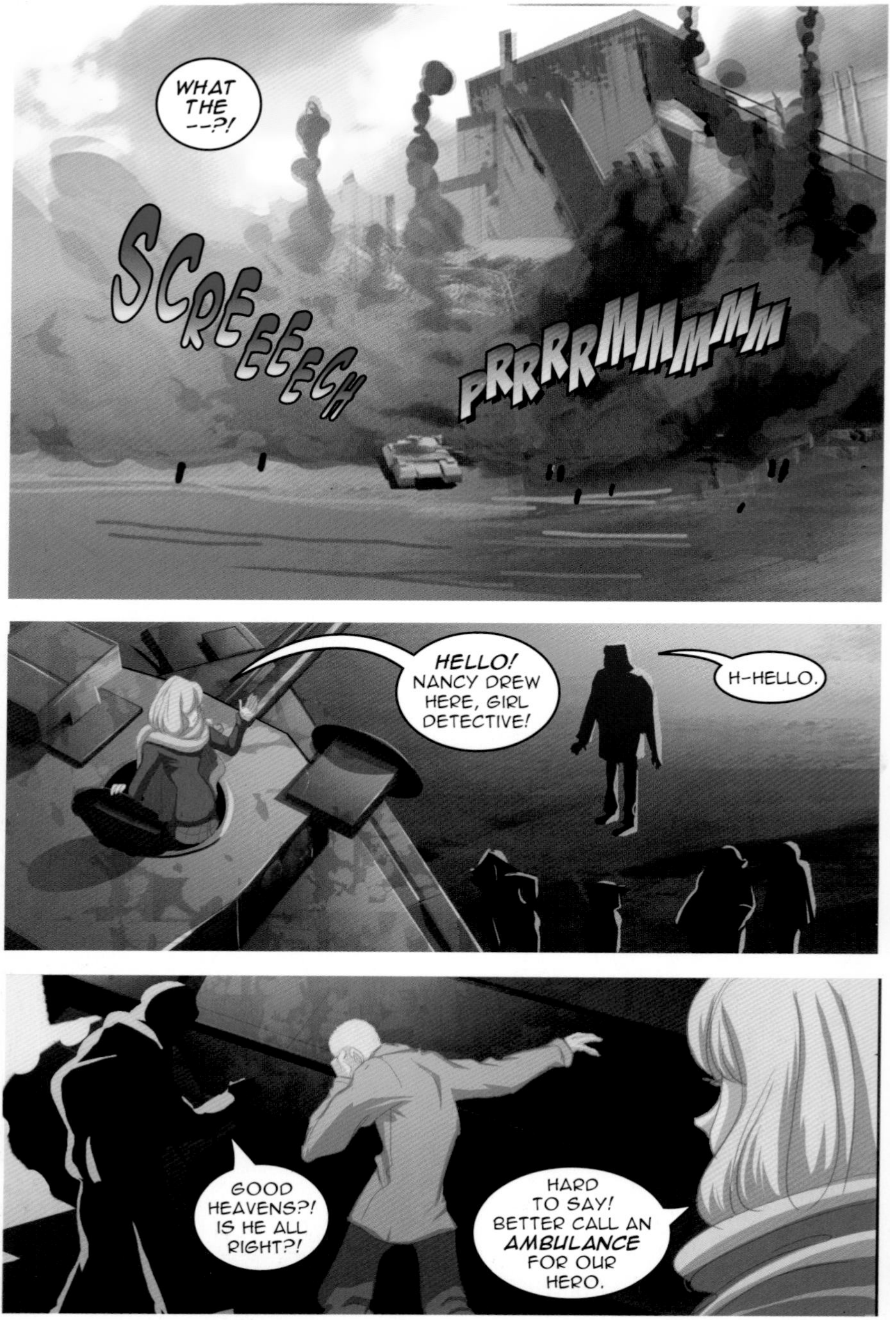
WHAT THE --?!
SCREEEECH
PRRRRMMMMMM
HELLO! NANCY DREW HERE, GIRL DETECTIVE!
H-HELLO.
GOOD HEAVENS?! IS HE ALL RIGHT?!
HARD TO SAY! BETTER CALL AN AMBULANCE FOR OUR HERO.

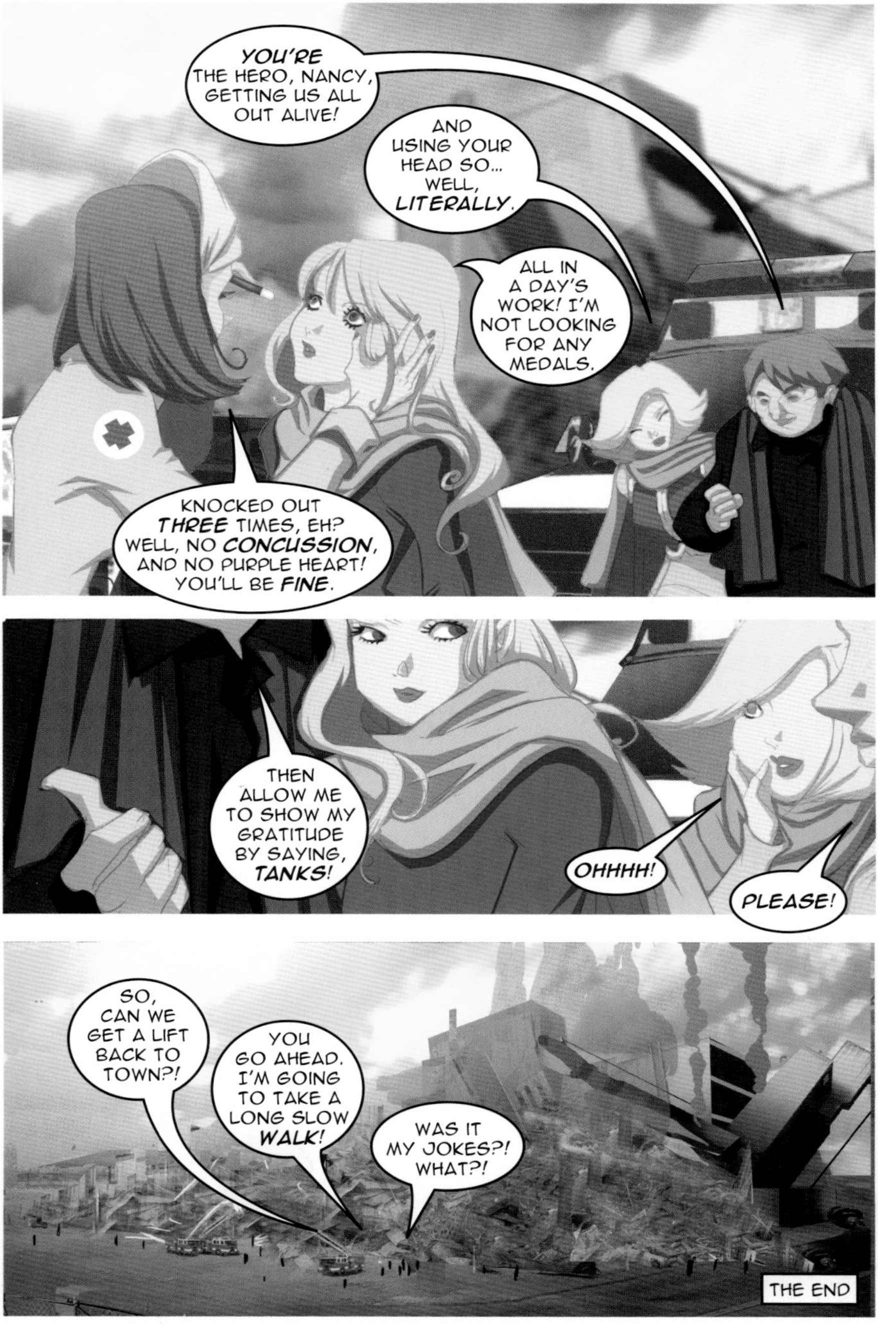
YOU'RE THE HERO, NANCY, GETTING US ALL OUT ALIVE!
AND USING YOUR HEAD SO... WELL, LITERALLY.
ALL IN A DAY'S WORK! I'M NOT LOOKING FOR ANY MEDALS.
KNOCKED OUT THREE TIMES, EH? WELL, NO CONCUSSION, AND NO PURPLE HEART! YOU'LL BE FINE.
THEN ALLOW ME TO SHOW MY GRATITUDE BY SAYING, TANKS!
OHHHH!
PLEASE!
SO, CAN WE GET A LIFT BACK TO TOWN?!
YOU GO AHEAD. I'M GOING TO TAKE A LONG SLOW WALK!
WAS IT MY JOKES?! WHAT?!
THE END

SPECIAL ADVANCE PREVIEW OF NANCY DREW GRAPHIC NOVEL # 10 – "THE DISORIENTED EXPRESS"

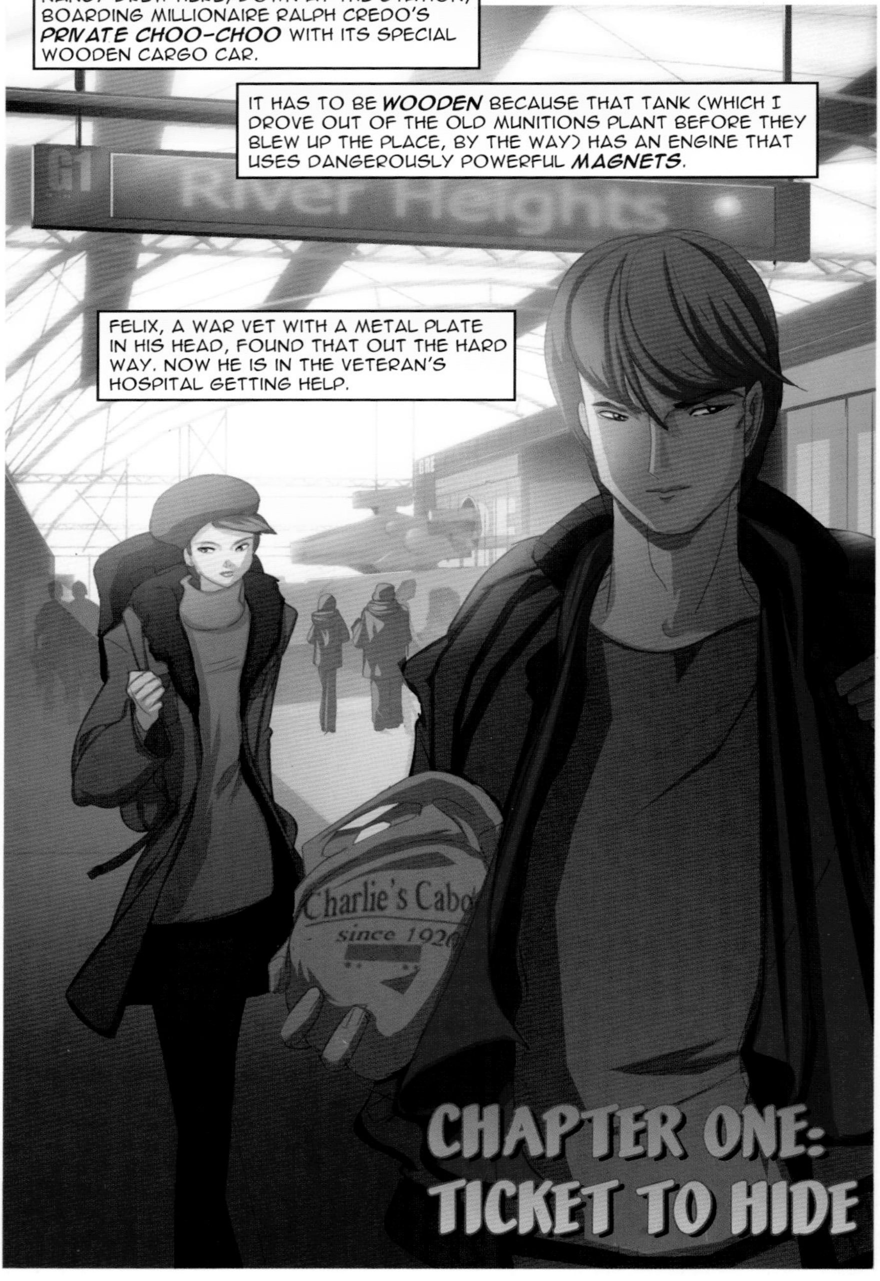
NANCY DREW HERE, DOWN AT THE STATION, BOARDING MILLIONAIRE RALPH CREDO'S PRIVATE CHOO-CHOO WITH ITS SPECIAL WOODEN CARGO CAR.
IT HAS TO BE WOODEN BECAUSE THAT TANK (WHICH I DROVE OUT OF THE OLD MUNITIONS PLANT BEFORE THEY BLEW UP THE PLACE, BY THE WAY) HAS AN ENGINE THAT USES DANGEROUSLY POWERFUL MAGNETS.
61
River Heights
FELIX, A WAR VET WITH A METAL PLATE IN HIS HEAD, FOUND THAT OUT THE HARD WAY. NOW HE IS IN THE VETERAN'S HOSPITAL GETTING HELP.
Charlie's Cabo
since 192
CHAPTER ONE:
TICKET TO HIDE

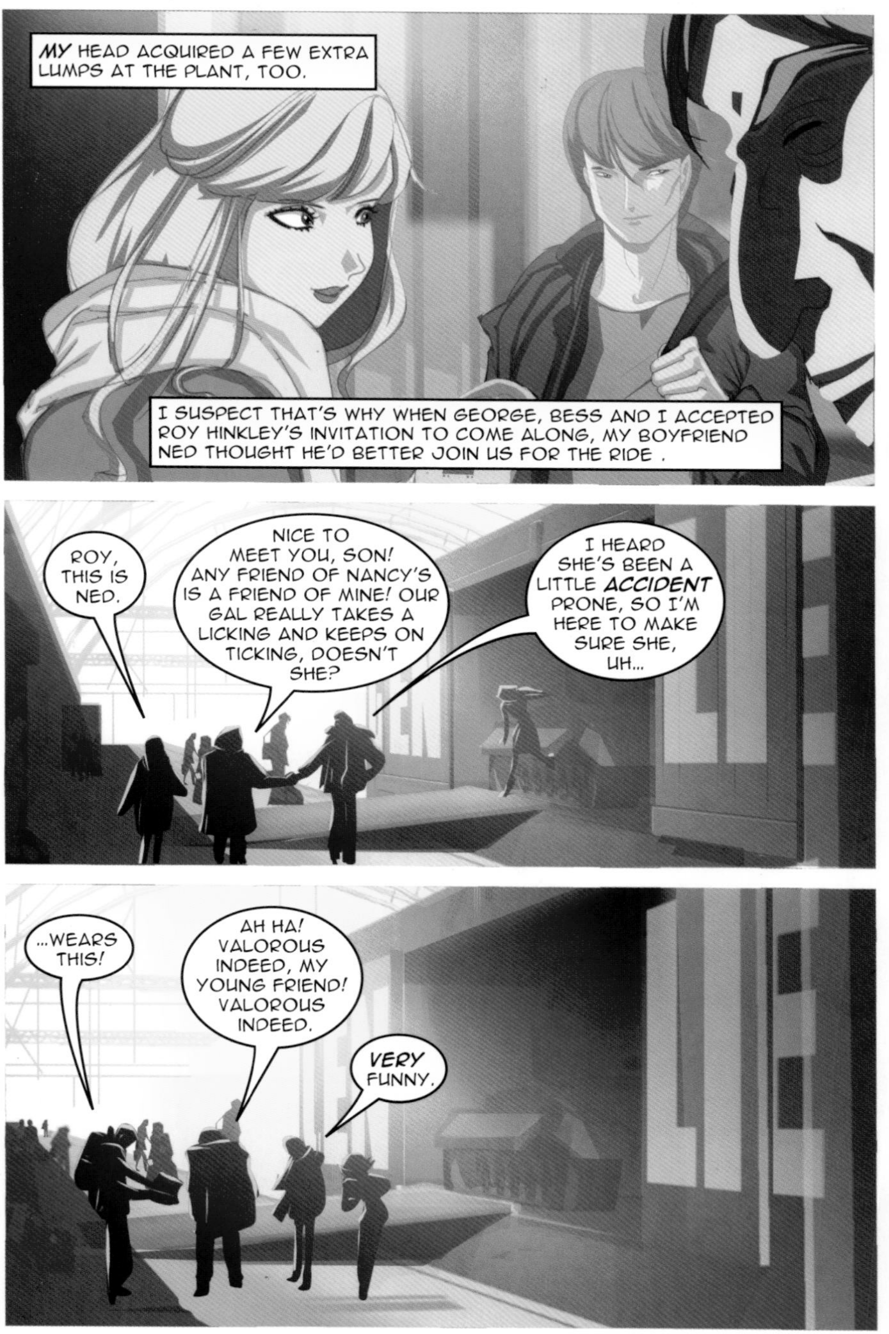
MY HEAD ACQUIRED A FEW EXTRA LUMPS AT THE PLANT, TOO.
I SUSPECT THAT'S WHY WHEN GEORGE, BESS AND I ACCEPTED ROY HINKLEY'S INVITATION TO COME ALONG, MY BOYFRIEND NED THOUGHT HE'D BETTER JOIN US FOR THE RIDE .
ROY, THIS IS NED.
NICE TO MEET YOU, SON! ANY FRIEND OF NANCY'S IS A FRIEND OF MINE! OUR GAL REALLY TAKES A LICKING AND KEEPS ON TICKING, DOESN'T SHE?
I HEARD SHE'S BEEN A LITTLE ACCIDENT PRONE, SO I'M HERE TO MAKE SURE SHE, UH...
...WEARS THIS!
AH HA! VALOROUS INDEED, MY YOUNG FRIEND! VALOROUS INDEED.
VERY FUNNY.

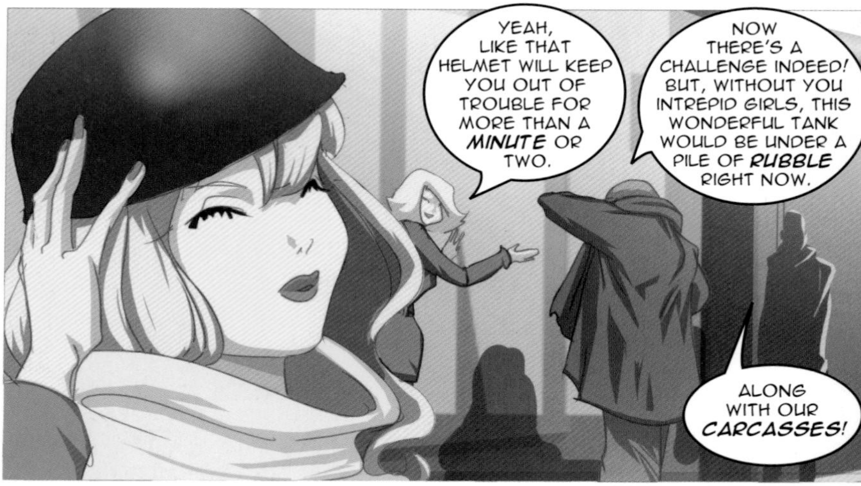
YEAH, LIKE THAT HELMET WILL KEEP YOU OUT OF TROUBLE FOR MORE THAN A MINUTE OR TWO.
NOW THERE'S A CHALLENGE INDEED! BUT, WITHOUT YOU INTREPID GIRLS, THIS WONDERFUL TANK WOULD BE UNDER A PILE OF RUBBLE RIGHT NOW.
ALONG WITH OUR CARCASSES!

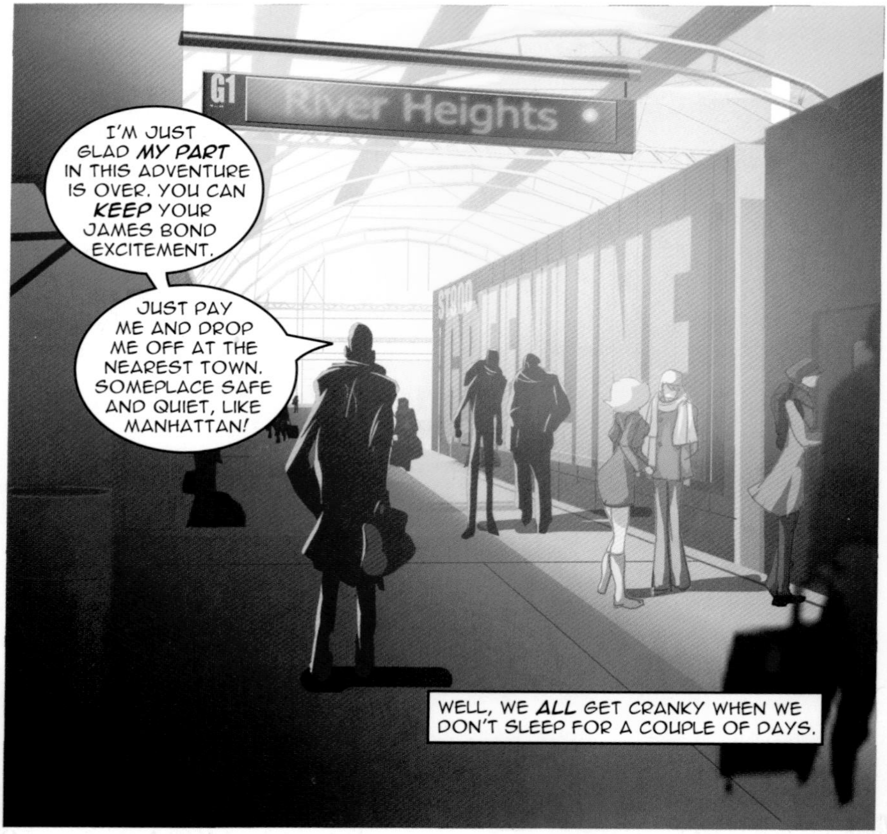
G1
River Heights
I'M JUST GLAD MY PART IN THIS ADVENTURE IS OVER. YOU CAN KEEP YOUR JAMES BOND EXCITEMENT.
JUST PAY ME AND DROP ME OFF AT THE NEAREST TOWN. SOMEPLACE SAFE AND QUIET, LIKE MANHATTAN!
WELL, WE ALL GET CRANKY WHEN WE DON'T SLEEP FOR A COUPLE OF DAYS.

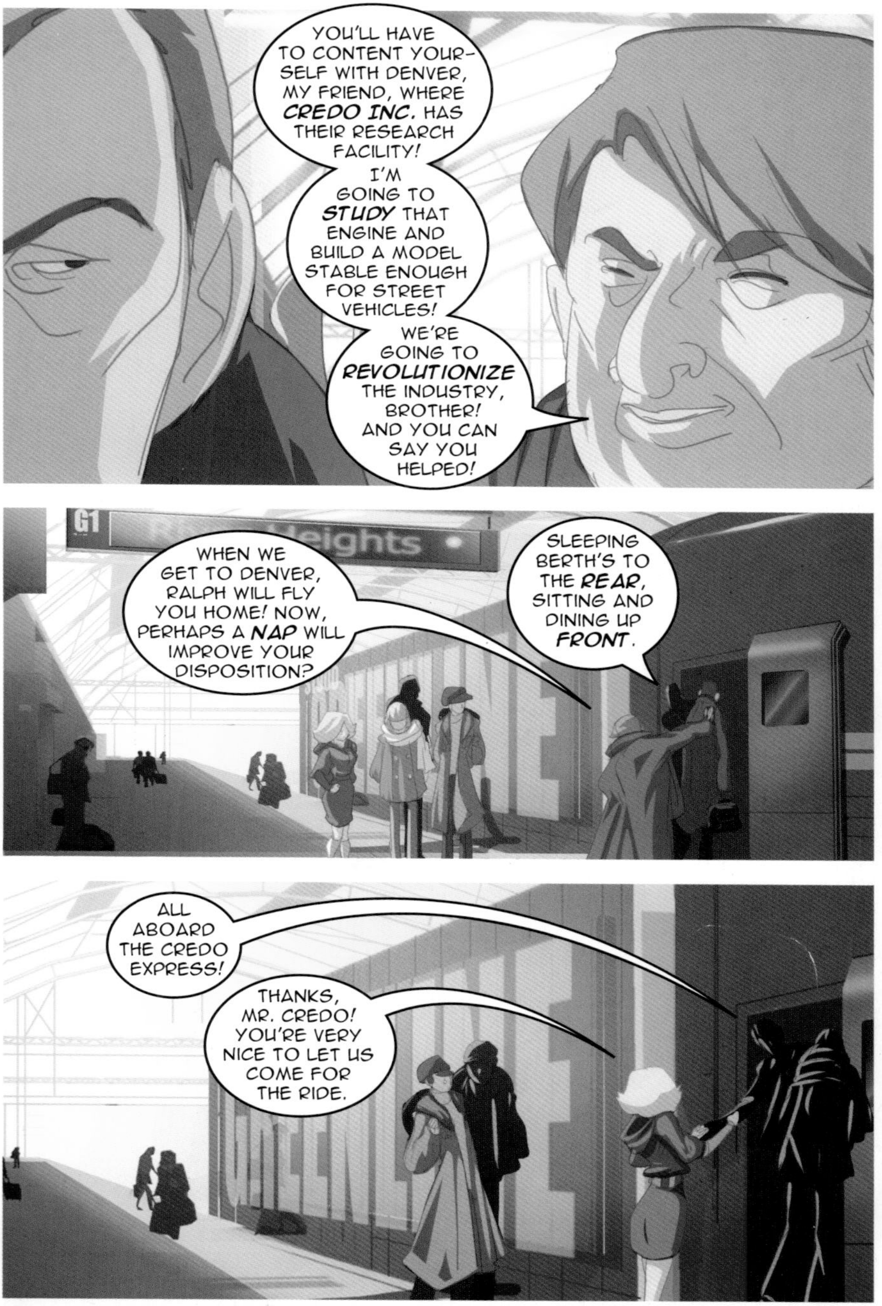
YOU'LL HAVE TO CONTENT YOURSELF WITH DENVER, MY FRIEND, WHERE CREDO INC. HAS THEIR RESEARCH FACILITY!
I'M GOING TO STUDY THAT ENGINE AND BUILD A MODEL STABLE ENOUGH FOR STREET VEHICLES!
WE'RE GOING TO REVOLUTIONIZE THE INDUSTRY, BROTHER! AND YOU CAN SAY YOU HELPED!
G1
WHEN WE GET TO DENVER, RALPH WILL FLY YOU HOME! NOW, PERHAPS A NAP WILL IMPROVE YOUR DISPOSITION?
SLEEPING BERTH'S TO THE REAR, SITTING AND DINING UP FRONT.
ALL ABOARD THE CREDO EXPRESS!
THANKS, MR. CREDO! YOU'RE VERY NICE TO LET US COME FOR THE RIDE.

DON'T MISS NANCY DREW GRAPHIC NOVEL # 10 – "THE DISORIENTED EXPRESS"

Go Undercover in Paris as Nancy Drew® in

Danger by Design

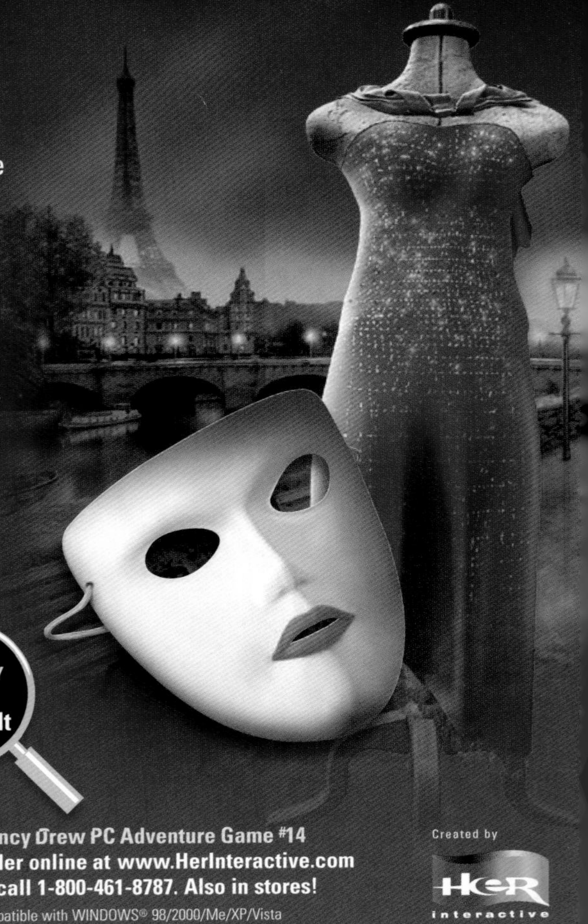

You, as Nancy Drew, are in Paris to work undercover for a prestigious fashion designer. Minette is all the rage in the fashion world, but strange threats and unwelcome guests are causing her to unravel. It's up to you to stitch the clues together and unmask the mystery in this PC adventure game.

dare to play™

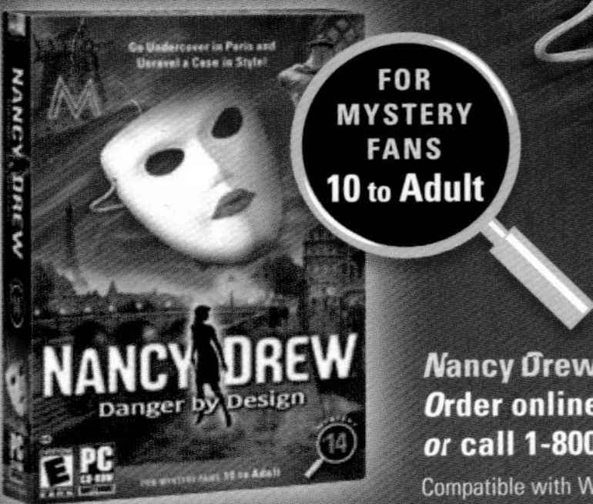
Go Undercover in Paris and Unravel a Case in Style!
NANCY DREW
NANCY DREW
Danger by Design
PC
FOR MYSTERY FANS 10 to Adult

***Nancy Drew* PC Adventure Game #14**
***Order* online at www.HerInteractive.com**
***or* call 1-800-461-8787. Also in stores!**
Compatible with WINDOWS® 98/2000/Me/XP/Vista

Created by HER interactive

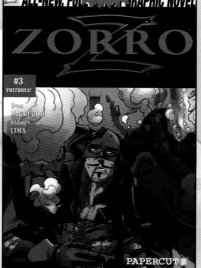

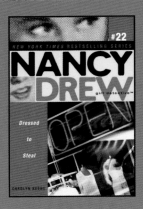

WATCH OUT FOR PAPERCUTZ™

Papercutz Editor-in-Chief Jim Salicrup here with something really important to say to you before we kick off this edition of the Papercutz back-pages: Thank you!

Thank you for picking up this Papercutz book. Whether this is your very first Papercutz graphic novel or your second, third, fourth, or sixteenth—we greatly appreciate it. We work around the clock to make each and every one of our books the very best we possibly can, so that you can get the absolute maximum amount of enjoyment from each and every page. But it's all for nothing without you!

And thanks to you, Papercutz has become quite a success story. We suspect that's because instead of offering more of the same types of comics that were already being published, Papercutz is devoted to bringing our own brand of fun and excitement to the world of graphic novels.

Thanks to you also for telling us what you like and don't like about Papercutz. That's been a huge help to us in choosing our new, upcoming Papercutz titles. By revealing how much you enjoy the humor in our mystery and adventure titles, such as The Hardy Boys, Nancy Drew, and Totally Spies, we knew our new series had to be just as much fun. We'll soon be adding a science fiction adventure series and a horror anthology to our line-up. And they'll both have that Papercutz sense of humor.

One of the new titles is revealed on the very next page...

But before you get to the big announcement, on behalf of all the Papercutz writers and artists, allow me to thank you one more time for giving us the opportunity to do what we love— create the very best comics we can for you!

Thanks,

Jim

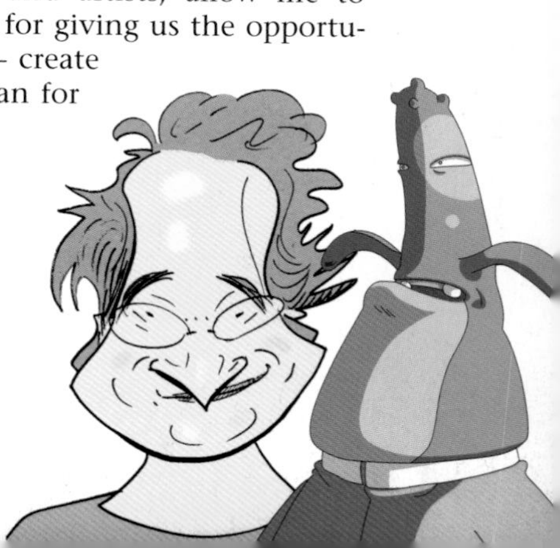

Caricature of Jim drawn by Steve Brodner at the MoCCA Art Fest.

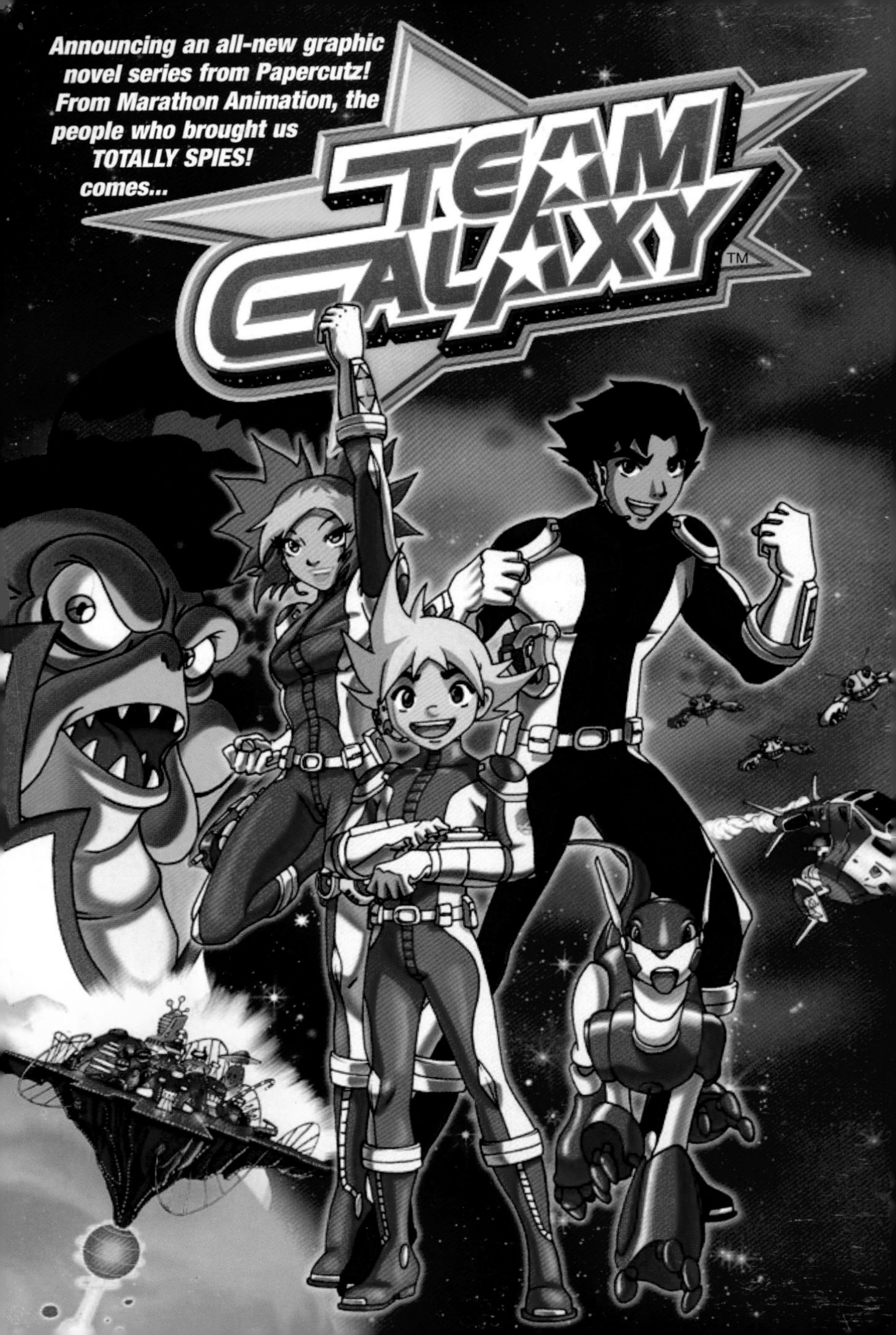

Announcing an all-new graphic novel series from Papercutz! From Marathon Animation, the people who brought us TOTALLY SPIES! comes...
TEAM GALAXY™

What happens when three outrageous teenagers are thrown into the most eye-popping space adventures?
TEAM GALAXY tells the story of friends like no others: Josh, Yoko and Brett. The three of them have been chosen to attend Galaxy High, the coolest high school on earth, where they are trained to become space marshals. Throughout their adventures, the heroes of TEAM GALAXY will have to multitask between the tribulations of their teen lives and fighting the craziest alien villains ever known to man.
Don't miss this exciting new series, based on the hit TV series, seen on Cartoon Network and YTV, coming this Fall from Papercutz.
Now let's meet the stars of TEAM GALAXY...

Josh

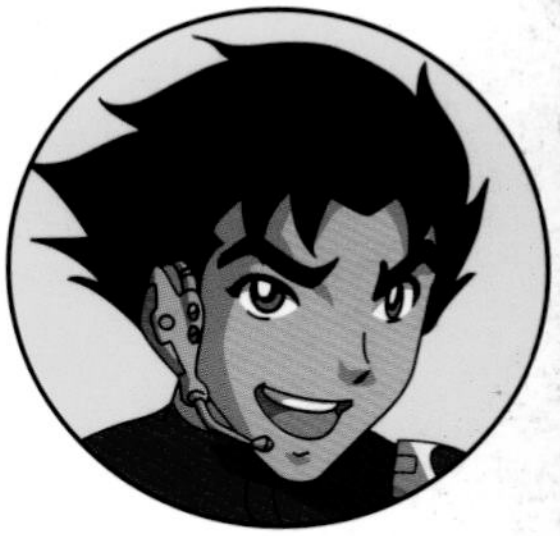

With his leather jacket, motorcycle and crazy antics, Josh has earned the reputation of the rebel of Galaxy High. He prides himself on being a professional slacker, and always seems to be in trouble with the principal – who also happens to be his father. But for all his wild stunts, Josh's independent thinking is a perfect fit for the team.

Yoko

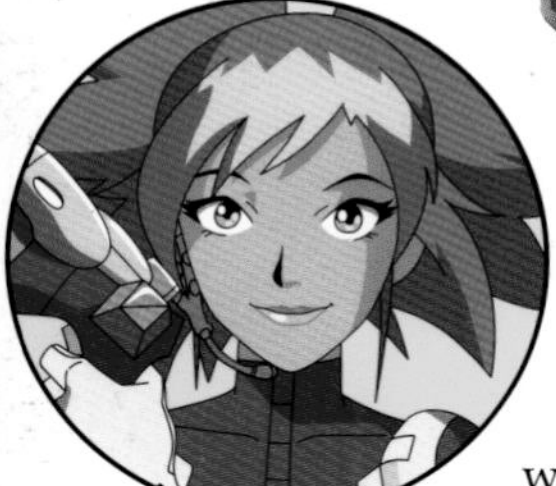

is a 15 year-old with a taste for the spotlight and funky fashion. Her wild streaked hair and colorful personality bring a unique element to the team. In addition to being amazingly talented (singing, dancing, writing, acting, playing guitar, painting), Yoko is a serious karate junkie, which helps when they have to battle with unsavory aliens.

Brett

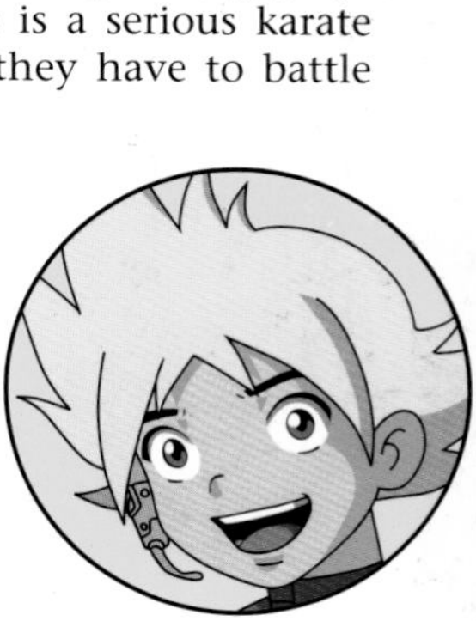

is the youngest, and smartest, of the students at Galaxy High. With a fascination for gadgets and all things sci-fi, he is labeled a true brainiac. He can fix almost anything that goes wrong with the school's equipment – but just don't call him a "kid."

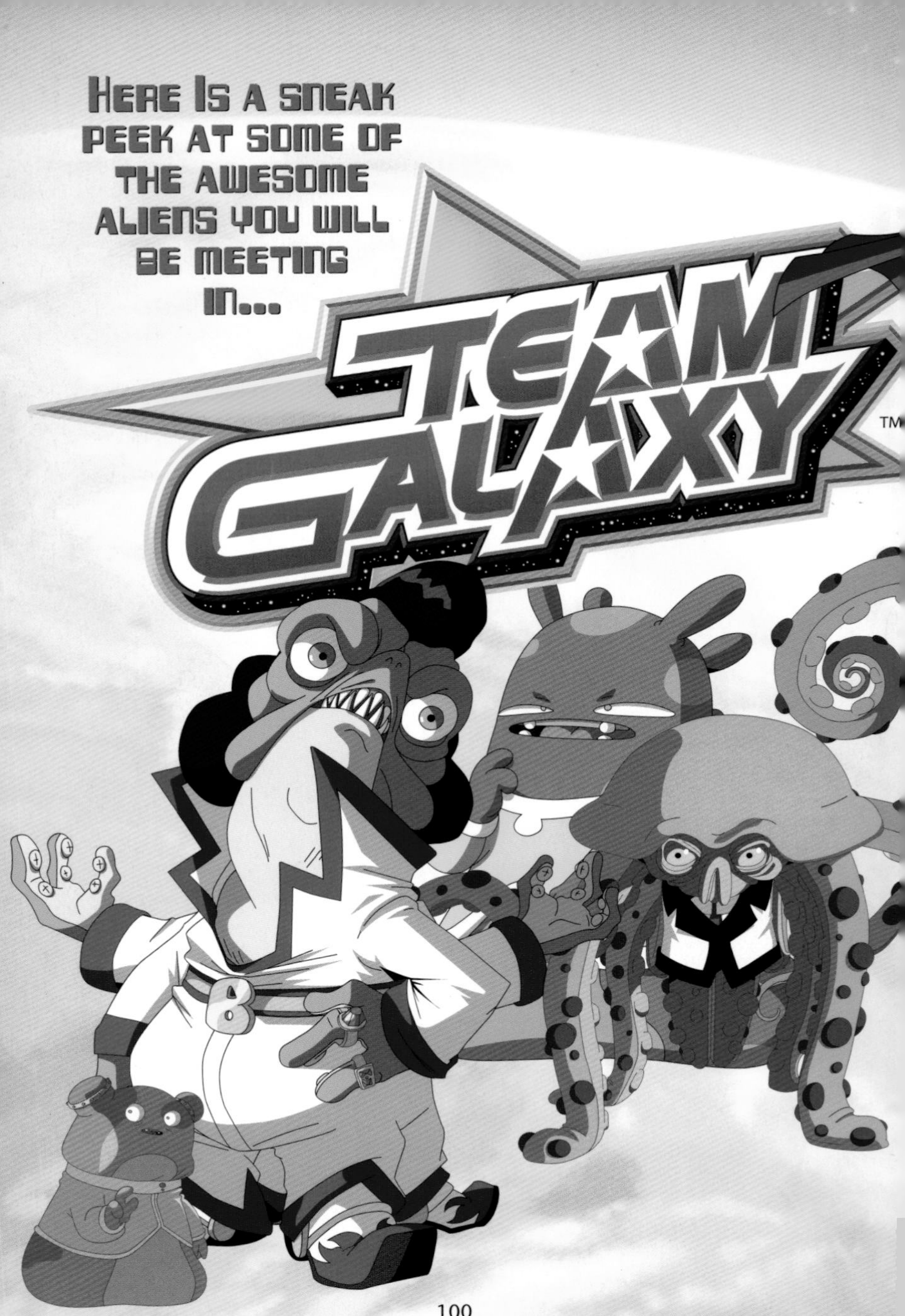
HERE IS A SNEAK PEEK AT SOME OF THE AWESOME ALIENS YOU WILL BE MEETING IN...
TEAM GALAXY™

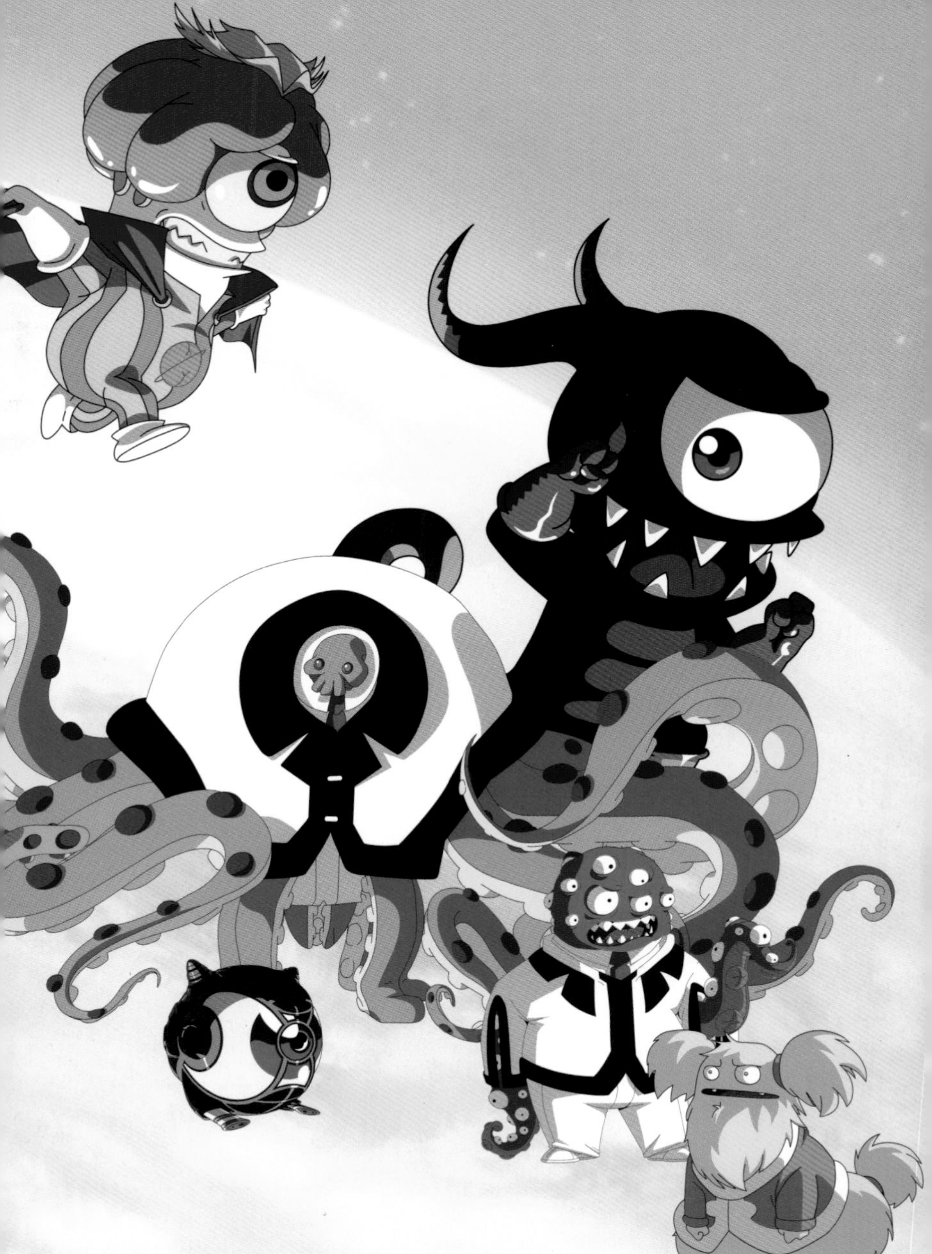

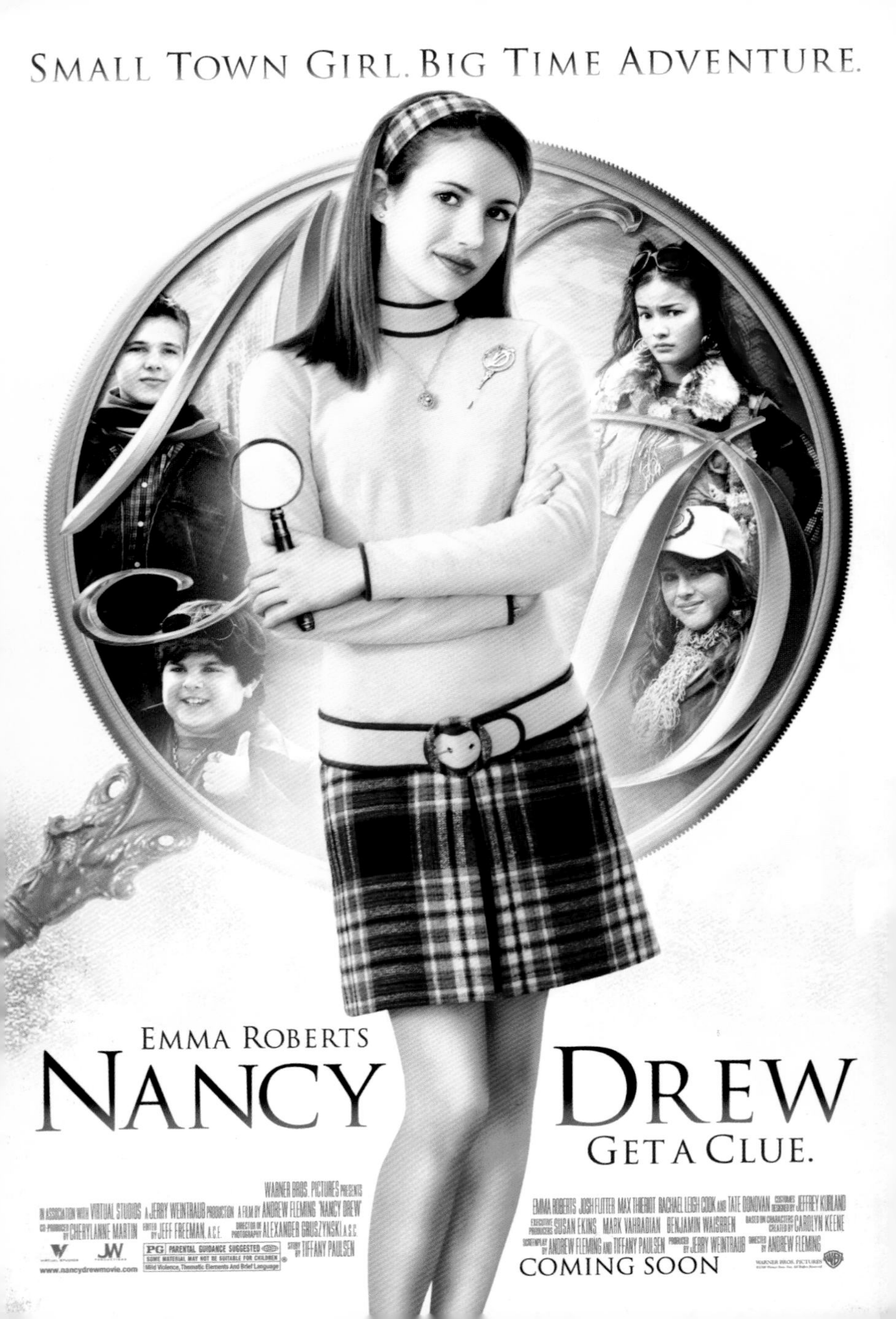

SMALL TOWN GIRL. BIG TIME ADVENTURE.
EMMA ROBERTS
NANCY DREW
GET A CLUE.
WARNER BROS. PICTURES PRESENTS
IN ASSOCIATION WITH VIRTUAL STUDIOS A JERRY WEINTRAUB PRODUCTION A FILM BY ANDREW FLEMING "NANCY DREW"
CO-PRODUCED BY CHERYLANNE MARTIN EDITED BY JEFF FREEMAN, A.C.E. DIRECTOR OF PHOTOGRAPHY ALEXANDER GRUSZYNSKI, A.S.C.
PG PARENTAL GUIDANCE SUGGESTED
SOME MATERIAL MAY NOT BE SUITABLE FOR CHILDREN
Mild Violence, Thematic Elements And Brief Language
STORY BY TIFFANY PAULSEN
www.nancydrewmovie.com
EMMA ROBERTS JOSH FLITTER MAX THIERIOT RACHAEL LEIGH COOK AND TATE DONOVAN COSTUMES DESIGNED BY JEFFREY KURLAND
EXECUTIVE PRODUCERS SUSAN EKINS MARK VAHRADIAN BENJAMIN WAISBREN BASED ON CHARACTERS CREATED BY CAROLYN KEENE
SCREENPLAY BY ANDREW FLEMING AND TIFFANY PAULSEN PRODUCED BY JERRY WEINTRAUB DIRECTED BY ANDREW FLEMING
COMING SOON
WARNER BROS. PICTURES

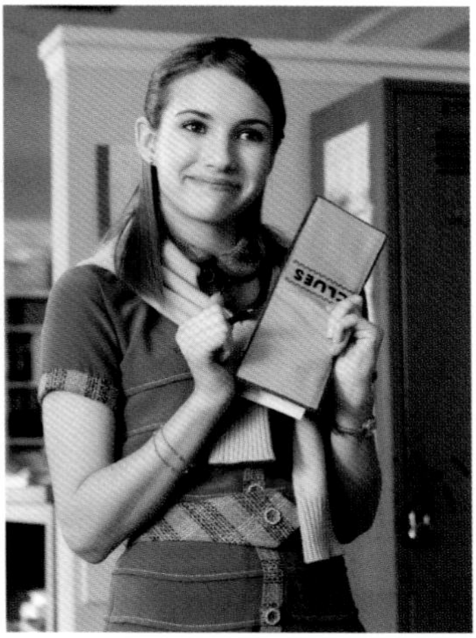

Nancy Drew (EMMA ROBERTS) in Warner Bros. Pictures' and Virtual Studios' teen drama action/adventure "Nancy Drew," distributed by Warner Bros. Pictures. Photo by Melinda Sue Gordon

The movie we've all been waiting for is almost here! To get a sneak peek, go online to: <u>http://nancydrewmovie.warnerbros.com/</u> and watch the fun-filled, action-packed trailer plus a lot more. You'll get to see Nancy Drew in action, in lots of scenes from her soon to be released major motion picture!

The film follows Nancy (Emma Roberts) as she accompanies her father, Carson Drew (Tate Donovan), to Los Angeles on one of his business trips and stumbles across evidence about a long-unsolved crime involving the mysterious death of a beautiful movie star. Nancy's resourcefulness and personal responsibility are put to the test when she finds herself in the middle of the fast-living, self-indulgent world of Hollywood.

Top to bottom: Ned (MAX THIERIOT), Nancy Drew (EMMA ROBERTS) and Corky (JOSH FLITTER) in Warner Bros. Pictures' and Virtual Studios' teen drama action/adventure "Nancy Drew," distributed by Warner Bros. Pictures. Photo by Melinda Sue Gordon

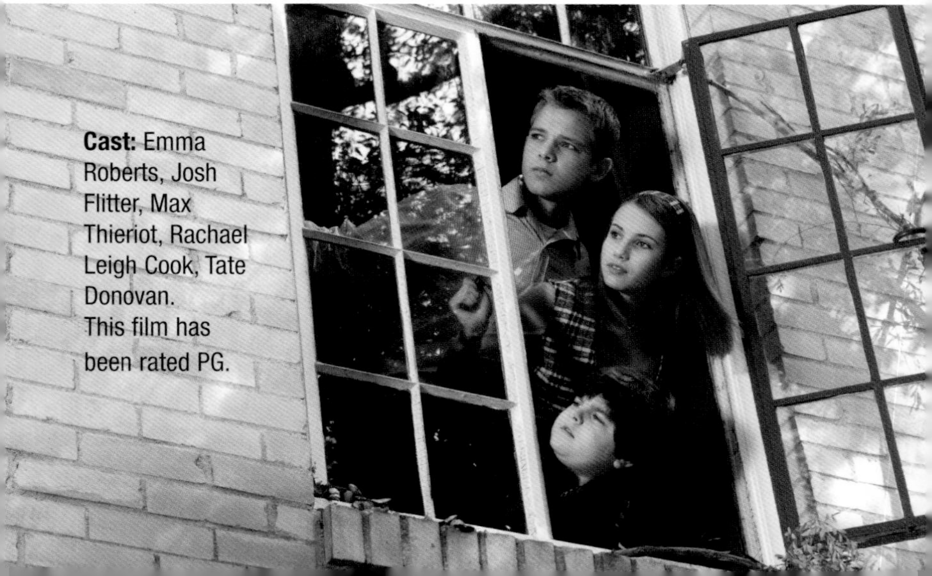
Cast: Emma Roberts, Josh Flitter, Max Thieriot, Rachael Leigh Cook, Tate Donovan.
This film has been rated PG.

Totally Spies!™

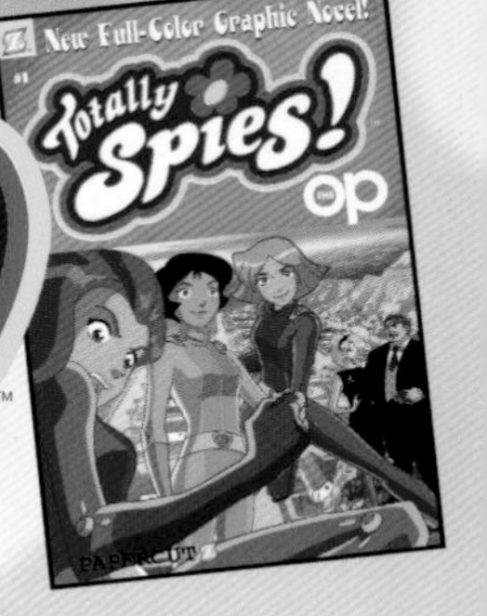

New Full-Color Graphic Novel!
#1
Totally Spies!
PAPERCUT

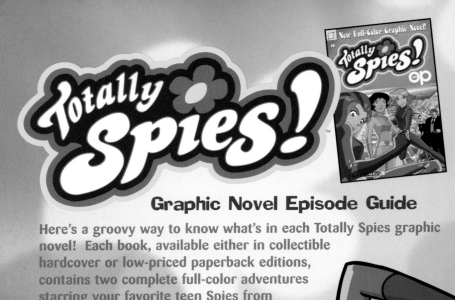

Graphic Novel Episode Guide

Here's a groovy way to know what's in each Totally Spies graphic novel! Each book, available either in collectible hardcover or low-priced paperback editions, contains two complete full-color adventures starring your favorite teen Spies from Beverly Hills...

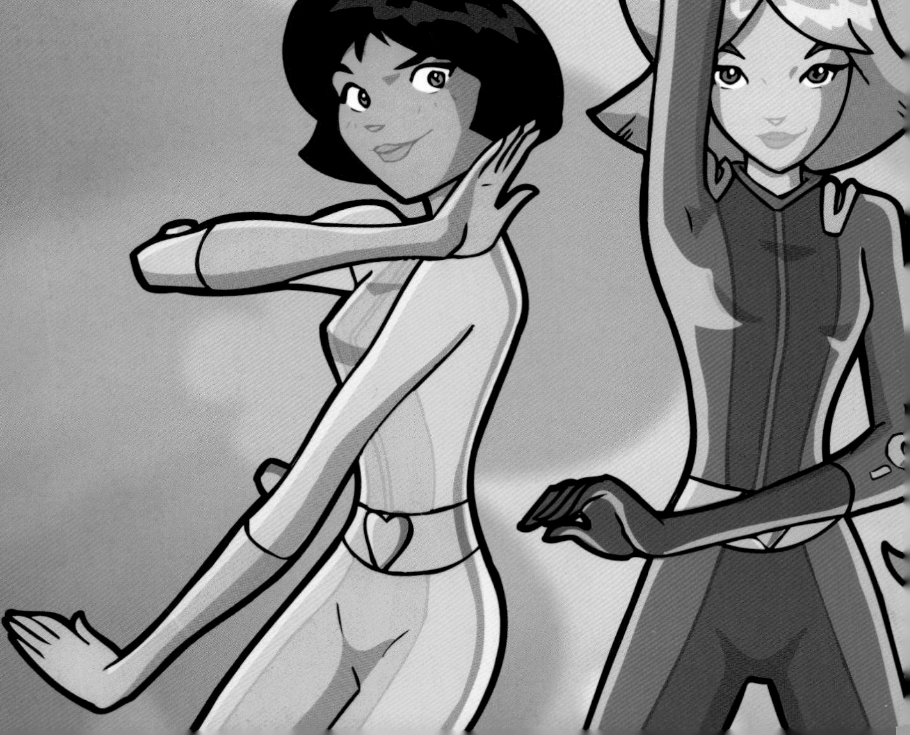

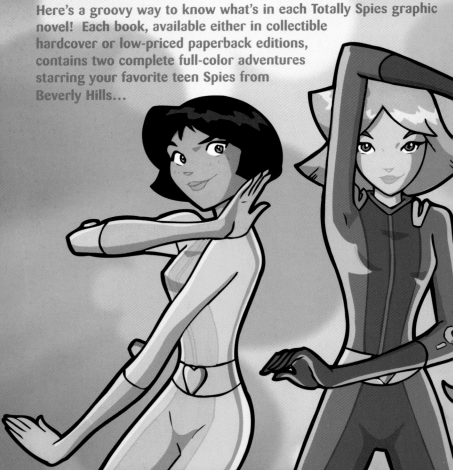

Totally Spies! Graphic Novel #1
"The O.P."

During a weekend road trip up the California coast, the girls' new car, a totally tricked-out, gadget-filled gift from Jerry to celebrate their recent success as super-spies, breaks down in a seemingly idyllic gated coastal town called Ocean Palisades – or "The O.P." for short. At first Alex, Sam, and Clover completely love it — the friendly, perfectly-tanned townspeople; the fancy, immaculate houses; the ridiculously scenic views – but, when they meet a few teens who seem to be too perfect to be real (they don't stay out after dark; they love spending time with their parents; they have sparkling teeth because they don't eat junk food), they start to get pretty weirded-out. Can the Spies find out what's really going on with the town's teens and save them from their crazy community – or will they be turned into perfect robot-like teens themselves and be forced to live in The O.P. forever?.

"Futureshock"

When the girls fiddle with Jerry's new time machine, they accidentally jet themselves 25 years into the future! At first they think it's way exciting – until they discover that Mandy is an all-powerful super villain who has control of all media! The spies are in awe when they see Mandy on the cover of every single magazine... starring in every single TV show and film... and dominating every single radio station – the whole time pushing her shallow Mandy agenda! And the worst part is, when the spies seek out their future selves, they discover that they're being held captive by Mandy! Desperate, present day Sam, Clover and Alex seek out future Jerry for help (he's the only one who knows how to work the time machine) — but to their shock, find that he's not exactly around anymore, he's had himself cryogenically frozen! The girls have to find a way to "thaw" him out, save the future versions of themselves from captivity, and stop Mandy before she totally "Mandifies" the planet!

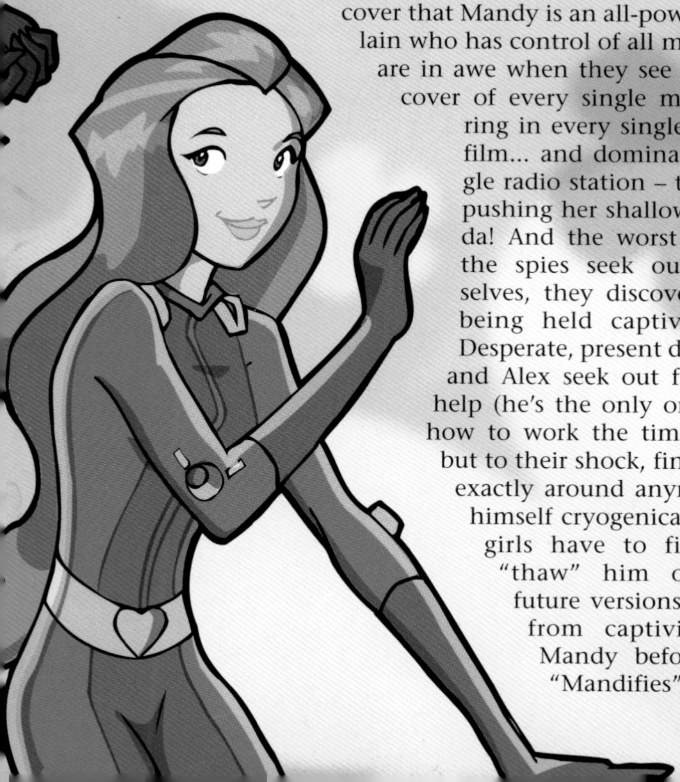

Totally Spies!
Graphic Novel #2
"I Hate The 80s!"

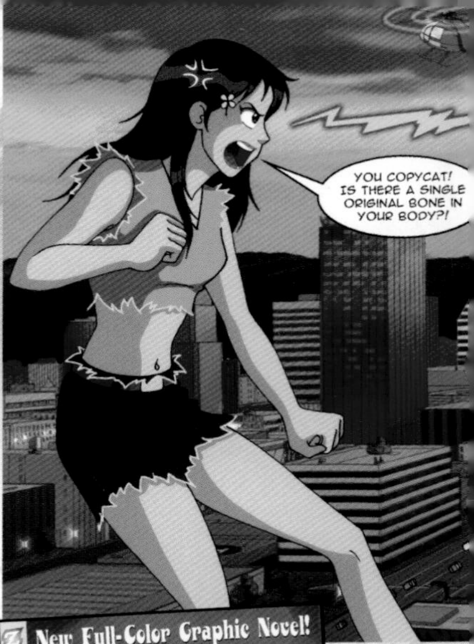
YOU COPYCAT! IS THERE A SINGLE ORIGINAL BONE IN YOUR BODY?!

Boogie Gus has updated his look a bit — unfortunately, not for the better. No longer a worshipper of the 70s, Gus has gleefully discovered the 80s. And he's bent on using his new device – "The Eightifier" to turn Beverly Hills into the ultimate 80s paradise. Can the Spies stop Boogie Gus before their home town goes retro for good? Can the girls deal with their complicated-to-maintain New Wave haircuts? Can they deal with all the synth-pop music at their school dances? Can they stop Jerry from wearing robin's egg blue sports jackets with the sleeves rolled up and pastel pink t-shirts underneath?!

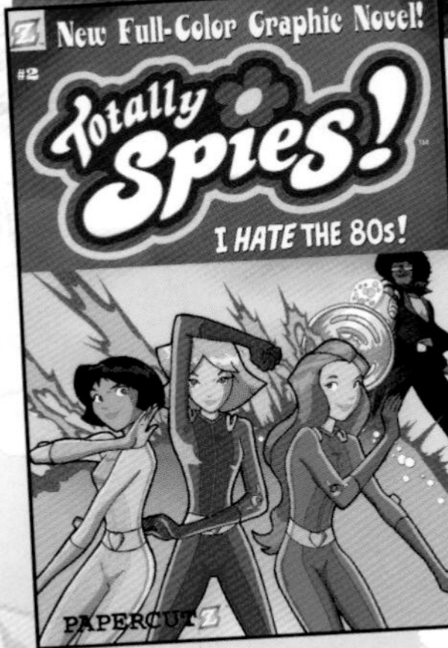
New Full-Color Graphic Novel!
#2
Totally Spies!
I HATE THE 80s!
PAPERCUTZ

"Attack Of The 50Ft. Tall Mandy!"
It's time to crown the new Miss Beverly Hills. Among this year's hopeful contestants are Mandy and Clover. In order to get that extra winning edge, they both unwittingly decide to get a special full-body makeover that promises to make their hair, smiles, eyes and even their attitudes bigger. Mandy: "And everyone knows that bigger is better when it comes to this type of competition." But as they are getting their treatment, both strapped into separate full-body machines, a shadowy figure sneaks into the spa and puts a microchip into Mandy's machine. Mandy is suddenly growing bigger in every way. As the Spies start to investigate a rash of disappearances among Miss Beverly Hills contestants, they find out that Mandy, who has now grown nearly fifty feet tall, is behind the crimes. They also discover that along with becoming bigger physically, Mandy's meanness has also become magnified. And in an effort to win the competition, she decided to take out the other contestants. Can the Spies stop this monolithic Mandy menace before it's too late?

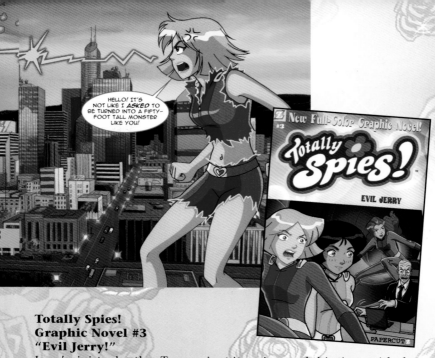

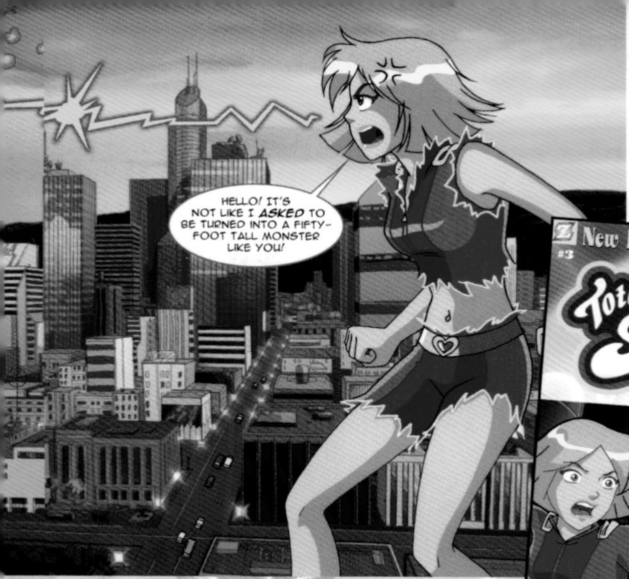
HELLO! IT'S NOT LIKE I *ASKED* TO BE TURNED INTO A FIFTY-FOOT TALL MONSTER LIKE YOU!

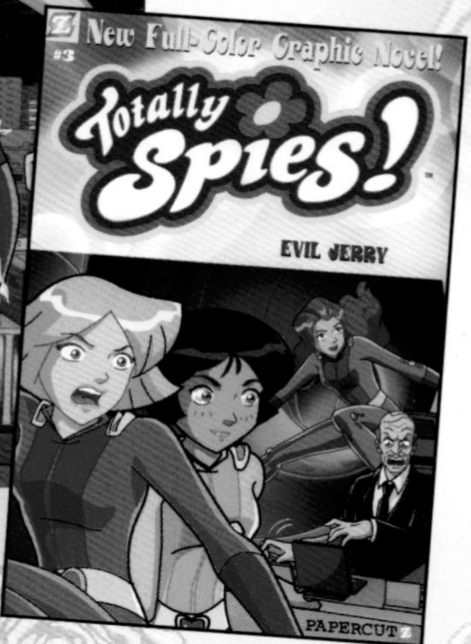
New Full-Color Graphic Novel!
#3
Totally Spies!
EVIL JERRY
PAPERCUT Z

Totally Spies!
Graphic Novel #3
"Evil Jerry!"

Jerry's sinister brother Terence is at it again – and this time, with the help of Tim Scam, he's created a crazy device that has the ability to gather half of the evil from him... and transfer it directly into Jerry! Luckily, the spies start to notice that Jerry's acting strangely. And even luckier, they figure out what's going on – Terence and a troop of ex-villains are to blame! Yes, the girls finally discover the LAMOS! Can the spies save Jerry and WOOHP before it's too late – or will Terence proceed with the rest of his wicked plan – moving himself and the rest of the LAMOS out of their submarine and into WOOHP (from which they can spread their evil all over the world)?

"Deja Cruise!"

The spies are totally psyched when Jerry informs them that he's offering them a little vacation on the new WOOHP Cruise Liner – a state-of-the-art, luxury ship designed to be a pleasure boat for overworked WOOHP agents! Once on the boat, the girls realize Jerry wasn't kidding, the ship is loaded with all sorts of amenities. Suddenly, the serenity of the vacation is broken as a gang of baddies, disguised as the ship's crew, take over the boat. Their plan: to destroy the ship with all of the WOOHP agents on it. The girls spring into action and try to defeat the villains, but their efforts only result in them accidentally causing the ship to sink. Or does it? The girls all wake up

and find that things are back to normal. Was it all a bad dream caused by eating bad sushi? Suddenly, just as things seem to be back to normal, the entire incident happens again. The spies try to stop the villains, but again destroy the vessel. And yet, again, they wake up on the ship. The spies realize that they are re-living the same day over and over! And the only way to stop this vicious cycle is to defeat the bad guys. Can the girls figure out what to do, or will they be stuck on this boat forever?!

Totally Spies!
Graphic Novel #4
"Spies in Space"

The spies are way psyched when they find out that their favorite new band, The Alpha Centauris, are about to make music history. The band plans to be the first performers ever to broadcast a concert live from the moon. The only problem is, it's just days before the gig and the band is nowhere to be found. Apparently, their space transport has completely disappeared from WOOHP radar. Jerry puts the Spies on the case (as if they would have it any other way) and after GLADIS outfits them with cool intergalactic gadgets, including awesome space suits, the girls head off to find the band. After finding their abandoned ship, clues lead the Spies to believe the band was abducted by aliens. Can the girls save the band before they are evaporated by the sun?

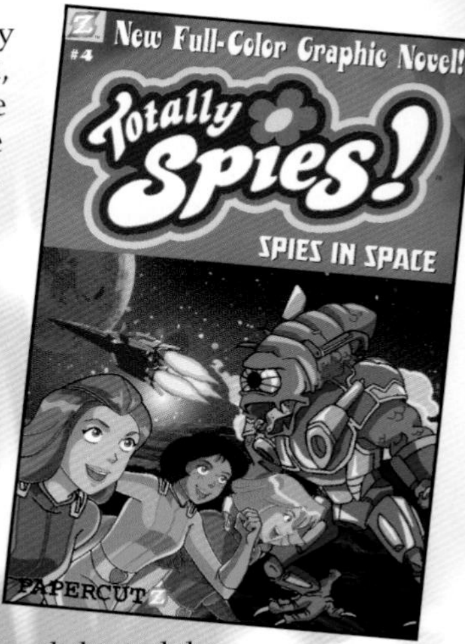
#4
New Full-Color Graphic Novel!
Totally Spies!
SPIES IN SPACE
PAPERCUTZ

"Spy Soccer"

It's the start of a new soccer season at Bev. High and Alex is psyched when her team gets a cool new coach. The only downside is that Clover and Sam feel a little snubbed because Alex is constantly busy with her team. Later, Jerry sends the girls on a mission to investigate a series of abductions. When the girls check out one of the crime scenes, they discover the place is totally trashed. And stranger still, one of the clues leads Sam and Clover back to... Alex?! When the girls confront Alex, she denies any wrongdoing, but can't explain or remember where she was at the time of the abduction. Then, seemingly out of nowhere, Alex's demeanor changes and she becomes very evil. She attacks Sam and Clover, and ultimately escapes. Sam and Clover discover that Alex's new soccer coach is using a special mind control ball to turn the Bev. High soccer team into her own private army – an army that uses their incredible, newfound, evil soccer techniques to get revenge on the coach's ex-teammates. Can Sam and Clover survive the final showdown – a death defying soccer match against the coach, Alex and her mind-controlled teammates?

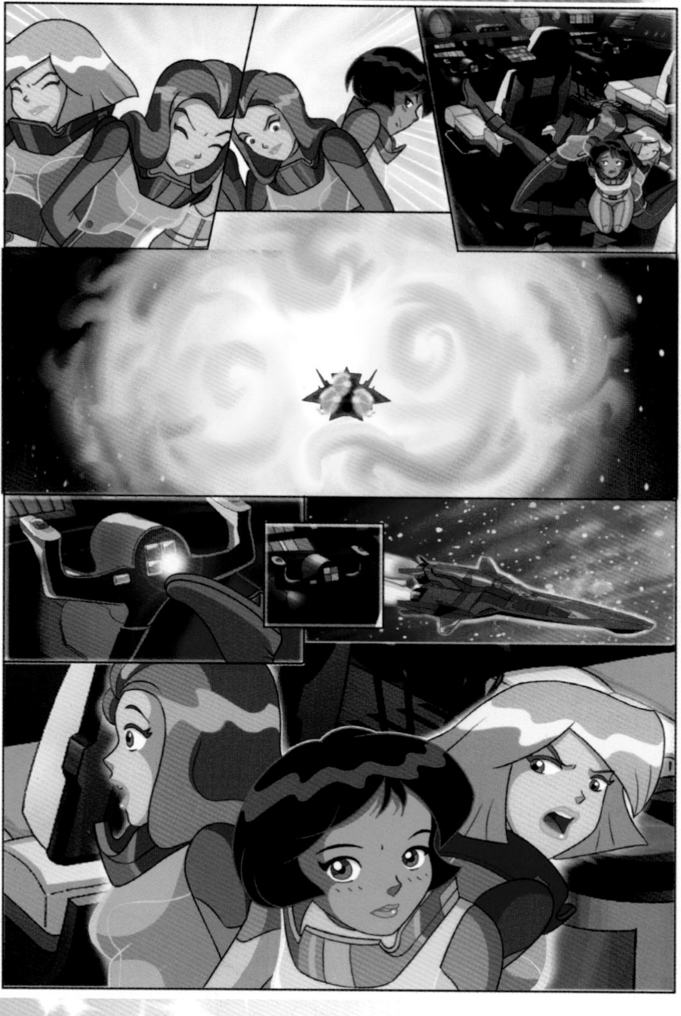

The Hardy Boys in Comics (and on TV and Vinyl)!

It's not that difficult to find an adult who remembers the late 70s live-action TV series, "The Hardy Boys Mysteries," with Shawn Cassidy and Parker Stevenson. And you can still find lots of Baby Boomers who recall the Hardy Boys serial, with Tim Considine and Tommy Kirk, which ran on the original Mickey Mouse Club TV series in the 50s. What's is almost impossible is finding anyone who might remember the Hardy Boys Saturday morning cartoon show from 1969. Like the Hardy Boys appearance on TV in the 50s, their animated TV series in the late 60s also inspired a four-issue comicbook series. But let's find out more about "The Mystery of The Forgotten Cartoon Series."

Back in the days long before entire cable networks were devoted to cartoons 24/7, the only place to see new cartoons on TV were on ABC, NBC, and CBS Saturday mornings. Back then Filmation Studios had a huge hit in the 60s with an animated series based on the Archie comicbook characters. Not only was it a hit on TV, but the songs performed by the animated Archies band became huge pop music hits — and you thought Gorillaz was the first cartoon band! But the technology didn't yet exist that could make it possible for a "cartoon band" to perform live on tour. The producers at Filmation decided to try to launch another cartoon series, based on characters loved by millions of children, but this time, they'd also assemble a live band made up of singers and musicians that looked just like the cartoon characters.

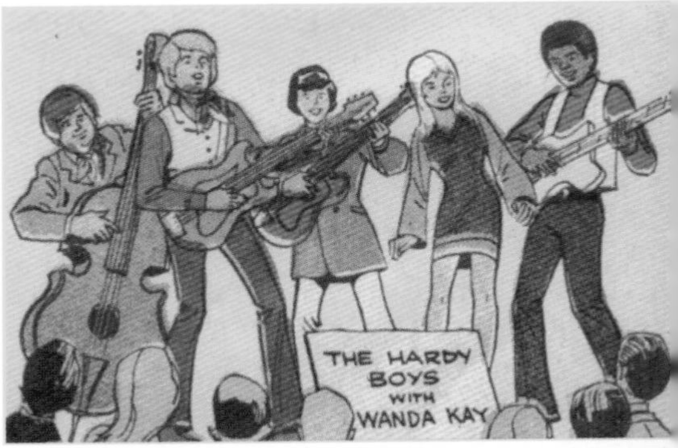
THE HARDY BOYS WITH WANDA KAY

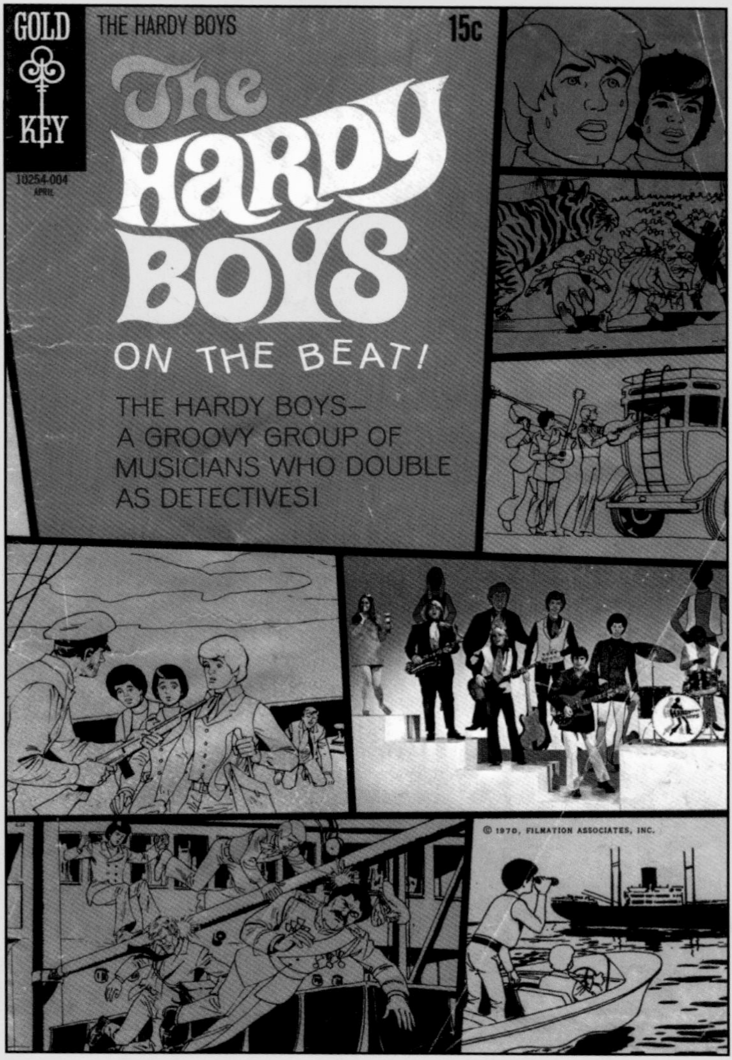
GOLD KEY
THE HARDY BOYS
15c
The HARDY BOYS
ON THE BEAT!
THE HARDY BOYS–
A GROOVY GROUP OF
MUSICIANS WHO DOUBLE
AS DETECTIVES!
© 1970, FILMATION ASSOCIATES, INC.

The Hardy Boys Gold Key Comicbook Checklist:

April 1970 – “Secret Of The Orinda Star,” “The Dart-Riddle Rumble”
July 1970 – “Mystery Of The Catacombs,” “Secret Mission”
October 1970 – “Mystery Of Wildcat Swamp,” “The Headless Horseman”
January 1971 – “Paddle Wheel Peril” “The Guise Of Medusa”

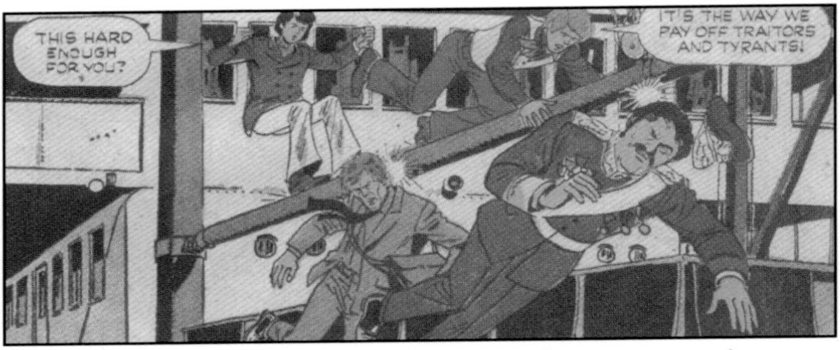
THIS HARD ENOUGH FOR YOU?
IT'S THE WAY WE PAY OFF TRAITORS AND TYRANTS!

The characters they chose to base this new show on was, of course, The Hardy Boys!

Filmation decided that in addition to solving mysteries, the Hardy Boys would be a touring bubblegum pop band. Joining Frank and Joe in this band, called The Hardy Boys Plus Three, were "Chubby" Morton, a character clearly based on Chet Morton, and new characters, Pete Jones (the first African-American character on a Saturday morning series*), and Wanda Kay Breckenridge.

For the non-singing parts of the show, actor Byron Kane provided the voices for Joe Hardy, Pete Jones, and Fenton Hardy; actor Dal McKennon did likewise for Frank Hardy and Chubby Morton, and actress Jane Webb supplied the female voices for Wanda Kay Breckenridge and Aunt Gertrude Hardy.

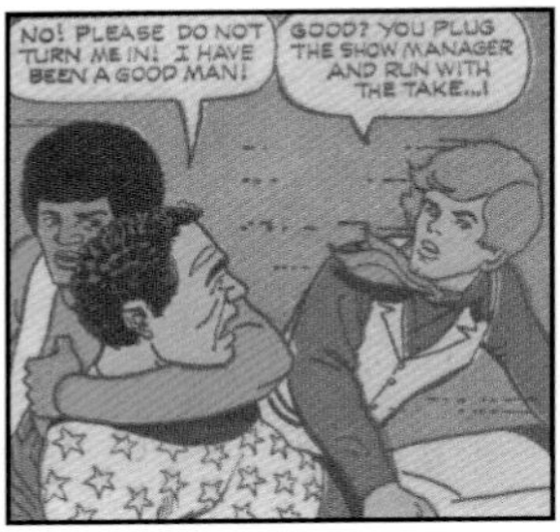
NO! PLEASE DO NOT TURN ME IN! I HAVE BEEN A GOOD MAN!
GOOD? YOU PLUG THE SHOW MANAGER AND RUN WITH THE TAKE...!

While the actual mystery/adventure stories were animated, the show did feature the groovy live-action band briefly at the end of each episode performing one of their songs. Two record albums were released, "Here Come The Hardy Boys" and "Wheels," featuring the musical Hardy Boys, and the first album even cracked Billboard's Top 200 Album Chart. About the only other place to "see" the live version of The Hardy Boys Plus Three was on the Hardy Boys comicbook's covers. Each of the four covers featured a mix of comic art and photos. The "live" band appeared most prominently on the second issue.

Oh, and the answer to "The Mystery of the Forgotten Cartoon Series" is that the show ran against the ratings blockbuster Scooby-Doo and everyone was watching the Scooby gang!

*While the prime time TV special, "Hey, Hey, Hey, It's Fat Albert," debuted in 1969 as well, "Fat Albert and the Cosby Kids" didn't become a regular Saturday morning series until 1972. Like The Hardy Boys it was also produced by Filmation Studios.

JE 1 4 '07